BEHIND THE CURTAIN

'Undress?' Tessa stepped backwards and stumbled over the chair. 'I'm not letting you near me.'

'Let me do it for you,' Sheila crooned, starting to undo the little buttons running down the front of Tessa's dress. 'I'll do anything for you, Tessa. You can punish me for hurting you.'

Tessa stuck her chin in the air, refusing to look at Sheila as the demure dress peeled away and her perky breasts pushed out from her chest. Sheila sat meekly down on the bed so that Tessa towered over her and she could feel really small. She undid the last buttons and pulled Tessa's dress off. The fabric was warm with Tessa's body, and she held it against her nose to sniff it. Then she pulled Tessa's knickers down.

'Give me your sweater,' Tessa said suddenly, kicking the knickers into Sheila's face. 'You take all that black stuff off.'

BEHIND THE CURTAIN

Primula Bond

This book is a work of fiction.
In real life, make sure you practise safe, sane and
consensual sex.

First published in 2007 by
Nexus
Thames Wharf Studios
Rainville Road
London W6 9HA

www.nexus-books.com

A catalogue record for this book is available from the
British Library.

Typeset by TW Typesetting, Plymouth, Devon

Penguin Random House is committed to a sustainable future for
our business, our readers and our planet. This book is made from
Forest Stewardship Council® certified paper.

Printed and bound in Great Britain by Clays Ltd, Elcograf S.p.A.

ISBN 978 0 352 34111 2

One

'So what's on the menu for tonight, Sheila?'

Maureen plonked one enormous, uninvited buttock on the edge of the desk and stretched her mouth at a grubby mirror. She scraped a blunted lipstick out of her handbag and squinted as if it was an artist's pencil.

'Menu?' Sheila resisted the temptation to glance at the clock. She started typing the last address label. 'What on earth do you mean?'

'Come on. We always like to find out a bit about our temps, especially the quiet ones.' Maureen tapped her lipstick on the top of Sheila's screen. 'So we did a rummage before you came in and found Nigella hidden in your drawers.'

There was a good deal of smothered tittering over by the door, where the others were already shrugging on coats and rustling shopping bags. It was Friday. They were all pissed after a long lunch. Now Sheila couldn't resist it. The clock above the water cooler said 16.58.

'I'm trying out harissa, if you must know.'

In her exasperation she inserted "harissa" on the label where Wolverhampton was supposed to go.

'Harissa, eh? Sounds like a belly dancer!' Maureen wiggled her bosoms and winked across at her cronies. 'We've a dark horse here, girls. All sorts go on at number 44, you know. Nigella, belly dancers – is that how your John gets his rocks off, then?'

Sheila pressed PRINT and lifted her head for the first time since lunch. The skin on her face drew tighter across her cheeks. 'How do you know about John?'

'Heard you cooing at him on the mobile when you thought no one was listening. I reckon he's stopped giving you one. Because you look to me like you need a right good seeing-to.' Maureen smirked and started colouring herself in. The thin, bloodless lips that chewed and sucked their way through phone calls and chocolate bars all day were now, as evening approached, turning a metallic purple. No colour in nature could ever match that. Could possibly be as hideous. Except –

Sheila stood up, automatically pulled her polo neck snug over her hips. It was a surreptitious way of touching herself even in public, just for reassurance. She patted a couple of pins more firmly into the tight chignon at the back of her head and resisted re-applying her own classic red lipstick.

'Just look at your mouth, Maureen. That ghastly purple,' she said, edging neatly round the immaculate desk. 'Have you any idea what it reminds me of?'

Maureen glanced up. Against the purple her teeth had a yellowish hue.

'Do you know, lady? Now that you're leaving us I think I'll say it. Our little Tessa thinks you look like that Katharine Hepburn. All black clothes and eyeliner and keep your knees together. But then she's got a crush on you. I just think you're prim like that because there's a carrot rammed up your jacksie.'

Sheila walked across to the coat hooks, careful to breathe slowly through her nostrils, not through her mouth, not show a thing, not reveal how exhilarated she could get at the prospect of a fight. She concentrated on flicking one high-heeled foot smartly in front of the other as they'd taught her years ago. Yes, balancing a book on her head. Imagine you're walking down a straight line in the middle of the room. Easy to pretend it was deportment or ballet if anyone asked why she moved like that.

Maureen and the other witches would never believe her if she told them the truth. And they were right. She did walk, and talk, exactly as if she had a carrot up her —

The other girls parted like the Red Sea in front of her. Tessa, the office junior, shyly handed her the long tweed coat with the fur collar.

'I actually said Audrey,' she whispered as Sheila pulled it on. 'You know, Hepburn.'

Sheila nodded, flicking her tongue quickly into the corner of her mouth. It was the nearest she could get to a smile, but she hoped that Tessa would recognise it as friendliness. She liked little Tessa. She got a kick out of the way Tessa blushed whenever she came near, the longing way she stared openly as Sheila stalked around the office. Tessa was cute and curly-haired, like a very young Marilyn Monroe in her Norma Jean days before she dyed her hair. Once in the ladies' loo Sheila had told Tessa that. And Tessa had revealed that this job was financing her through drama school.

But Sheila couldn't stand the other harridans in the office. And they couldn't stand her.

'Excuse me, madam!' Maureen roared across the room. 'What were you going to say about my lipstick?'

Sheila buttoned the coat up at the neck then opened the door, holding her time sheet ready to be signed in Human Resources. Her heart hammered in her chest. It wasn't fury, or fear. It was frustration. Every so often she had to let fly. See the shock in their eyes.

'Now that I'm leaving you I think I'll say it.' Sheila tapped the time sheet thoughtfully against her lips. 'Your mouth is the exact colour of a baboon's anus.'

Two

When she turned into her street Sheila Moss slowed down. She didn't want the neighbours to see her running, maybe tripping over the wet leaves that had turned gold and fallen during the day. But it was so hard to keep calm. John would be home, waiting for her. She could hardly bear the suspense. He'd been gone so long, chasing jobs and money and prospects.

As for her side of the bargain, she'd sorted out the house and persevered with those god-awful temping jobs. Now, thank God, she could give all that up. Now he was back it was up to him to take care of everything.

And what about the biggest sacrifice? Her secret challenge? That she hadn't touched herself, not once, in all those months. Not once had her fingers dived beneath the lavender bubbles in the claw-foot bath to feel for that delicate part of her, to make it open and slippery with soap. Not once in the night had she blown out the candle she kept beside her bed and instead of sleeping in the darkness pushed its sturdy length, still warm and melting with wax, up between her smooth thighs, up towards her aching, empty sex.

No one else had touched her, either. Not man, not woman. She'd lived, as always, like a nun. Fat Maureen was spot-on when she reckoned Sheila needed a good rogering or whatever vulgar way she put it. But Maureen couldn't guess just how horribly close she was to the truth, because Sheila was indeed saving herself, the sex was always far better that way, the feast after the fast. Except that lately she was nearly always fasting . . .

Tonight was the night, and she would make John see it, too. He would greet her on his return, take one look at the look in her eyes, maybe throw her onto the floor, right there on the Persian runner in the hallway, right there in their new home, and take her from behind, again and again. He would be mad for it because he had waited as long as she had and men went mad, didn't they, if they didn't get it. This time she would show him she could scream out loud until she was as abandoned as any streetwalker.

She put a gloved hand over her mouth to smother the gasp of excitement. Lights were coming on in the square-fronted, identical Edwardian houses in her street. Figures moved about, visible above hedges or between cherry trees, framed by stained or clear windows, curtains not yet pulled in a last nod to the summer. She flicked aside a dripping branch. A heavy green fruit bumped at her face. All this foliage had a sharp, ripe aroma. Her senses were singing. She just had to think of John and what he looked like naked and her nerve-ends shrieked. Oh, if those perfect neighbours could read her mind . . .

In number 44, as Maureen had sneeringly called it, she and John could at last be left alone. They could cook up whatever scenario they liked. No one could shake their heads or follow them around with their tongues hanging out or try to twist their story to make it dirty. No one knew anything about them.

The properties really were finished beautifully, especially now the autumn had started to weather the work. You'd never think they had only been completed in the summer. And the quality and the individual quirks he'd designed for each one were all down to John's skill and vision. The project had given John a

5

reason to come back to England after years of exile, and of course she had followed him.

And how different these suburban dwellings were from the swanky, sprawling, white-painted apartment they'd shared in Paris, situated, as it turned out, above a high-class bordello. It was years before she clicked. So innocent. So frigid, Maureen would say. If only she knew! She'd even befriended some of those girls, the gorgeous whores whom John actually *paid* when she was away from home. And once word got out about her and John, and clients started taking the lift up to their floor, thinking it was an exotic extension of the brothel, she'd had to give up her work, yank John out of there before she lost him for good in that decadent world . . .

How different number 44 Spartan Street would be. Here they could be Mr and Mrs Respectable at long last. She smiled, rebelliously kicking open their gate. Disreputable, more like. Master and Mistress, behind closed doors.

She fitted the key into the lock. Phallus easing into vestal virgin. She bit her lip, tasting blood. What would John say? Oh, she could do decadent, when it suited. Just watch. Even the way the ridges of the Chubb key snagged slightly against the polished brass hole made her stomach tighten.

'John! My darling, I'm home!' she called, falling back against the front door. He was early. This wasn't the plan. Her legs started to crumple. 'I can't wait a minute longer! Come and get me! I want you now!'

There was no answer. He was playing with her. He hadn't even turned on the lights. But his jacket was slung across the polished banisters and she could hear faint music coming from somewhere upstairs. Already the ambience of her silent house was altered. He must have brought a CD player back with him. He used to like jazz, when they lived in Paris.

'I'm doing something special later, with chicken!

6

Your favourite!' she called again. 'Your reward if you're a good boy!'

She pulled her coat off and tossed it on to the floor. There was still no answer. She hung the coat up. Her office clothes felt too tight. Her body wanted to burst free. She put her hand over her left breast. It bounced with each thump of her heart, seemed to grow bigger with each beat. She squeezed her breasts together, those sensitive mounds habitually concealed from the world under black cashmere. The long-awaited contact was too good, nipples springing up like beacons at the slightest touch. She stopped. *Save it for John. Save it.* She held on to the banisters with both hands and started to climb.

Her lips parted, she could hear the rushing of her breath. *Not long now.* Just up the stairs and then she could have him. He'd promised. He was singing up there, his deep, tuneless voice. Now he was trying to imitate the high notes of the saxophone. He sounded like a girl.

And see, there were his suitcases, still zipped up, hulking in the centre of her, their bedroom. Some suitcases she didn't recognise. And certainly more than he'd taken with him.

'Where are you, Johnnie? You can't hide from me forever!' she cooed, tiptoeing across the floor towards the bathroom. 'I'll give you one more minute.'

She kicked off her shoes. Her toes sank into the circular pink rug which she'd recently bought, thinking it would look welcoming for a boudoir, but now she wasn't sure. Too feminine for his taste, perhaps? John liked things simple, and masculine. The flat in Paris had been all his. That's how come it was so chic. She listened. She could hear the splashing of the shower.

'If that's the way you want it – I'll come in there with you!'

She giggled and reached under her skirt to unclip her stockings. The months of abstinence had made her bold.

7

Or perhaps she'd caught the crudeness of Maureen and her friends, like a new, pleasant disease.

Her fingers brushed her thighs and the skin shivered. She changed her mind and pulled the skirt off instead, leaving the stockings on. She felt sexier partly clothed. John could do the rest. He could take off the silky black sweater, a version of which she always wore as if in mourning. It was her uniform; the simplest way of concealing her real self. Except that over the years it had *become* her real self.

When he'd done that, he'd see her once-famous breasts, a bit smaller since he'd been away; her appetite for food, for everything really, diminished when he was away. He'd laugh at her if she admitted that, tell her she was skinny like a lovesick puppy. But maybe this time he would touch them, as she burned for him to do and never dared demand.

He would see her legs in the sheer black stockings, raise his eyebrows at her knickers. Maybe too sensible? But men liked all the schoolgirl stuff, the big knickers and the skirts and the socks. She'd read that in one of Maureen's magazines, left in the canteen. The magazine had also said, confusingly, that men liked the dominatrix stuff, the teacher, the black gown, the cane, the punishments. So which would it be? How long would it be before John would be pulling her knickers down, maybe putting her across his knee – or asking her to whip him?

She stepped nearer. In the few short weeks she had worked at that horrible office, Maureen, if she but knew it, had given Sheila a right good educating –

At last, a voice. A groan, perhaps in response to her teasing. Her chest tightened as she tiptoed across the rug. She could hear him, the slight thump and squeak of his body in there, but he wouldn't be able to hear her above the music. *Let him play his jazz.* She would loosen up, he'd see. She'd wised up. All those magazines, all that solitude, had taught her how to keep him happy,

8

stop him wandering. She didn't want to waste any more time. He could do what he liked, now he was back. He could do what he liked to her.

The transparent walls of the shower unit were steamed up, but she could see them being bent from inside, fleshy-pink shapes flattening against the streaked panels, then being sucked away again. There was some kind of struggle going on.

'Are you all right, John?'

There was a snorting giggle, definitely female, and Sheila stiffened. Above the basin there was a round chrome mirror shaped like a ship's porthole. She'd brought that from the flat in Paris. Screwed it into the wall herself. Reflected in it she could see his naked body. No, not his body. She knew it better than she knew her own. This was a curved, female rump. A big fat woman, a total stranger, was in her shower!

Sheila looked around for a weapon. The only thing to hand was the hair dryer. She slipped slightly on the tiled floor to reach for it, and as she did so she saw the woman stagger slightly and part her legs. Her hands were pressed against the wall to keep her balance as she threw her head back, curling her toes to grip the uncertain surface.

And kneeling between her legs was a man, his tanned skin and dark hair streaked by water and soap bubbles. He'd put on weight. Someone else had been feeding him up. He grappled at the woman's thighs, pulling them wide, revealing the woman's secret lips nestled there, plump and open and lined with bright pink. Despite being paralysed with shock, Sheila felt herself twitch in reaction. Or was it a kind of recognition?

And now the man's fingers were stroking and gripping and digging into the woman's flesh as if he meant to hurt her. Then he buried his face between her legs.

Sheila left the hair dryer where it was. Her throat was tightening with a harsh groan of what, desire? Despair?

9

But her hand had a different agenda. As the man's nose and mouth made contact with the woman, Sheila's hand copied. It slid straight down towards her knickers and she gasped. She'd forgotten she wore no skirt. The gusset of her knickers was damp. She dabbled her fingers against the fabric. The crevices of her body seemed already to be tensing and straining.

Now the man's head was moving slowly up and down, and the woman was shaking with growing pleasure. He withdrew for a moment. He pulled her plump labia further apart so that pink delicacies peeped out. His long red tongue curled out as if he was about to lick a particularly delicious ice cream.

The man's hair and the woman's dripping bush merged as he fastened his mouth back onto her, and their bodies were glossy in the steamy little room. It was difficult to work out, in Sheila's confusion, what was real and what was reflected.

So it was easy to wonder, as she let her hand rub dreamily back and forth over the thick cotton, gradually speeding up to keep time with the man's head, if sex would taste like it smelled. As she felt herself moistening under the work of her own fingers, how would such sweet droplets taste on her tongue? What flavour would another woman's excitement be?

He had never done that, with his tongue, to her. Never even spoken of it, not even during those debauched conversations they used to have when they lived in Paris and he was home from a trip; when they drank the family Burgundy until dawn and dared each other to be outrageous, describing what they might do to each other even though it was forbidden; goading each other to a frenzy until they couldn't help it and they succumbed to yet another brief, wild coupling.

She'd never done that thing to him, either. They'd never talked about what he would taste like. His penis and its own juices. She could do that thing, couldn't she, to him, now that they were free? A blow job. That's what Maureen would call it. Sheila wanted more than ever to see him clearly, his penis erect for her so that she could do that for him if he really wanted. She could suck on it, if that's how you did it. But something told her – the woman in the mirror told her – that she'd been too slow. Someone else had got there first.

Once, in a way that left her strangely cold, John had said that she was sacred to him. Maybe that was why they'd never sucked each other like that. But how could sucking be less sacred than fucking?

She fell back against the bathroom wall, feeling sick. She was appalled by the fury ripping through her. She ought to be shouting at them now to stop. He was *her* man. But they were at it in front of her, and they wouldn't take any notice of her if she did shout, and she was weak from watching. She could almost feel as if he was licking her now. That part of her was like a sponge (here they were in the bathroom after all), a little sponge that she was squeezing, releasing, squeezing restlessly.

Her hands rubbed more and more frantically, wishing it was his tongue that was doing this to her, straining to scale that desperate point, just out of reach.

But her watch must have flashed in the mirror, because suddenly the woman in the shower with John looked round and her reflected eyes met Sheila's. Sheila expected a shriek of embarrassment, a grabbing of a towel, but the woman just smiled, red lips like cushions spreading into a filthy grin wide enough to split her face. She kept on smiling as John's head and tongue pushed her and simply dragged Sheila with her into her world of sensation.

Her eyes held Sheila's for a minute or two but then started to glaze over, eyelids flickering but not closing, her obscene mouth slackening, and then she gave a gentle moan, crashed heavily against the shower and buckled to the floor.

11

'Enjoy the show, honey?' the woman asked a minute or two later, barely out of breath. Her arm was draped loosely round John's shoulders, but she was staring straight at Sheila. 'I can see you did.'

John turned. He caught sight of Sheila's hands, trapped between her legs but thwarted now in their task. There was no embarrassment for him, either. For some reason he, too, started to smile.

'Who the hell is that?' asked Sheila. She used the moment to spring her hands free and point at the woman lolling there, large breasts dribbled with water and soap suds, legs sprawled open. Now that John had rolled sideways, Sheila could see that the woman's pubic hair was waxed into a neat, curly line. 'What are you doing in my shower?'

'Sorry, Sheila. Didn't mean you to see all that.' John reached out of the shower and took a towel. 'I should have known you'd be back home on the dot.'

In all the confusion and steam Sheila hadn't had time to catch sight of his nakedness. His prick, as Maureen would call it. A better word to use right now, especially as everything was going so horribly wrong. A good word. Sheila watched him knot the towel quickly round his middle. He was definitely chunkier. More manly. It suited him. And changed him. She'd always thought of him as a boy . . . She yearned to see his penis. His prick. Was it hard, or was it soft? She'd longed for it all these months. Years, to tell the truth, because she knew she couldn't keep him to herself.

Well, at least he hadn't shoved it inside that woman just now. It would still be clean. He was keeping it ready for her after all.

'You can't bring a stranger here!' Her voice was shrill. 'You can't do – all that licking and sucking – to a stranger in my house.'

'*Our* house –'

'I hurried home especially, John. You know how I look forward to seeing you.' He was coming towards

12

her. She stared at the bulge under his towel. The urge to snatch the towel and grab at him was overwhelming. But she could still just about contain it. 'I've got supper planned. Harissa chicken. Baked in yoghurt and coriander.'

'Always thinking about food!' John patted her shoulder in a fatherly way he'd never used before. 'Wouldn't think it, would you, to look at her?'

'*I* usually poach it in stock first. But it sounds delicious.' The woman licked her lips and twisted her hair to get out the water. The American accent and the balloon lips reminded Sheila of Monica Lewinsky. 'I'm starved.'

'I've only catered for two.' Sheila bashed her arm at the shower. 'Could you please get out and leave us alone?'

'Sheila, this is Roxanne. Toby's wife. I've brought her over, to see a bit of little old London.' John's jaunty American accent was new, and fake. 'And to help me pack up.'

'Toby? Little Toby? What's he got to do with anything?' Sheila froze. 'And what do you mean, pack up?'

'You don't know about Toby? The money man behind this great development?' The woman, Roxanne, stood up. She was curvaceous, not as fat as she'd looked squashed up against the shower. In fact she was graceful, like the burlesque dancers Sheila had seen in Paris, with harem skirts swirling round their hips and tassels twirling on their nipples. 'And what do you mean, *little* Toby? He was pretty damn big last time I saw him.'

'I just meant I didn't know Toby was around again, let alone involved in your business.' Sheila's jaw was tight with anger. 'And I didn't know he had a wife.'

'Ex-wife. Oh, John, but she's sexy, huh? A librarian on the top half, with that high-neck sweater and the

13

prissy hairdo and the white face.' Roxanne stepped out of the shower. 'And a hooker down below! Check out those legs. She's not at all like you said.'

'That's because I've never seen her posing before. This must be what you looked like when you were modelling that lingerie in Paris.' John cocked his head. His eyes were half shut and gleaming with a familiar lustful expression. Despite everything it made Sheila's breath quicken. Now she had his full attention. 'I think I like it.'

'Don't you dare talk as if I wasn't here.' Sheila backed into the bedroom, fumbling for her skirt. She was certain "the white face" was turning red. 'I want you to leave!'

'Don't worry, that *is* the plan.'

'Not you, John. No, oh, no. I've been waiting for you. I've made this predictable little house in this anonymous little street our very own home. The *plan* is that it's just us now. You and me.'

The fire inside Sheila was frightening in its intensity. The image of John and Roxanne crashing about in the shower, skin shiny with water, the gradual, passionate silence, John lapping at Roxanne's – what would Maureen call that glistening red gash? – Roxanne's eyes glazing over. All of it flickered like an old film across Sheila's vision. Kept her burning.

They both followed her into the bedroom.

'You're very possessive, honey. And I can understand that.' Roxanne picked up a long silk dress flung messily over the wardrobe door, and sat down on the bed just behind Sheila. 'That's so sweet.'

Sheila whirled round. 'Haven't you got a husband to be sweet to?'

'Ex-husband.'

'Well, you can get your hands off mine.'

The curtains suddenly blew out from the window. White muslin with devore ivy design. Romantic, see

14

through, sleeping beauty curtains. No old-lady netting. And framing the window were the main curtains, a thick dark-pink brocade. They were still open, and a chill draught rushed across the room.

'Oh, we both know you don't have a husband. So that makes two of us!' Roxanne flung herself back on the bed. 'But we're not going to talk about all that ugliness, are we?'

'No.' A rictus grin blotted the shadow that had crossed John's face. 'Come on, Sheila. Chill out. I'm here now. There's food. We can all still enjoy our evening, can't we?'

Sheila closed her eyes as John came up behind her. He used that soothing voice when they were younger, because he was the older one. It's what made her fall for him. The words sounded foreign now. He'd been away a long time. She leaned against him, keeping her eyes closed. She didn't want Roxanne in her face, as Maureen would say. Puncturing the precious moment.

John was still. His hands rested on her shoulders. The place where he normally touched her at first. So respectable, you see. He always started there, as if refusing to allow himself to go further. Shoulders were so bony, but the pleasure of anticipation still shivered through her, triggering instant responses in all the other parts.

'That's right, honey,' the American woman drawled. 'You English should learn to chill. I hate to see you so uptight, girl. See how relaxed we are, after making out in that lovely shower. So I'm feeling generous with my man. I think she needs a little TLC, Johnnie.'

'Tell her to leave, *Johnnie*.' Sheila mimicked the accent.

She glared at her unwelcome guest, but Roxanne had moved away and was dropping the silk dress over her head so that the material clung briefly to the points of her nipples, even the hairs on her pubes, before settling

15

into a tight sheath. Sheila's eyelids fluttered in keeping with the fluttering in the pit of her stomach as John's hands started to move.

'Show her what you can do to a woman.' Roxanne was sitting on the chair now. She crossed her legs and started to brush her hair. It was drying into gold spirals. 'Go ahead. Show her what you've learned, Johnnie. She looks all dried up.'

'Dressing like this suits me fine.'

'I'm not talking about the sweater. Black is very elegant on you. But I'm talking about the sex, girl. The pussy. You're all shrivelled in there, aren't you?'

'I promised myself I wouldn't do this again.' John was still behind her, so Sheila couldn't possibly look him in the eye. 'But Roxanne is so persuasive.'

Sheila could see them all reflected in the darkened window. Her thighs glowed very white against the shadows of the room. She tried to move past the bed.

'I should draw the curtains. The people at number 43 can see us.'

The shadow was back across John's face. 'Maybe we should have taken the show home when we had the chance,' he muttered.

Sheila frowned, confused. 'This is our house, John. You picked it especially when I was stuck in Paris. You said it would suit me perfectly.'

'Anyway, what does it matter? They'll just love their new neighbour. These little English houses are all so close by.' Roxanne's voice was gravelly with amusement. 'They'll see you in a whole new light. Go on. It looks to me like you've waited way too long already.'

John paused, then laughed, too. Sheila could hear it rumbling in his chest. His hands moved down her shoulder blades, down her back. She went rigid. Her knees knocked slightly against the bed.

'Nearly fifteen years, isn't it?' he whispered, and before Sheila could form a reply he'd taken the hem of her jumper and plucked it right off, dragging out strands of her black hair as he did so. 'Since we first met?'

The draught from the window licked at Sheila's skin. 'Why are you talking about that now?'

'Because you're trapped in that long, hot summer, don't deny it. You still count up the days. Maybe I'm trapped, too, if we really analyse it. Because it was the time of our lives, wasn't it? You were seventeen. I was twenty. So young. So gorgeous.' John stroked down her ribs to her hips, moved on south to wrap his fingers round her thighs. No way could she stop this now, even if the whole of London was the audience. She heard the sharp rasp of Roxanne spraying perfume.

'This isn't how your homecoming should be. We can't – with her here –' moaned Sheila, powerless as his fingers reached her knickers and paused as they probed the dampness. 'Let's just get rid of this woman, and go eat and talk. Harissa chicken. You'll love it –'

'None of us could believe our luck when you showed up in the south of France. Such a surprise. Everyone had the hots for you. My mate Toby. Even Dad. How kinky was that?' He started to press harder, to rub his fingertips ruthlessly back and forth so that the fabric of her knickers crept into the crack. Sheila fell forwards, landed on her elbows on the bed. Instinctively she ground herself against his fingers to guide them towards the spot burning just inside, until he grazed it and sent shock waves through her.

'Your Dad? Now what's going on?' Roxanne's voice sounded miles away.

John went on speaking right into Sheila's ear, but she wasn't listening. She glanced again at the window, the curtains clapping gently together as if in applause. A flash of triumph sliced through her. She could see the figure of Roxanne, hovering in the background of the room. She wasn't so chilled now. So let her watch. She might regret prancing in here when she finds out about her precious John-boy.

He was leaning right over her now, thrusting his knee between her legs to part them. She tilted herself to reach him, and he yanked her pants down. 'You wanted me then, you little bitch on heat, and you want me now.'

'Whoa, Johnnie.' Roxanne jumped up with a little shocked gasp. She came and stood beside the bed. Very close. She was holding the hair dryer as if it was a gun, the silk of her ridiculously thin dress moving with a life of its own as the breeze blew it across her skin and trapped it right up between her shapely legs. Sheila watched as Roxanne hitched the dress right up and bent her knees on to the bed. She was either preparing to pray, or to join in the game.

Sheila closed her eyes. Roxanne could clearly see John's fingers, exploring inside her, fingernails excruciating on the sensitive flesh, making her jerk and moan afresh into the duvet.

'Oh, I'm not done yet. This conversation is long overdue.' John's fingers were working faster and harder now, sending electric shivers all over her. 'Why don't you go and fix us all a drink or something?'

By now Sheila didn't care whether Roxanne stayed or left. In fact, she wanted her to stay so John could work out whom he really wanted. She gripped the duvet as if it was a cliff face, as if the waves were coming up to drown her.

'Oh, I'm the one who's not done.' Roxanne was going nowhere. 'You're saying that Sheila here – this is so weird – I thought she just kept house for you, had a secret crush on you, sure, that's why she wore black and chased all the chicks off like some guard dog, but I didn't expect her to walk in here half naked, then she's watching you licking me out in the shower, now she's turned into a doggie wiggling her butt in the air all ready to take it up the ass –'

18

'She's all that, and a whole lot more, Roxie. So I guess it's time to introduce you properly.' The slightly American drawl matched a new laziness in John. Slowly he started to draw his fingers out. Tiny muscles right up inside Sheila panicked and gripped to keep him in there. She could hear, they could surely all hear, the saliva sounds as he drew her moisture out with him and wiped his hand casually on her leg. 'This is Sheila. My sister.'

Three

The growl of an approaching car fractured the stunned silence. Nothing odd about that. Several cars had come and gone since Sheila had unlocked her front door and gone inside. Spartan Street was designed specifically for executives, and this was the time of day that they came home to roost. But the menacing purr of this engine as it cruised, and the clanging statement that John had just made, made all three of them glad to have a reason to glance out the window. Because this was a car that would only be satisfied when it was unleashed at 120 down a long, empty road.

'Aston Martin,' murmured John, rolling off Sheila to lie back on the bed. 'I told you this was a classy area.'

'Only after you'd rebuilt it –' Sheila was breathless. She sat upright and tapped his chest. She leaned closer to sniff at him. 'Your vision turned a slum into a dream area.'

'You said it was predictable and anonymous!' John was smiling straight into her eyes at long last. 'You sure I picked the right house after all?'

'I loved it the minute I set foot in it.'

'Bravo! My God. What a pair!' There was a patter of clapping hands. 'And I thought I'd seen it all!'

Sheila had almost forgotten about Roxanne. It was so easy to slip back into the easy dialogue she and John shared when no one else was around; the mutual admiration. But Roxanne was around all right. In fact, Sheila was sandwiched between the two of them. They were both lying on either side of her like the recumbent lions on her fire grate in the living room. Comfortable as you like. On *her* bed.

Automatically she snapped her knees together. Her sex lips and the curls of hair there were still damp, but at least they were hidden now. All that covered her was her bra, and seeing the outline of Roxanne's breasts beneath the silk reminded Sheila that the bra, too, was far too sensible.

'Perhaps you can see why it's best that you leave,' she said to Roxanne, reaching up to pin the loose strands of hair back into place. 'Now that it's out in the open.'

'This is unfinished business I have to hear.' Roxanne was looking across Sheila at John. 'She's your *sister*?'

John raised his eyebrows at Sheila. Was he going to deny it, shove it back into the closet where they'd tried, and failed, to keep it hidden? She wouldn't let that happen. But the blatant lust still gleamed in his eyes.

'Half-sister.' He spoke first, stroking Sheila's thigh. 'Technically. Same father, different mothers.'

'You must be disgusted, Roxanne. I don't know how you can sit there.' Sheila crossed her arms. The sooner they could explain the scenario, the sooner Roxanne would be gone. 'Who'd want anything to do with a pair of perverts like us? We've been lovers for years. But we didn't know about each other till we were grown up. So for us, that makes it OK.'

'That makes it OK? My, my.' Instead of leaping away like a scalded cat, Roxanne stretched out on the bed, still holding the hair dryer. Behind her was the open window, and voices in the street. Roxanne smiled. Her mouth was as big as a slice of melon. '*Now* what would the neighbours say?'

'Oh, they'd never guess we're related. We act different. Dress different.' John's fingers were wandering

21

further up Sheila's leg. The car outside gave a final rev before killing the engine, and his head jerked towards the window. 'Sheila was so determined to fool the world she took the demure image a bit too far. No way does she look like a woman who shags her brother –'

'Don't make it sound so dirty, John.' Sheila leaned away from him so that she was hanging over Roxanne. 'You must be so jet lagged, Roxanne. Let me phone for a taxi.'

'She stays right here, Sheila.' John's fingers stopped stroking, started pressing warningly into her leg. 'I'm sorry, but she's part of the picture now.'

'The picture?' Sheila stayed where she was, hunched over the other woman. She liked this position. She was in charge. Roxanne's melon-slice smile was still in place, the red moist lips, cute white teeth, very blue eyes. 'Oh, there's no room for anyone else in this picture, I'm afraid.'

'Paint the picture for me, Sheila.' Roxanne said. 'Please.'

John was silent. Sheila could see herself reflected in the window, bare except for the narrow straps of the bra. It looked as if she was alone in the room. The sounds in the street had stopped now, and there was just a sliver of light coming from the opposite house.

'You won't like it.'

'Try me.'

Sheila leaned lower. Roxanne's perfume in her nostrils was thick and musky. 'We've never been able to tell this story to anyone, have we?' She glanced across at John. 'Sometimes I've wanted to explode with keeping the secret.'

'Explode away, honey.' Now it was Roxanne's hand on Sheila's leg.

'My mother didn't want me around once I was old enough to leave home,' Sheila began. 'She went off to the South of France with an old flame, Frederick, and when I heard they were married I decided to turn up to congratulate her. It's the only rebellious thing I've ever done. I'm really very shy.'

'You don't say.' Roxanne's hand was strangely soothing. Her other hand rested on her own leg and she was stroking it, under the silk.

'They were all busy with some grape harvest or something, and once I'd arrived they couldn't exactly chuck me out. She and Frederick barely noticed I was there, anyway. It was revolting –'

'At it like rabbits. They didn't care who saw them humping. On the balcony, by the pool, in the vineyard. In the end it was catching.' So John wasn't asleep after all. 'Actually, it was deliberate. They were trying to scare us all off.'

'I just pitched in to help.' Sheila glanced at him. The long bulge under his towel was growing. 'John used to watch me through the vine leaves. They shimmered, those leaves, in the sun.'

'Toby was staying with us that summer. He was her little stalker. That's why we called him little Toby.' John leaned over to Roxanne. 'She wore these crotch-eater shorts and tiny vests, you know? All that stretching and bending to pick the grapes. She was a walking wet dream.' He edged round behind Sheila and unsnapped her bra. 'Look at these. They were worth a fortune, once. On every advertising hoarding in France one season.'

As her breasts perked up into the air, Sheila saw them glowing white in the window. Still curving upwards, demanding the attention he never gave them. Not the way she *really* wanted it . . .

'I can see why you were a brassiere model,' remarked Roxanne, shifting further up the bed to lean on the pillows. Her dress wrinkled right up over her pubic hair, covering the neat line dividing her lips. 'What a pity to hide those tits in that plain outfit –'

'And you see why her mother didn't want Sheila around. Too much like competition. In the end she paid Sheila to quit the modelling. But that wasn't the real reason she tried to keep Sheila away from us that summer. She must have known we'd start to wonder why we looked so alike. We both look like our father. Black eyes, black hair –'

'Peas in a pod, now you're naked!' Roxanne parted her legs a little. 'How did I miss that just now?'

As Sheila watched Roxanne's fingers crawling up her own thighs, John started to touch her all over again. Sheila's stomach tightened with fresh desire. He was stroking down her spine where her bra strap had been, and her nipples hardened. There was nothing she could do about that. And Roxanne was staring at them.

'I was a virgin when I arrived in France. May as well tell her that.' Sheila was getting breathless again. Her nipples tingled, alerting her. She liked the way Roxanne was looking at them. It made her feel powerful, and defiant. 'I was never really interested in boys until that summer.'

'That's because you set eyes on John, and he looked like you,' Roxanne remarked, tapping her leg with the hair dryer. 'The ultimate ego trip.'

'I suppose so. I used to lie out on the parched earth of the vineyard to sunbathe, wait for him to find me.' She let her voice go girlish. 'You know. Waiting for him to deflower me.'

'That's so sweet!' Roxanne giggled and let her knees flop open.

'Imagine it,' continued John, bringing his hands round to the front and cupping Sheila's breasts in his hands as if offering them to Roxanne. 'She was the colour of golden syrup by the end of the summer, though you'd never think it to see this porcelain skin.'

'You wouldn't think it, no. Does it feel hard and cold, too, like porcelain? Or is there warm, red blood running

24

under there?' Roxanne stretched out to flick a hard red nipple, and Sheila jumped. There was a sizzling connection, and down inside there was an answering low throbbing. John never touched her there. He liked fondling her breasts as he took her from behind, squeezing them until she whimpered with the promise of pain, but no more. Would sucking her nipples be too much like a mother thing? The tip of Roxanne's tongue poked out between her big lips. Oh, Roxanne would know.

'There's warm red blood running in me, as you know,' John laughed, lightly massaging Sheila's breasts so that they seemed to expand in his hands. 'So I had to have her, didn't I? At the time I thought a holiday romance would cover it –'

Sheila reared up. 'I never knew you thought of it like that!'

'She was driving me wild. Just like you do, Roxie.'

'Go on. This is making me so horny,' Roxanne breathed, grabbing hold of the hair dryer. She started stroking the smooth plastic nozzle as if it were a phallus. 'Tell me how you did it.'

'In the wine cellar, after the bottling party, our parents started arguing so everyone was distracted. This one was standing in front of me. She was wearing the tiniest little sundress. But even then she nearly always wore black.'

John blew on Sheila's neck, another favourite trick. His body was warm and heavy behind hers. He wrapped one arm firmly round her and with the other threw the towel on the floor. As the functioning fragment of her mind nagged her to pick it up, Sheila felt a long hard shape thumping down on her bare buttocks.

'I'll never forget it,' she moaned, her body a tingling mass of nerve endings now, nothing more. 'I still dream about it every day.'

At the other end of the bed Roxanne had opened her legs wide and was angling the end of the hair dryer towards the livid red slit revealed there. She tapped the dryer idly on the soft, parted lips, twiddling the narrow nozzle in circular motions until she realised she was teasing herself, because her tongue came out again to slide across her mouth and she pushed the phallic shape further in. And now Roxanne's long fingers were burrowing in, easing her wider to manage the tip.

'Tell me how you fucked your sister, John.'

John parted Sheila's legs again with his knee. She felt him guiding the blunt end of his penis, his prick, under her. She tilted herself so that he could find the place, it must be flaming enough to see in the dark by now. He moved slowly back and forth between the cushions of her buttocks, separating them to move closer to the warm dark place where she wanted him to be.

'I didn't know she was my sister, remember,' said John. His voice was hoarse. 'She was bending to pour wine out of a barrel. We were all very drunk, but not so drunk that I couldn't get hard at the sight of these white panties she had on. I pushed her further into the cellar, between the barrels, the party was only a few feet away. There was only one way to do it, and I've liked it like this ever since –'

'I was so innocent. I didn't know you could take it from behind –'

'But you were already wet, like you knew what was coming,' he cut in, 'those cute white knickers practically dripped right off you.'

'It was tropical in there. We were sweating –'

'This story is so hot – I'm feeling so hot –' Roxanne was pushing the very tip of the hair dryer in and out of her crack, her fingers holding her open but her body kept closing over her fingers as if to eat them. Sheila had never seen another woman's bits, let alone so open and red and moist and releasing an achingly familiar scent like an exotic flower.

But John was nudging inside her now, keeping in time with what Roxanne was doing to herself, perhaps. And this was what Sheila wanted, above all else. First the tip, now more of him, inches of solid muscle.

'Everyone was partying, just the other side of these barrels, you know? We thought we were invisible. It was so wicked, doing it in the dark like that, they could see us if they just looked hard enough. And so I bent her over, such a sweet arse, my favourite bit of her, those knickers on the floor in no time, her long black hair flowing over her face and she's arched at me like a little minx, arms round this big fat barrel, bottom up, spreading her legs for me.'

Roxanne started rocking her buttocks on the bed, dancing about on her bottom as John spoke. The hair dryer looked as fascinatingly brutal as any cock, its blind nose burrowing at Roxanne's shocking-pink slit whenever she let it, but she kept holding it away as if to torment herself. Her head started to sway, her hips rotated on the bed, her tanned thighs fell further apart as the nozzle played between them, hovered over her pubic mound, still only flicking and stroking, but with each nudge her hips rocked more wildly.

John pulled at some pins in Sheila's hair, actually hurting her as he tried to loosen it.

'And then I fucked her. Just like this. With everyone standing around, drinking and chatting probably about us.'

John was the only one speaking now, his voice low and quiet, but they could both still hear him. Sheila saw Roxanne's pussy lips parting, heard the damp slick of the juices, knew hers sounded, felt, smelt the same.

But she was the one holding the solid length of male muscle inside. She let John ram her to and fro, feeling her muscles grip him tighter with each thrust until the peak approached again and as it did so she allowed herself a long hard look in the window. John's head bent beside hers, he was muttering into her neck now, Roxanne was in some kind of self-induced trance, but

27

she, Sheila, stared straight across the road at the tree branches waving back.

'And that's when they caught us.'

'Who caught you?'

Roxanne was drowsy and breathless. Sheila felt as if she was floating above the scene, apart from the glorious sensations of lust and triumph crackling inside her. She mouthed at whoever in Spartan Street might be watching.

'This enough for you? Enough of an eyeful?'

'Apparently it was poor little Toby.'

'Not so little,' Sheila murmured. 'He was cute.'

'Poor, because he had the hots for you. Little, because he was only sixteen.'

'My brute of an ex? Cute and sixteen?' Roxanne snorted.

'Well, he saw Sheila's bare feet. She used to paint her toenails pink. He thought she was stuck between the barrels, or something. He was going to help her, but then he saw my feet planted there between hers, and he yelled out, but we couldn't stop, just like we can't stop now –'

'No, don't stop now,' Roxanne groaned, burrowing her fingers into the curling nest, too many crowding in, pulling back, tangling in the line of blonde hair springing over her labia. Sheila could tell that keeping her thighs apart would heighten the pleasure, everything would be that much more exposed to pleasure and sensitivity so she spread her own legs a little wider, too.

'Can you imagine being caught rutting, right there in front of the grown-ups? We felt just like naughty kids. Can you imagine that awful silence, feet shifting about on the dusty floor, someone trying not to laugh, and something made us go on and on with it –'

'You're such a stud, Johnnie –'

'– we just kept on and on, there in the darkness, reeking of spunk and Burgundy –' John was enjoying this.

And so was Sheila. 'But Toby punched John, right out of the blue.'

'He didn't speak to me again for nearly ten years, not till we went into business over Spartan Street – that's how come I hadn't met you before, Roxie –'

'And then my mother had no choice, she had to tell us that her precious Frederick was actually my long-lost father so whoops, Johnnie, you can't have her, she's your sister –'

'And do you know what this hussy said to them all? Tell her, Sheila.' John's voice was gruff with approaching climax. 'It's so hard to believe. You were such a rebel back then.'

Sheila looked directly at Roxanne, saw her eyes glazing over again as she started to bring herself off. The nozzle grazed at the dark-pink slit as she held herself open, flicking it up and down.

'Tell her, Sheila.' John rammed inside her again.

She couldn't stop herself. She started to work herself frantically up and down John's shaft, he was being too slow, too much talking, her clitoris was raw now, she could do nothing except buck hard against him and moan it out.

'They're the ones who wanted to keep it in the family,' she gasped, not sure if either of her companions were listening any more. 'We used to chant it at school. I didn't know what it meant.'

The orgasm was rising, rising inside her.

'Go on, Sheila,' urged John, thrusting so hard they both shifted right up the bed, practically on top of Roxanne. 'Go on.'

'I just yelled back, I can't believe myself, I shouted, "Haven't you heard? Vice is nice, but incest is best."'

John whooped with laughter and Sheila knew he was hers. They were like pistons of the same engine. He rammed himself once, twice, as she slid up and down in front of him, heat building through her, crashing and burning, her arms collapsing under her own weight as he thrust inside her once more and then fell on top of her as the flood broke for all of them, all over the clean white duvet cover.

Within seconds the others had fallen asleep. Jet lag. Not surprising after a performance like that. Sheila had fallen across Roxanne's leg. She lifted her head and whispered right into the other woman's ear, 'Don't get comfortable, *honey*. You see, they were too late to stop us then. And you're too late to stop us now.'

She unhooked her dressing gown from the back of the door. She shivered with utter pleasure at the memory of what they'd done. They'd relived that first time all over again. Their secret was out in the open.

Outside the window the twigs of her wisteria scratched at the glass, scattering the last of its purple petals. There was quite a wind out there. Someone was walking along the pavement, bent against the weather.

Her stomach rumbled, and she ran down the darkened stairs. The lights came on and lit up the creamy new units, a smart new farmhouse kitchen right in the middle of London. She opened the built-in fridge and for a while she was too busy to think. She shredded coriander leaves and smeared the russet harissa and yoghurt mixture over the pale chicken breasts, ready for the oven.

Then she went to stand by the living room window, piercing a cherry tomato with her teeth and letting the juice spurt on to her chin.

Her mother was dead. Frederick was in Australia with his sixth wife. Not even poor little Toby could stop them now. And Roxanne would soon be gone. Everything was going to be just perfect.

Four

'And that's when they told me, after they'd eaten my harissa, after I'd pulled out all the stops to forgive them for the horror, the sheer *insolence* of finding them like that in my shower, after I'd actually made them *welcome* – after I'd made the house so perfect for John, after all the plans we'd made – that's when they told me they were leaving.'

Sheila leaned back, exhausted by repeating her sorry tale out loud. She closed her eyes. Her head was thumping. But the oversize calico cushion was so soft. Softer than anything she had on her sofas at home.

In fact, Cherie Vixen's house at number 51 might as well have been a million miles from hers. Oceans away from Spartan Street. Sheila had only travelled a few yards down the wet pavement from her own front gate, but it was like she'd arrived at an oasis. The temperature was tropical. Mysterious music – lutes plucking, cymbals shivering, the odd piano note – played from room to room, softly and with no real melody so that you thought you were imagining it. It drifted in and out of her ears like a breeze.

'Ambient music.' Her new neighbour hummed vaguely and she, too, sounded as if she was floating about somewhere in the air. She pronounced it in the French way, like *ambience*. 'We brought the CDs back from the Maldives. They play it everywhere there. In your bungalow when you arrive. They play it when they're massaging you. It pipes out of the palm trees on the beach. It plays in the bar. Totally dreamy, isn't it?'

Sheila nodded, and forced her eyes open again. As well as the music the air was filled with lovely fragrances. Everything was so bright. She especially liked the way you could catch the weak rays of autumnal sun in here. She wished she had a conservatory extension like this filled with white wicker furniture, raffia blinds and glass tables. It made number 44 look positively medieval.

'So you're saying that the bastard left you there and then? In the middle of the night?' Cherie put her coffee cup down carefully so that it wouldn't rattle on the saucer. 'Excuse my French. I'm so upset for you.' She moved up the sofa and patted Sheila's leg. 'But it's healthier to share it. Don't be a stranger. You can confide in me.'

'He left the next morning, actually. So you see, he'd never had any intention of playing house with me.' Sheila looked down at Cherie's hand, resting on her black skirt. Small, evenly tanned, not a single freckle, several diamond and sapphire rings sparkling away to match her bracelets, and white-tipped nails manicured in the new, shorter style. Not those evil chipped talons which the girls in the office favoured and kept snapping off on their keyboards.

'Playing house? What a childish way of putting it!'

Sheila glanced up into Cherie's wide-apart, pale-blue Bambi eyes. Actually it was *her* expression. That's exactly how she saw her life with John. Playing house. Angry tears pricked at her eyes. 'I don't know what I'm going to do all on my own over there!'

Cherie's thin eyebrows were very slightly puckering across her unlined brow. It was hard to tell under the caramel powder dusting the pretty face, but surely she was too young for those Botox injections Sheila had read about in Maureen's magazine?

'So you're saying that after all this insult, after you'd come home after a tough day at the office, you poor thing having to work, only to find them shagging in your shower –'

Sheila's stomach tightened. Cherie's language summoned up that same fluttering sensation sliding down her stomach, down between her legs. How could she still feel aroused by it?

'He was giving her – I can't say it – you know, oral sex. They weren't actually having intercourse. Not then, anyway.' She bit her lip, saw John's dark head ducking and diving, the water streaming off him. 'You know. He was just – he was licking her.'

'He was *just* – You caught your husband with his tongue in another woman's muff? It's like one of our – it's like a dirty movie!' An appalled squeal escaped Cherie's frosted lips. 'We're talking full-on cunnilingus?'

'It was terrible, Cherie. He belongs to me!' Sheila felt the words tumbling out more easily, the more she described it. Cherie Vixen was right. It was helpful to share. Little by little the heartache was receding, and it had only been a week. Like the tide going out, leaving the beach exposed. And something else, she couldn't work out what, was already stirring, waiting to replace it. Something hard, like pebbles, not soft, like sand. She leaned a little closer to Cherie. 'How would you feel if you saw your husband –'

'How could you forgive your husband and this tart? After seeing him sticking his tongue into her? You must be some kind of saint!' Cherie pushed at a stiff, white-blonde curl bouncing over her temple. 'How could you calmly go ahead with the harissa dish?'

'I had all the food in. I'd already marinaded the chicken in olive oil and lime. It would have been a waste.' Sheila wondered why she was the one comforting Cherie. 'You should try some of my cooking some time.'

'You could think about food at a time like that?' Cherie had jumped up and was shaking her head into one of the many mirrors around her house. She gaped at her reflection. 'And these two adulterers just bunked down for the night and carried on screwing the living daylights out of each other?' Another stiff curl of hair joined the first one, as if in protest.

'They were in my bed, actually –'

'I don't believe it! All this happening in this very street!' Cherie covered her mouth to hide the shriek of outrage, then turned to face Sheila and slapped her hands down her white wool trousers. 'And you were under the same roof, down the hall, sobbing away in your own spare room? Why did you let them do it to you?'

'What else could I do? Call the police?' *And be found having a threesome with my half-brother, because I thought that was the way to keep him?*

Cherie was searching for the answer to that one when the doorbell chimed melodically into the scented atmosphere. Both women jumped. Cherie gave up fussing with her hair and waggled her fingers at her guest. 'Stay right there, Sheila. That's Flora from number 33. She's another one who's been gagging to get a good look – I mean, you must meet her –'

'Amazing how you've all got to know each other so quickly,' Sheila mused, sitting down again. 'I thought nothing ever happened in this neighbourhood.'

'Lots of time on our hands!' Cherie trilled. 'We're the English desperate housewives, didn't you know? Without the kids, thank God.'

Sheila took another sip of vanilla and mocha coffee. 'I'm so sorry, Cherie. You shouldn't have to hear such degrading – I won't burden you with any more detail.'

'Hush, hush. I'm glad to help.' Cherie's heels clacked across the terracotta tiles of the conservatory then sank into the white carpet of the living room as she trotted to answer the door. 'And believe me, from what you're saying, plenty goes on in this neighbourhood!'

Guilt poked at Sheila. She wasn't being straight with this kind woman. But how could she possibly tell the truth? Cherie Vixen's false eyelashes would drop off if Sheila told her what really happened at number 44 – that she and her "husband" and his American floozy had all three gone back to bed full of harissa chicken and several bottles of Californian Chardonnay and she'd been dragged into being their willing pupil for the night.

No talking this time, no stories to tell, just heavy breathing in the candlelit silence as they got her drunk and showed her it didn't always have to be doggie-fashion, and how many times three went into two.

'Come through to the kitchen, Sheila!' Cherie called from somewhere miles away. 'Come and meet Flora Fox!'

Sheila sighed. She'd been reluctant enough at first to be ushered into Cherie's house. And though talking about it was easing the pain a little, she wasn't in the mood to be polite to another bright perky neighbour.

She followed her hostess's voice through the quiet cream and white house and realised why the cold reality of John's defection hadn't yet hit her. It was because every time she moved, her legs still ached. The muscles at the top of her thighs twanged like guitar strings to remind how she'd balanced herself on her heels, gritting her teeth as she obeyed Roxanne's order to sit on her face because John would love her for it. Roxanne parted her sex lips and lapped at her until Sheila forgot why she was squatting there, why she would want to be anywhere else, wanted to trap Roxanne's warm wet tongue inside, but it just got better, because the tip of Roxanne's tongue had located the bud of her clitoris and started to encircle it so that Sheila couldn't stop jerking about as if she'd been electrified. Then Roxanne closed her big lips around the clit and started sucking mercilessly so that tiny ripples of fire followed her tongue, flicking like several snakes to build up the pressure.

There were peals of high laughter from Cherie's big kitchen. The two women were busy carrying shopping bags in through the back door. Sheila leaned in the doorway for a moment, feeling dizzy. She could barely remember where she was. This white house full of light and air was so different from the velvets and dark reds and green luscious plants of her own.

On her bed Roxanne had pulled her down and her tongue pushed right inside, flickering from side to side as Sheila's body tried to suck her right in. She didn't think the pleasure could get any more intense, and John was somewhere in the room, watching or filming she didn't know which. He would never want to go back to New York now. They'd watch it together, perhaps it would show how Roxanne inserted one finger, then another, into Sheila's pussy until she was filled with jabbing fingers and the relentless sliding of her tongue . . .

But John had gone back to New York.

And this wasn't Roxanne dumping a bulging Waitrose bag on the granite work surface of the kitchen island and coming towards her. This was another blonde woman, smaller and slimmer than both Roxanne and Cherie, her silky hair pulled back in a neat ponytail, like one of those Russian tennis players, and like a tennis player she was wearing a white velveteen tracksuit which she was slowly unzipping.

Behind her Cherie was running her finger round the lid of an ice cream carton and licking off the chocolate. Roxanne had licked the cream from her just like that.

'This is the poor creature I found outside on the pavement,' Cherie was saying, hitching one neat buttock on to a bar stool. 'Sheila's from number 44.'

'So good to meet you at last.' Flora didn't shake her hand, but smiled as she tossed her track top to one side. She sniffed her armpits and giggled, then ran her hands down her ribs, tightening the tiny vest to the texture of cling film so that her sharp nipples were clearly visible. Her face was less made up than Cherie's, but had the same evenly tanned skin and zero wrinkles. 'Excuse me for undressing. I'm so sweaty. Been working out at the gym, then had to do all this shopping for lazybones here.'

'Only because Jamie took my Merc to play golf today,' Cherie piped up, peering inside one of the bags. 'Did you get the black olive hummus?'

'I ought to go. I've got an appointment at the agency.' But Sheila couldn't move. The two women danced about like a couple of pale blooms, and their pretty, air-headed friendliness was like a balm. Like lilies of the field, she thought wearily. They toil not, neither do they spin.

'Agency?' the lilies both queried.

'Now that John's left me to run the house on my own I've got to find another job.'

Cherie and Flora stopped pulling asparagus out of elastic bands and cocked their heads questioningly.

'To pay the bills?'

'You poor, poor thing.' Flora's pretty face slid downwards in a pout that was meant to represent sorrow. 'Cherie's told me about your disaster. Your husband's just buggered off?'

'That's why I dragged Sheila in here.' Cherie kicked off a high-heeled ankle boot and curled one foot under her. These two seemed anxious to rid themselves of their clothing. Sheila tweaked the cuff of her blouse as Cherie threatened to re-run the entire morning's saga. 'I found her, absolutely distraught, standing by the gate of number 44 just staring into space –'

'Actually I was trying to see into number 43 –'

37

'Oh, it's still empty.' Flora stepped closer to her, unscrewing the lid of a mineral water. 'Was it another woman?'

'Worse than that!' Cherie nearly clapped her hands with the thrill of it, and quickly diverted them to unpacking the aubergines. 'Poor Sheila caught them at it in the shower.'

A flush spread across Flora's high cheekbones as her little mouth dropped further open. 'You saw your husband screwing another woman?'

'Licking her –' Cherie corrected. 'Do excuse her French as well, Sheila! We don't want you to think we're downmarket or anything!'

'Look, I'm not such a victim.' Sheila sighed again, not knowing whether to laugh or cry at the way they couldn't seem to get enough of the gory details. 'It was my fault just as much.'

'How is it your fault?' Cherie wagged her finger in the air, and Flora, still fixing Sheila with a caring expression, nodded vigorously. 'You're the saint around here. No one deserves that kind of behaviour. I mean, bringing your mistress to your new house, just when your wife wants to make a good impression, and making her watch while you –'

'I'm sorry if my sordid business lets down the tone of the neighbourhood.' Sheila wanted to go home now. She wanted to lick her wounds in private, if there was no one else to lick them for her.

'*Au contraire*.' Flora tipped water into the back of her throat. 'It livens the place up no end.'

Cherie examined her nails. 'Don't forget we're all new residents around here, Sheila. Maybe there isn't a "tone" to the neighbourhood yet. It was condemned before it was redeveloped.'

'I know that perfectly well,' Sheila said before she could stop herself. 'My brother developed it.'

'Your brother is John Moss?' Cherie stretched to open her Smeg and put two bottles of wine inside.

38

'Yes.'

'So he has the same name as your rotter husband? How confusing.'

'So what Cherie means to say,' said Flora, sniffing at a bar of peach soap, 'is that no one's lived in Spartan Street before. At least not for decades. There's no old lady twitching her net curtain, no busybody organising the Neighbourhood Watch.' She giggled, and glanced back at Cherie. 'So maybe I'd better appoint myself the one to look out for scandal!'

'There should be plenty of frisky ghosts around.' Cherie popped the lid off some Pringles. 'There was a brothel on your side of the street, you know.'

'My house, to be precise. That's why John chose it.' Sheila tried a hearty laugh. They hadn't noticed her near slip-up. Cherie and Flora both had the same dimples in their mask-like cheeks when they smiled. 'So I'm on the wrong side of the tracks, you see.'

'Ah, but your properties are slightly higher up than ours, didn't you know, so actually you can see right over our rooftops on a clear day.' Cherie shook back her hair, and there was a faint whiff of hair spray. 'Your house may be narrower, and you've got that kind of garret at the top, but look at the view from there!'

'And the view from here is everything going on in your house, if we had telescopes!' Flora took a handful of Pringles and crunched them in her teeth. Was that a flash of malice in the preternaturally cornflower-blue eyes?

Sheila started to back out into the hallway. 'You should be an estate agent, Cherie.'

'Funny you should say that!' Her hostess reached over and gave a little nudge, her knuckles digging into the softness of Sheila's breast. 'For my sins I ran the site office here. You know, showing prospective buyers round the show home. It almost kept me out of mischief. Didn't I show you round?'

'There was no need to look around. I – we – came here straight from Paris. Obviously I knew whatever John designed would be perfect.'

'I can see the resemblance, now you mention it. Of course! Those beady black eyes. Your brother, eh?' Cherie put her finger up to her lips again and tapped the nail against her teeth. 'Tall, dark guy barking orders into a mobile phone –'

'That sounds like him.' Sheila gave a tight laugh. 'Though I've never seen him at work.'

'Probably a good thing. He sounds like a right stud.' Flora elbowed Cherie in the ribs. 'You wouldn't stop talking about him, Cherie! It was one of the first intimate conversations we ever had.'

Cherie blushed and picked an imaginary piece of thread off her immaculate trousers. 'A bit incestuous talking about him in front of his sister, isn't it?'

'What about your reputation, trollop! Talk about the tone of the neighbourhood –'

'What do you mean, "stud"?' Sheila sidled back into the room. Cherie jumped off her stool and offered it to Sheila. She climbed up awkwardly. It was still warm. 'Did he harass you in the show home?'

Both the women let out squeaks of amusement and just as quickly stifled them.

'I've never heard it called a show home before!' squealed Flora. 'Go on, Cherie. At least let the lady know her brother wasn't a sexual harasser. You were just as up for it as he was.'

'Yeah, but don't for God's sake tell my Jamie.' Cherie lowered her eyes and actually battered her lashes at Sheila. 'Do you really want to hear what happened? Really, he was the perfect gentleman.'

'And an eye-watering lay as well!' Flora snorted through her nose like a naughty schoolgirl. 'I'm getting out the Penis Grand.'

'She means the Pinot Grigio,' explained Cherie,

increasingly flustered. 'You must excuse her. Face of an angel. Mouth like a sewer.'

'Pot and kettle, darling. Just get the screwdriver.'

'My brother's always had a way with women,' Sheila said, accepting a glass after all. It seemed the fastest way of joining their curious little club.

'You should be proud of him.' Cherie slung one leg over another stool and sipped at her wine. Flora jumped up on to the granite work surface and wiggled her ankles, ready to listen. 'He's incredibly well hung!'

Sheila's wine went down the wrong way and she choked, making the others laugh. 'Is he?' Well, she'd had precious little to compare him with?

'It can be fucking boring sitting in those show homes. Lovely, you know, dusting the surfaces and handing out those little bags that look like shower caps for people to put over their shoes to stop them mucking up the carpet, but –'

'Don't be such an old woman. She's obsessed.' Flora poured herself another glass. Her ponytail was slipping. She winked at Sheila, her eyelid descending very slowly like a doll's. 'I'm an absolute slut when it comes to housework. Thank God for cleaners.'

'And at weekends business was slower still. So they made me spend my time photocopying brochures and particulars, you know, plans and so on.'

'So you were bending over the desk –' Flora prompted her, but Cherie had gone bright red again and was dabbing at her top lip. 'Like a Carry On film.'

'It's the first job I've ever done. And definitely the last. You mustn't tell Jamie. Ever. He thought sitting in that show home all day would be good for me.'

Sheila just raised her glass in solemn promise. If vengeance was to be hers, this Jamie Vixen would surely join her.

'It *was* good for you!' Flora butted in. 'You said it spiced things up no end –'

Cherie gave a little shake of her head. 'Anyway, it was back in the summer, and I was wearing a gorgeous kaftan dress, not really businesslike, but he didn't care about that, I just had to look smart. And he marched in, jetted straight in from Paris, so glamorous he is, and we were chatting. I was sitting on the edge of the desk a bit nervous, you know, and my dress kept riding up.'

'Did you know he had a fiancée?' Sheila mumbled into her glass.

'No, but he knew I had a husband. He'd met Jamie several times, poring over the plans. Didn't stop him, did it?' Cherie tilted her chin. 'Didn't stop me, either. I know I was shameless, but he was so impressed by my sales figures.'

Flora snorted again and wriggled matily up to Sheila. 'She's obsessed with her figure all right. Won't be truly happy till she's shed that stubborn stone.'

'Well, the sun was blazing on the double glazing, and we couldn't get the windows open, and I couldn't leave the office in case the phone rang, and actually it did ring and I leaned across him to answer it, he was in my chair, and he suddenly pulled me over. So I was straddling him. You know, in his lap.'

Sheila sat very still in her own chair. 'It was the heat. It overcame you, I suppose.'

Cherie was near the end of her glass. Her blue eyes were less innocent now. 'He was already overheated, I can tell you. Boy. He started stroking up under my dress, right up my legs to my stomach, and he had the smile of a man used to getting his own way, a bit like my Jamie, and he said something about working his way through all the princesses in the street, but I could hardly speak by now, my skin was crawling with excitement, you know?'

Sheila and Flora nodded wordlessly, their glasses hovering in the air in front of them.

'I did say that I should get back to work, someone might come in, but all the while his fingers kept swiping and stroking across my hips and stomach, never going higher or lower. I kept glancing at the door, and he just kept murmuring, he's like a horse whisperer. A woman whisperer. I was so, like, hypnotised that he was able to kiss me, and I let him, because actually I was waiting for him to do something more exciting.' Cherie slumped slightly in her chair. 'How evil is that?'

'And you were the one so outraged about him doing all that in the shower,' Sheila remarked, taking a long swallow of wine. She regretted staying around to listen to this.

'Your husband, you mean?'

Sheila didn't reply. Her thoughts had scattered.

'I know I'm awful, but at least this time it was me that was being unfaithful. I can't be outraged at myself, can I?'

Flora spluttered into her drink while Sheila tried to work out the logic.

'Well anyway, there wasn't any time for thinking. There I was, plonked on to his lap, I must have creased his suit trousers, but under my dress his hands were busy and do you know what he was doing?'

'Fingering you?' begged Flora.

Please stop, thought Sheila. Her John, straddled by this mannequin. How many other "princesses" had there been? The last of the wine in her glass burned down her throat.

'Undoing his trousers! Very businesslike, I don't think! But the woollen of his trousers was already rough on my – thick fabric for summer, and I wasn't wearing any knickers, you see.'

'Ooh,' said Flora, tipping the bottle over Sheila's glass.

'All that friction made me wriggle about on his knee, it was turning me on, but he lifted me away while he was

43

trying to get it out, and I had to balance on my knees, but the urge to lower myself onto his groin was almost irresistible.'

Outside her kitchen window rain was falling on the perfect privet hedge.

'Then he said, "Does your husband have one like this?" and he lowered me back down on to him and there was this enormous cock. I was sitting on it like some kind of rocking horse and it was a great thick thing spreading open my pussy lips. I had to bite my lips. I had to feel it. It was vast. Already slippery from where I'd been sitting on it, it was all swollen and stiff, it was as big as a, as big as a –'

'Rolling pin?' Sheila crossed one leg over the other to try to still the quivering of her own pussy. Now she knew why whenever she rolled out pastry she'd thought of John.

'Almost! And the end of it was already beading up with spunk, you know, like a teenager's! They're always so keen, aren't they, when they're young, they're always ready to burst!'

Cherie drew breath. Her legs spread wider on the stool seat. She'd forgotten to be ladylike now. She was sitting like a cowboy, and rocking very slightly to and fro.

'There was a boy at school we used to call Duracell,' snuffled Flora, wiping her mouth with the back of her hand. 'Because he was Ever Ready!'

The two girls cackled. Sheila had to smile. She really had to. She didn't want to look like the prude Maureen thought she was. She remembered little Toby was like that. Ever Ready. He'd pulled her aside one hot day in the vineyard, and told her so.

'Anyway, he told me not to be so gentle with it, it wouldn't break. So I'm afraid I didn't need much more invitation. I put the tip against me, and the second it touched me there I made this groaning noise, so filthy,

44

and he pushed me down so that his cock was right inside, every throbbing inch of it. I wondered how much room there was, I'd never seen anything so enormous, but I was expanding to let him in, I was impaled on this great rod –'

'Sounds agonising!' Sheila remarked. Her voice came out in a hiss.

'Oh, Sheila. Do you mind me talking like this? He is your brother and everything. Perhaps this is a bit too much –'

'I think it makes you sound like a gymnast. But you can't stop the story now. You're telling it far too well,' chortled Flora, dropping to the floor and ripping open a bag of peanuts. She sketched a dance move with several pelvic thrusts. 'We're almost creaming it ourselves!'

'Did he do it from behind?' Sheila had to know.

Cherie shook her head a trifle impatiently. 'We didn't have time to experiment with positions!' Her knees were opening and closing. 'He just sat back, his hands still loose on my hips, and down I went, right down to the base of it. It just got bigger and bigger inside me –'

'Like one of your home-made loaves!' Flora knocked at one of the metallic instruments dangling from a rack above the hob.

'Did he touch your nipples?'

Cherie slid off her stool and had started pacing about the granite flooring. Now she was too absorbed to be surprised at Sheila's question. 'No. It was like his cock was all there was. And it was addictive. Once I'd started I couldn't stop. Even when the phone rang again, he didn't stop. He braced against the back of the chair and took the call. Actually it sounded like he was having a row. In French, maybe so I couldn't understand. I was just getting wetter, jerking about like a puppet, watching his cock going at me and he was saying, "You'll keep your hands off my house!" or something, into the phone. All these property tycoons shafting each other – anyway he cut the call short and just reared at me and grabbed me, pumping up so hard it nearly threw me to the ceiling and then I was coming, and goddammit he lifted me off him, it took ages to slither out and it was still hard, but he plonked me on to my feet and somehow packed it away in there, zipped himself up, and do you know what the rush was?'

Both the others were agog. Flora was astride Cherie's stool and she and Sheila were both quite obviously rubbing themselves up against the leather seats. 'Why did he push you off?'

'Because I'd clean forgotten about the clients who'd been looking round upstairs! They were standing in the doorway, clutching their particulars! They'd seen everything!'

Flora waved the packet of crisps around, screeching wildly. 'They'd probably been bonking in the bedroom!'

'And your brother, Sheila, he was so cool. So cool.' Cherie returned to the fridge and leaned against it. 'He just rested one arm on the desk, crossed one leg over the other and said "Thank you, Mrs Vixen", for all the world as if I'd just taken the minutes.'

Sheila's head was spinning. This was the time to spill the beans. Tell precious Cherie Vixen that she didn't have a husband at all. Just a well hung brother.

But instead she turned to walk, one foot directly in front of the other, towards the back door. She wanted to get out. She wanted to re-run that story again, in the privacy of number 44, and vent her anger.

At the door she turned and sniffed. 'At least one of us has a decent love life.'

'Oh, now you're offended,' gasped Cherie, her hands over her face again. 'It never happened again. I'm so married to Jamie –'

'Enough said,' added Flora. 'We're sorry. So tactless.'

The girls moved closer to each other, wrapping their arms round each other's tiny waists and assumed identical expressions of sympathy. 'Have some more Penis – Pinot.'

'I really have to get down to the agency. I don't know how I'm going to manage –'

'Think of us as your friends, Sheila. Friendly neighbours.' The blonde, white-clad women nodded eagerly. 'Anything we can do to help. Can't bear to think of you slaving away in some dingy office.'

'Or a shiny show home?' Sheila did up the buttons on her tweed coat. A nasty streak in her enjoyed Cherie's blush of confusion. 'Actually, you've done me a favour, Cherie. A big, big favour.' A strange, girlish perfume on the collar reminded her suddenly of little Tessa from the office. 'Put me off men for life, in fact!'

They echoed the laugh uncertainly. No doubt thinking of their own poor husbands.

'I'm sorry about your brother. Please don't think badly of him.' Cherie remembered her manners, saw Sheila to the door. The back door, admittedly.

'Quite the reverse, I would have thought,' added Flora, looking at her watch behind Cherie's back.

'And I'm sorry about your husband, too. Oh dear.'

'Don't worry about me and John.' Sheila patted her hair, her serenity restored. 'We're permanently estranged.'

Five

The temperature outside had taken a dive and suddenly job hunting was the last thing on Sheila's mind. For all her cool dismissal of her brother and his antics, her composure was, as always, mostly on the surface. Inside, this latest revelation about him had left her reeling.

She clicked briskly down Cherie's rubbish-free path, aware of two pairs of perfectly mascara'd eyes trained on her posterior. She'd been on a mission this morning before Cherie had accosted her. Now she was too distracted to focus on her list of duties for the day ahead. Was it having John rammed into her face again, hearing about his antics with Cherie Vixen (while just across the road she, Sheila, was probably lovingly blending mangoes for his supper)?

Or was it the weird fact that Cherie describing the scenario in the show home was so graphically sexy, it was like watching a film? Her John, screwing the comely and willing Mrs Vixen in broad daylight. Did the clients get horny when they walked in on them? Sheila flushed. She stopped dead at the end of the path. Because she was horny, just thinking about it. Did that make her a voyeur? Because it was sexy to watch? And watching was safer, because you were removed from the action and under no obligation to perform. Was that why she'd been turned on by that display in her own shower, too, even while it broke her heart?

She pinched herself hard on the arm, her habit when she deserved a chiding. Thoughts of John could wait. It was her visit to number 51 that was distracting her. She'd basked in all that unaccustomed attention. Cherie and Flora clucking round her, pressing her to talk. Two people, strangers really, expressing an interest in her life, her situation. OK, so they'd tittered about the dirty bits, but then she needn't have been so precise about those, need she? She'd wanted to tell all, stop being so mealy-mouthed about it. Had they encouraged her? Whatever. It was totally natural for a wronged woman to spit it all out, warts and all!

So they'd listened, made all the right noises. Maybe it was feigned. Maybe they were laughing at her. But it was a hell of a long time since she'd felt any kind of solidarity with anyone, especially female.

Even in her modelling days, when she and the other waifs huddled their bony bodies for warmth in freezing studios and warehouses dressed in scraps of satin and lace while their innocence fled, she always ran back to John for comfort. And look at how miserably she'd got on with Maureen and the girls in that horrible office, for God's sake. Other people were like so many mosquitoes buzzing and whining around her, never actually getting a bite. Because her whole life had revolved around John.

She wondered what her new neighbours were saying about her, right this minute. She tensed up. Was this embarrassment? Had she gone too far, telling them? Or self-pity? Was this a new kind of satisfaction she was feeling? She was only walking down a garden path, but it was almost as if she was stepping out of some long dark shadow.

She pulled her coat closer round her as she reached the gate. They might think she was some kind of alien landed in their pampered world, but if they *were* so intrigued by her and the way she'd been abandoned, why not give them more? Exaggerate a little. Anything to hide the incestuous truth, after all. And that way, if she was really destined to be on her own from now on, maybe they'd befriend her, ask her round for coffee or cocktails one day, let her into their perfect little lives once in a while.

She let her shoulders droop and turned to lift her gloved hand. Cherie and Flora showed identical dimples as they smiled goodbye through the kitchen window, then in a mirrored movement waggled their fingers back at her. Their cheeks were pressed together like two soppy little girls in one of the pastel Victorian postcards she liked to frame and stick around her fireplace.

She was about to turn away when Flora suddenly grabbed the big breasts swelling under Cherie's white mohair sweater. Sheila blinked to be sure. She might look plain peculiar now, hovering about by the gate, but not as peculiar as these two. Flora was definitely fondling Cherie's breasts. Cherie continued smiling and waving as if Flora's hands were new kitchen utensils.

Then Flora obviously decided to give her prim new neighbour a little more for her money. She shifted behind Cherie, and her little hands came up round Cherie's throat. A friendly touch, perhaps, but then she started squeezing, so that Cherie's eyes went wide, but then so did her mouth, into a toothsome grin. Flora dipped her head and started to lick Cherie's ear lobe, her fingers closing round Cherie's throat. Cherie tipped her head back on to Flora's shoulder. Flora was licking and biting her way down Cherie's arched throat. Her frosted lipstick must be leaving a sticky trail over the pulse going in Cherie's neck. Cherie started to sway as if she was slow-dancing. Perhaps she couldn't breathe. Flora looked as if she was trying to strangle her. But then why were they both maniacally smiling? And why was Cherie now sensuously kneading her own breasts where Flora had left off, rubbing the flat of her hands over the white mohair sweater, letting it ride up over her generous white stomach?

So much for neighbourly interest or admiration! If Sheila's eyes weren't deceiving her, it was each other they were into. Not her. Sheila was a stupid, stupid fool. As she gaped, Flora stared brazenly out at her. No more cute dimples. Cherie's eyes closed and she started to rub her white-trousered crotch against the stainless steel sink. The same gaping crotch that John had pushed his cock into until Cherie was spinning on it.

Sheila was shaking now. She wanted to run, be sick, but she couldn't move. Flora let go of Cherie's throat, leaving four fingerprints on each side. Smiling, she lifted the white sweater right up and yanked Cherie's bra downwards, so that her enormous breasts lolled forward, totally bare. Cherie stuck her tongue out with pleasure. She caressed her breasts lovingly, moulding the soft white flesh like so much dough while Flora pinched the large brown nipples into thick hard points, rolling and pinching them between her fingertips, pulling them viciously into longer points. Sheila's own ultra-sensitive nipples hardened and tingled in response, knowing how good that would feel.

There was something loose about Cherie, like an overblown schoolgirl, the way she swayed about, wound up by Flora but now knocking her smaller friend sideways, lost in her easy ecstasy. The way she ground herself against the kitchen sink, her breasts flopping about for all the world to see. Sheila was pretty sure she'd forgotten she was being watched. But Flora hadn't. She calmly slid her hand down the flat front of Cherie's white trousers, where a dark wet patch was growing. Cherie's thighs folded round Flora's fingers. Still staring straight out of the window, Flora gave another one of her strange winks, her eye closing very slowly while the rest of her face remained motionless.

51

Then she reached up, released the ruffled blind, and the two perfect neighbours scrolled out of sight.

Talk about being left out in the cold. Sheila left the gate swinging and broke into a run, dashing across the road and causing a dark car to brake violently. Back into a silent, dark, cold number 44. Her nest. Up the stairs. Go to your room. Time to face it. She was alone now.

She was about to fling herself down on the bed when the curtains rippled out in a kind of greeting. She glanced outside. The house opposite, number 43, looked back blindly.

She unbuttoned her black coat. She was going nowhere today. Her nest was the safe house where she would always return. The oasis of Cherie's picture-perfect interior had shattered, like a kaleidoscope. Reformed itself into something quite else. The set of a porn flick. A club to which she didn't belong. A club where women touched each other's breasts and pussies at elevenses. She thought of Flora's little hands tweaking and fiddling with Cherie's huge nipples. She couldn't help it. She slid her own hands up her jumper.

She was lonely up there in her bedroom. And jealous. That was the surprising truth of it. Pure and simple. And the truth, as Oscar Wilde said, is rarely pure and never simple. The knot in her stomach was nothing to do with being hurt over John now, not really. She would brood about him later, probably, and what he'd done with Cherie, and Roxanne, and the tarts in the apartment in Paris, and all the others, but right now she couldn't get those perfect housewives out of her head. She wanted Flora, or someone like her, someone cool and immaculate, to touch her like she had touched Cherie. Casually, and often, just like swapping recipes. *Come round for skinny latte and a grope, darling. Come and see my show home.*

A weak bubble of mirth popped somewhere in her chest, surprising her. So she was able to laugh about it now, was she? Why wasn't she totally, utterly shocked? Two women groping and fondling like that? Wanting to try it herself? Sheila tossed her coat on to the bed and sat down heavily. She smoothed her hand over the duvet. This is where the three of them had romped the other night. ("Romp" was how Maureen's magazines would describe what she and John and Roxanne had done the other night.) She nodded as if agreeing with an internal audience. The reality of that scenario was hitting home. The reality she'd kept from her nosy neighbours. John assumed he was the leader that night, swallowing down her delicious supper then coaxing her into their cosy threesome. She thought that meant he was back for good. He thought he was sugaring the pill, sharing the insatiable Roxanne for one night. But actually it was Roxanne who had initiated it. Roxanne who was the first woman to touch her. Who was now a fading memory, a tropical bloom planted at the head of her bed with her Venus flytrap mouth opening to snatch at her.

And now she was curious to know more. Those two women over the road weren't a couple of overheated schoolgirls, for all their giggling. Or a pair of love-starved models, such as she'd known when she was young. They were housewives with kitchens and conservatories and, for God's sake, husbands. Groomed women with hard faces and filthy minds. She could have been like that, couldn't she, if John hadn't moulded her from the start into a spinster? So was it a woman she wanted now? Had her life with John ruined other men for her? One day she wanted fingers to peel away her clothing to expose her swelling breasts nestling in their expensive lace bra. Female fingers, male fingers, any fingers to touch her.

Sheila shivered and kicked her shoes off. She liked to feel pleasure stirring under her clothes. She liked to keep something on. She liked finding her way in through lace and cotton and wool until she made contact with bare skin. The barrier of clothing made anticipation all the sweeter. John used to take her doggie-style, push her down on to her knees in the hallway when she was still in her business skirt. His favourite position. His favourite place. He just shoved her skirt up, pulled her buttocks apart to get quickly and easily into her and they grunted, brother and sister, skin of their knees squeaking on the polished parquet floor of the Paris apartment.

But he took Cherie across his lap, didn't he?

Sheila was light-headed now. She opened her blouse and let the cold morning light crawl over her breasts. She looked down. Her pride and joy. They were bigger than you'd expect, not as cumbersome as Cherie's but juicy, swelling out from her slim ballerina's body. Excitement sliced inside her. How impressed would her neighbours be? She pinched the dark red nipples, just as Flora had pinched Cherie's, and instantly her cunt twitched in response.

She paused, touching herself, reminding herself. That tug of pleasure behind her navel. Then she walked right up to the window, pressing her nipples against the cold glass. That felt good. Cold hard glass on nipples, making them shrink with excitement. *Come on, everyone. Take a look. See what I'm doing. See my gorgeous breasts, such a feast, so sensitive, so desperate for attention, wouldn't you like to take a handful, squeeze them till they hurt, suck them till they burn? See how I'm going to pretend I'm joining in Cherie and Flora's little game, marching back into their house, making their mouths drop open as I unbutton my blouse and show them my bare breasts, offer my tits to them to bite and suck, arch myself towards them while they circle me, uncertain, then let their fingers wander over me, probe and prod my pussy too, see how their tight-lipped new neighbour looks when she's disrobed. See how she tastes.*

Her pussy contracted as she pressed herself hard against the glass, rubbing her breasts against the cold pane so that the friction hurt and made her nipples rigid. She pushed her breasts together so that the nipples jutted like blunt arrows, how sexy that looked.

Then she saw the bright red of the postman's bag, wheeling past her hedge.

She moved more exotically, rubbed herself even more frantically. If she pressed any harder she'd crack the glass. What if he saw her? She wanted to laugh as the postman bent his head so seriously to sift through his handful of letters, ready to shove them through the letter box. The postman always rings twice. She could see uneven streaks of grey in his windswept hair. Now, how would that be, if she rushed downstairs right now, flung the door open, grabbed him by the lapels of his ridiculous fluorescent jacket –

She wanted to be watched. Never mind that she picked on the first human being who crossed her path. She crushed her breasts viciously against the glass just a few feet above the postman, tempted to call out so he'd look up and see her breasts flattened as if someone was pushing her from behind, trying to push her right out of the window, so he'd see her face flushing with the new pain singing through her, such pleasure to be found in the most mundane things. *The most mundane people, Mr Postman.*

Maybe he'd also see her fiddling with her tight skirt, so eager to catch his eye that she stumbled into the corner of the bay and the curtain hanging there got caught between her legs. She tore at her flimsy knickers and got them down, kicked them away, and then she was still tangled up with the billowing curtain. It wound round her, and the thick fabric caught right up in her crack, right in between her wet sex lips, scraping against her clitoris so that her pussy clenched at the new plaything and she crossed her legs to keep it stuck there, fed it through her hands to make it rub so hard and fast that it was as if she was trying to start a fire, but not so hard and fast that she'd pull it off the curtain pole above her head.

The threading and beading of the intricate pattern scratched and scraped, steadily driving her crazy, and all the while she was right there in the window, like it was some kind of pedestal, inviting everyone to watch her, to see her, to get turned on seeing what she was doing to herself, see Sheila Moss with her blouse gaping open, skirt up round her thighs, fingering herself, dancing round her curtain like the horniest whore.

The unmistakeable scent of her arousal pricked her nostrils. It was like flicking a switch. Things were really cooking . . .

Look up, Mr Postie, look up. See what I'm doing. Stop whistling. Let your mouth drop open because there's Mrs Moss rubbing her tits against the window up there. Drop everything, bag, letters – Put your hands over your crotch to hide it, but there it is, your cock getting so big and so hard inside those faded blue trousers that I can see it all the way from my bedroom window.

Ring the doorbell, throw your bag of letters on the ground while you grab and rub at your thickening erection through your flies. Ring twice. You don't know what to do with this hard on. I'll tumble down the stairs and you'll crash through the door, shove your way into the house. I don't even know what you look like, I can only see a dark stubble on your face, but I think you'll do, you're thick-set, polite enough but more of a rough diamond than a gentleman. Your breath smells of cigarette smoke perhaps, saliva bubbling at the corners of your mouth, your eyes watering because you want to fuck something, me, get this load off, my skirt's up round my waist, the pale sweep of my thighs above the silk stockings and then between them my open wet pussy is thrusting at you, inviting you, ordering you to fuck me, I'm opening my pussy up wide for you on the stairs, spreading myself open with my fingers, and you leave the door open, leave it swinging, I want everyone outside to see, every passer-by, look, there's a man with his trousers pulled right down showing the crack of his bum, his big hairy thighs, shoving his jacket to one side, scrabbling to get his knees on to the bottom step, pulling at me so I'm half sitting, half lying on my staircase, holding on to the banister pole while your great grubby hands dig into my arse cheeks to yank me up to you, they're the fattest part of me and you spread them open like I'm spreading my cunt. Your fingers are digging right into the crack and Sheila Moss, this new Sheila Moss, oh think what Maureen would say, Sheila Moss tenses up tight as wire when your fingernails scrape at the tight hole where no one should go, but you don't care where your fingers go, the little hole flinches shut then gives a little, but that's dirty surely, too dirty, putting fingers up there, but the flinching of that little virgin hole felt good, surprising, it's stopped me in my tracks, dirty but good, that little hole agreeing to open up, take something in.

Sheila was talking to herself, her voice growling and urgent. And she was still alone, up in her bedroom like Rapunzel.

But you're a rough kind of guy, Mr Postie, no point licking the tip of your finger to flick paper over on your clipboard, you're going to ask Mrs So-and-So along the road to sign something, aren't you? No point keeping your eyes averted as you wander absent-mindedly away down my garden path, I know that you'd be the kind of guy with no preliminaries, that's how you treat your women, you get them home from the pub or wherever and you push them on to their backs and feel for them with one hand while you pull your cock out of your pants with the other. Show me, show us both what it's like. What do your women see before you're banging away at them? It's short and stubby, isn't it, and dark like your hands, the end swollen and bluish, and the veins stand out under your hand as it moves up and down to try to relieve that pressure, the same busy hand that delivers everybody's letters up and down this street, dear God.

Up that thick shaft, down again, practically tugging it off at the roots. The papery foreskin closes over then wrinkles away from the bulb, everything pushes out as blood pumps, as you, Mr Postie, bully your own cock, your shady face intent on what you're doing, don't you dare masturbate here in front of me, Maureen would call it wanking, but you read my mind and there's a glint in your eye under your thick eyebrows and I know you're getting yourself ready for something a whole lot better.

You barely touch me but that's OK, I'm touching myself, but now your knob is pushing at my sopping cunt, no ceremony, just pushing and shoving like you might with a rusty gate and do you know, I let go. I just spread my legs, let them flop open because I'm a rag doll, and you, Mr Postman, walk your knees up in between mine then spread your thighs until I'm doing the splits there on the stairs, you kneel there and your weight crushes me and the breathlessness makes me dizzy.

(That must be how Cherie feels when Flora squeezes her throat, what turns Cherie on and makes her fondle her own breasts the moment she senses pleasure.)

I grab your great fat buttocks, feel the muscles in them clench and thrust as I dig my long red nails in there, edge them into your crack like you did into mine, it's warm and damp in there. I'd find your bum hole, wouldn't I, if this was real? What's real is the climax rising, rising just here where the curtain and my fingers are teasing me, where I'm dancing in the window.

Your teeth are gritted, Mr Postman, I can just see two slits where your eyes are, but thank God you have very white teeth, that's good, good teeth, that shows hygiene, and they flash as your cock goes in, slams in like the key in my lock and I feel my body gripping, closing round it like one of those clam shells you see under water, the ridged walls of muscle inside me gripping the cock. It's even shorter than I expect but so thick it pushes out the sides, fills me, so much better than my own flimsy fingers and as my head falls back I fancy I see someone passing along the pavement behind us, stopping to watch us through the front door as we fuck on the stairs –

Who could it be? Sheila's eyes closed to picture it. John, perhaps, come back for her. Well, she didn't need him any more. She could get what she needed from the postman. Cherie, or Flora, come to call. Or those handsome husbands of theirs, immaculate in tennis whites perhaps, jogging past the gate back from the club and getting a good look at what the hell was going on at number 44.

Whatever the postman did, it would be hard and fast. No games, no positions, just basic rutting, complete with grunting, he'd angle his cock right up her, and slam it and she'd feel the crunch of his groin on hers, bone on bone and his face would get redder and darker with the effort of holding on, and then he'd swear blue murder and come, pumping into her, her head knocking back against the stairs, and now she wanted to come, swaying on her own in the window, with her buttocks twitching and the curtain and her fingers rubbing and poking her dark wet crack.

The postman was gone from her garden and from her fantasy, had zipped up his trousers without so much as a thank you. But a movement caught her eye. A car door slamming shut. A powder-blue Aston Martin, as John had said, parked outside number 43. And a fair-haired man, who may or may not have been watching her, walking up the garden path and through the gothic arch of his front door.

So her neighbour was wrong. Number 43 was no longer empty.

Again a sharp smell was released as Sheila peeled her wet sex lips apart. Her cunt was like a greedy mouth or grabbing hand, snatching at her fingers, dissatisfied with this, wanting something huge and hard to fill her, the postman, anyone, anything. Her knees were too feeble to carry her across the room to find a hairbrush, hair dryer, shampoo bottle, to the kitchen with its cucumbers and bananas.

So she opened her eyes and for the last gasp imagined who might be watching her between the winter twigs of the trees, someone peeping, his long thick telescope matching the bulging erection as he watched what Sheila Moss at number 44 did to herself at lunch times.

As her cunt squeezed she started to come, rapidly, in a rush of tiny impatient movements, but it was all over too quickly. She staggered back to the bed. It wasn't nearly enough. Maybe John had spoiled her – a cock on hand, as it were, whenever she wanted it. When he was at home, at least. And the way he could make it last for hours. But there was a suspicion sneaking through her that even John might not now be enough.

She sat with her knees splayed apart, juices sticky on her thighs. She was the rag doll tossed aside. No one wanted her. Her nipples, which had darkened to blood-red, were fading again to pink. She had to do it all by herself.

Where would Cherie and Flora be now in their house of pleasure? Sheila scratched at herself in frustration and tears stung her eyes. They'd have all the luxury of foreplay, of course. Ladies of leisure, nothing else to do. They'd have staggered as far as the hall, perhaps, or be sprawled on the stairs, groping and fondling, their sexy, familiar regime set up long ago, tongues flickering in and out of each other's mouths, high-pitched squeals and moans drowning out the exotic music. Cherie the one being chased and fondled, Flora, for all her girlish ponytail, taking the lead. Sheila had no idea how such a lesbian scene would work. Who would do what to whom? Would it go further than kissing and fondling, would they find something to penetrate each other, really do the fucking thing properly, grab a suitably phallic cucumber from the fridge, perhaps, a banana from the fruit bowl? She shivered. Those playful hands with their diamond rings, waving their implements around like toys. Or would they be deadly serious? Flora looked pretty mean when she lowered that blind. How did it work? Would their roles depend on whose house they were in? On who was hostess for the day?

Sheila groaned, wanting more, cursing herself and John and Roxanne and her neighbours for rousing this sexual curiosity and downright envy in her just when she thought she could live without it. In her silent bedroom she wanted all of them here to finish what they started, to do to her every which way they pleased until she screamed for mercy.

But it wouldn't happen, because none of them would ever know about her half-formed, dirty little desires. How would they possibly know what was going on in her mind when she kept it all so well hidden?

She took an ironed hankie out of her pocket and dabbed her dripping nose. She stood up, her legs shaking. She started to mop the juice off her pussy and her legs with the hankie but then she swiped her fingers through her damp bush again, shivered some more, and held them up to sniff each fingertip, licking off every trace of sweet wetness. Then she swiped herself again, slowly, cleaning into each crease with the hankie. She sniffed the hankie now, and put it in her pocket. She went to the basin to wash her hands but she could, whenever she wanted, take out the hankie, spread it over her face, and breathe in the heady scent of her own come.

And that, for the moment, would have to do.

Six

It was while she was waiting in the offices of Smart Secs, employment bureau for the very best secretaries, that Sheila saw the advert. *Room required for single working girl.*

It hit her like a bolt from the blue. That could be the answer to her problems, now that John had left her. She hadn't checked the account, and he'd promised to look after her. Even so. If she didn't want to work full time she could make money without moving an inch or lifting a finger. Take in a lodger. Two lodgers, three even. She had the four bedrooms, for heaven's sake. She glanced out of the window at the darkening high street, where a zebra crossing flashed its orange warning. And it looked odd, didn't it, a single woman rattling round in a house the size of number 44. It wasn't exactly a mansion, certainly not as big as the odd numbers on the other side of the street, but it was a family home, not a spinster's bedsit. She may have thought she'd be perfectly happy alone in her nest, and she was getting very used to it, but really it wasn't healthy. And this was especially noticeable since she'd quit the last job and didn't have enough to do other than clean and clean and clean again.

It would be good to have someone to cook for again, if that was part of the deal. But what sort of "working girl" might this be? There was only a mobile number.

She could be anyone, couldn't she, someone dodgy, someone dangerous.

Sheila crossed her legs, releasing the faint scent of arousal. She had been at it again, this morning. She'd made herself late for her appointment, this time fantasising about a traffic warden she'd spotted nosing around Spartan Street looking for improperly parked cars just as she was pulling up her stockings. She'd imagined herself actually *in* one of those cars, let's say the powder-blue Aston Martin, the cream leather seats tilted right back, her feet up on the walnut dash, so that when the warden peered through the windscreen he would see her straddling the two front seats, positioning the knob end of the gear stick right into her puss . . .

She rustled her newspaper unnecessarily, crossed her legs. Then again, the girl was taking a risk placing an advert. I mean, Sheila Moss, putative landlady, could be dodgy and dangerous, too.

A woman sitting next to her, wearing an extremely well cut chalk-striped trouser suit and filling in an application form, turned very slightly, her nostrils flaring. She looked straight at Sheila's knees in their black stockings. Sheila started to swing her ankle, aware of how elegant her court shoe looked just slipping off her toe.

'What do you think? I might just be looking for a lodger,' she asked casually, tapping the newspaper advert with her Biro. 'But what does "working girl" say to you?'

The woman studied the advert. She had very full lips, painted blood-red. The rest of her face was difficult to see behind a cascade of claret-tinted ringlets. But the mouth was enough. Sheila couldn't take her eyes off it. Those were the kind of pouting lips that would wrap round a choc-ice on a billboard and make it look like fellatio. And the pouting lips were parting slowly in a wide smile.

'Hmm. It says professional. Alone in the world. But has a job. Has money.' The woman spoke with a foreign accent and gave a deep smoker's chuckle which came from somewhere behind the middle button of her tight jacket. She angled her elbow and nudged Sheila in the curve of her breast. 'But you're thinking it could say hooker.'

'Was I? Maybe I was.' Sheila bit her lip as her face flushed slightly. 'In that case I couldn't possibly – I mean I live in a very respectable street.'

'I can tell.' The woman flicked her hair back to give Sheila a quick glance, but looked away again before Sheila could see her face properly. 'Relax. I'm sure it's totally innocent.'

Annette, Sheila's usual recruitment agent, crooked a finger through the glass wall of her office to say I'm ready for you. Sheila stood up, smoothing her skirt down. The woman watched her hands running down her hips, down her slim thighs. Her red tongue ran across her lips, making them glisten. Still on a high after her morning's fantasy, Sheila had a mad urge to bend down and run her own tongue across those sexy, inviting lips. What was wrong with her? All this business with John, her neighbours' interest in her affairs, the explosive pleasuring she kept giving herself for the benefit of postmen and traffic wardens and the drivers of Aston Martins – it was quite simply getting to her. Turning her head, as her mother used to say.

She folded the newspaper, dropped it on to her vacated chair. But the woman stretched out and picked it up again.

'Go for it,' she said, handing the paper to Sheila. Sheila found herself mesmerised by a pair of tawny eyes, sizing her up like a watchful lion before half closing in a smile. 'What have you got to lose?'

What did prospective landladies usually wear? Sheila turned this way and that in front of her three-way mirror, wondering if the all-black ensemble made her look more like a French governess than the kind of woman who might, after all, be something of a mother figure to the waifs and strays.

In fact, as she glanced past the mirror into the dark sheen of the window, she reckoned that since John had left her she was dressing even more severely, not less. She couldn't deviate from the black, except for the odd silk scarf, and except, obviously, the palette of jewel-bright colours of her lingerie drawer. To think that she'd even considered letting her hair down, cutting it, even, to celebrate her new domesticity with John.

But now she was back in her black uniform, her suit of armour, her shield. Designed to repel all comers. Surely that wasn't the intention. She didn't want to scare the poor lodgers off! But she couldn't help it. It was as if she was preserving herself in aspic.

She heard footsteps on the pavement outside, and her heart gave a little flutter. They were a woman's steps, surely. Tripping across the stones, almost dancing, on high heels. Sheila glanced down the road at Cherie's house, and rather wished she'd taken up Cherie's kind offer, when she'd gone round there a couple of hours ago, to come over to number 44 and vet the lodgers.

'Sounds like a new parlour game, *n'est-ce pas*?' Cherie tittered, waggling her newly manicured fingernails. There was little sign of the woman she'd last seen a few days ago fondling her own breasts while her friend left love bites on her neck. 'Let's play vet the lodgers. I must tell Flora.'

'I just wanted to run the idea past you,' Sheila ventured, standing awkwardly in the hallway. 'I just wondered, as a friend, you know, if you thought taking in paying guests was a good one?'

This time Cherie didn't ask her in to the airy conservatory. In fact she kept looking at her watch and peering over Sheila's shoulder into the street behind her.

'Expecting someone?' Sheila asked, backing reluctantly on to the doorstep.

'Jamie. My husband. He's been overseas for a fortnight, and I'm getting all twitchy. You understand.' Cherie looked at Sheila, and her face softened. She stretched out both her hands, took Sheila's arms, and pulled her until their bodies were touching. 'Oh, how tactless. I'm sorry. To think you were waiting each evening for John to come home, not that long ago.'

Sheila shrugged. 'I'm getting over it. I'm thinking that maybe having lodgers will be a big help, actually. Financially, obviously. And I won't be so lonely, then.'

'And we won't *let* you be lonely!' Cherie hugged Sheila then, pressing her cool cheek against Sheila's. 'What kind of lousy neighbours would that make us?'

As Cherie enveloped her in Chanel and feminine warmth, her big breasts pressing softly into her own, she wondered what would happen if she did what Flora had done the other day. Stroked Cherie's powdered neck. Untied today's white cashmere wrap-over to expose those big breasts. Took one in each spread-out hand, squeezed hard until Cherie squeaked –

'So it won't lower the tone, then?' Sheila murmured into Cherie's neck.

Cherie left a wet kiss on Sheila's cheek, and held her out at arm's length. 'Oh, how I'd *love* to see you lower the tone, darling,' she said.

The footsteps seemed to be continuing past the house. Maybe this lodger girl, Marilyn, had mixed up the address, was going the wrong way. Sheila hurried downstairs but there was no one at the door. She ran out to the gate in time to see a tall figure in a white fur Cossack hat and long white coat crossing the road towards Cherie's house.

'Excuse me! Over here!' she called, just as Cherie hurtled out of her house and flung her arms round the newcomer. Sheila fell back, embarrassed. It must be

66

Jamie Vixen. What camp clothes he liked to wear! This was something not even Maureen could have dreamt up for Spartan Street. Cross-dressing husbands –

But then Cherie dragged the figure under the dull gleam of a lamp post and kissed it full on the lips. Now Sheila could see that the person in white was actually yet another, beautiful, perfect blonde female.

'Mrs Mop?'

Sheila was still staring as Cherie unbuttoned the long white coat and wound her arms inside, pressing her cheek against the other woman's chest. The taller woman nodded down at her. She didn't seem to be particularly overjoyed. But then no one could be quite as effusive as Cherie. And now she was lifting her face and pressing her lips against her friend's mouth again, right there in the street, and her tall friend wasn't stopping her. Apart from the kissing, the pair of them looked like something out of a Persil advert in their perfect whites.

'Is this number 44 Spartan Street?'

At last Sheila turned at the interruption, and Marilyn Monroe was standing there. All Sheila could make out in the autumnal night was a huge blonde wig, a very obviously false beauty spot, and heavily made-up eyes.

'Marilyn?' She clutched her head. Everything was becoming surreal. 'You've come about the room?'

'Oh my goodness!' The Marilyn figure stepped closer, her little cape falling off her narrow shoulders. She'd freeze in this weather, wearing the iconic white halter-neck dress as if they were on the sidewalk in sultry California. 'Is that really you? I didn't think you needed to let rooms. I thought the woman on the phone said Mrs Mop! I thought it was too comic a name for a landlady! Oh I thought I'd never see you again!'

'It's Mrs Moss. There must be some mistake.' Sheila stalked up the path. 'Now, if you'd care to see the room –'

67

She went back in, and stood aside to let the girl pass.

'It's lovely. Really lovely. Just like home.' Marilyn peered round the gloomy hallway. There was a faint whiff of cheap perfume, perfume Sheila had smelled before. 'Oh, Sheila, this is like a dream come true!'

'How do you know my name?'

'But Sheila, don't you recognise me?'

And then with no warning the girl clawed at her back-combed hair until it came right away from her head and, throwing what transpired to be a hideous yellow wig so that it landed like a dead animal on the stairs, she burst into tears.

Sheila kicked the front door shut and folded her arms, raising her eyes to heaven. As if she hadn't got enough problems. What wouldn't she give to think up some polite excuse to go over to Cherie's house, invite herself in, see what was going on with this latest of gorgeous, sexed-up neighbours of hers. Get them to accept her into their club. Show her exactly what they liked to do to each other –

But then Sheila saw the sobbing girl's soft caramel-coloured curls falling limply round her contorted face, and recognised, as the tears smeared through the pancake make-up, the freckles peppering the snub nose. The serious little face she'd seen countless times illuminated by the flashing lights of the photocopier. The childish cheeks blushing scarlet as Maureen roared out some filthy joke about arseholes. The soft arms that had carried heavy piles of files from desk to desk, the fingernails that had just scratched into the groove at the back of Sheila's neck, tweaked a stray hair from her scalp, as she helped her on with her tweed coat that last day at the office.

'Tessa?' she breathed, unfolding her arms. 'What on earth has happened to you?' She dragged the bedraggled starlet towards her, intending to shake her gently, but Tessa flung herself dramatically at her, knocking against

68

Sheila's sharp chin. Sheila could feel her breath hot on her throat. Tessa's pert breasts pushing against hers. The halter-neck dress was only very thin, and she suspected Tessa had failed to find the right bra to wear under it, so she'd gone without. She started to stroke Tessa's baby-soft skin under the insubstantial little cape. She must be frozen. She could feel the girl's bare shoulder blades, the little hairs down her spine tickling under her fingers.

Tessa shivered, but she didn't pull away. Sheila moved her hands up under Tessa's tangled hair, massaging her scalp, moving her hands round the girl's neck and cheeks. Tessa tilted her head back, her long eyelashes stuck together with tears, eyes closed as Sheila warmed her up.

'It all went wrong at the other place. It all got complicated and he chucked me out and now I'm homeless!'

'We're both in luck, then. I've been abandoned. You can come and live with me.'

All at once Sheila's empty world looked more inviting. She carried on stroking Tessa, remembering something she'd read about how handling pets could reduce stress levels. Certainly Tessa was calmer, and had no urge to move away, either. But the hallway was not the place to comfort the girl or make her feel at home. She kissed the top of Tessa's head. Tessa pressed against her, tilted her face up, so Sheila gave her another kind of soft peck on her cheekbone.

'I always liked you so much, Sheila.' Tessa's lips parted in a big smile, showing her glistening tongue. She kissed Sheila quickly on the mouth then blushed. 'So sophisticated. So mysterious –'

'That's better.' Sheila looked down at Tessa, overcome by all this adoration. 'Can I take it you've got over your little crisis now?'

'Crisis? What crisis? Never a crisis when you're

69

around, Sheila.' Tessa tossed her hair back. Totally recovered, indeed. 'Can I see my room now?'

Sheila led Tessa up the stairs, aware of the girl close up behind her practically twittering with excitement. She decided to give her the little room at the end of the landing, almost a cottage room with eaves. Apart from her own extravagantly decorated boudoir, none of the bedrooms had been touched.

'You can do whatever you like in here,' Sheila said, leaning in the doorway as Tessa threw her bag and coat and horrible yellow wig on the single bed and twirled over to the window. This room looked over the garden at the back.

'Ooh, does that mean I can have, what do you call them – gentlemen callers?'

Sheila pursed her lips. 'I mean paint it, decorate it, put up pictures, scatter toys – I'm thinking you like pink.'

'You know me so well, Sheila! And I'm only teasing about the gentlemen callers!' Tessa bent over at the waist to unzip her bag, then reached up to undo the halter top of her dress. She stamped her little foot. 'Can you help me get this bloody dress off? I won't be needing it tonight. They cancelled the booking.'

Sheila's legs felt stiff as she walked across the creaking painted floorboards towards her new lodger.

'I'm not sure that moonlighting as a look-alike is very suitable work for you, Tessa,' she said, lifting the baby-soft curls to get at the knot. 'Although I have to say with that wig you looked exactly like her. But Marilyn Monroe was a sex kitten, wasn't she? And you're –'

'Just a kitten?'

Tessa giggled. She mewed and wiped her paws over her freckled nose, and Sheila's stomach drew tight.

'A very cute pussy, darling.'

'Fuck me, Sheila! What would Maureen say? That sounded so naughty!'

70

Tessa's little shoulders wriggled as she giggled. The halter knot was coming loose, but Sheila went on worrying at it, breaking one of her nails in the process. She found herself counting the little bones in Tessa's neck, the golden hairs meeting over her spine. Her fingers were shaking. Tessa's cheap perfume was clogging her senses.

'What went wrong at your last lodgings? Were they horrible to you?'

Tessa shook her head. 'Yes, and no.'

Sheila waited, holding the two ends of the undone knot. She'd learned as a kind of agony aunt to the Parisian hookers that the less you say, the more they open up. So to speak.

'My landlord tied me up.'

'He kept you prisoner?' Sheila bit down on her lip so that she could taste blood. She kept her eyes fixed on the groove in the back of Tessa's child-like neck. 'So he *was* horrible to you. Worse. Barbaric! You should call the police. That's abduction. False imprisonment –'

'Not prisoner, exactly, Sheila. I let him do it. I wanted him to do it. And it was only at night, when I got back from work.' Tessa glanced over her shoulder, caught Sheila's eye. She must have seen something there, because her face flooded scarlet. 'I liked it, Sheila.'

'Was this going on all the time I knew you? You were coming in to that ghastly office every morning, so sweet, so shy, all neat in your little skirts, and that very night, every night, you were – he was –?'

'Living a double life.' Tessa bowed her head. 'You're shocked. You hate me. I shouldn't have told you.'

'I'm glad you told me. I want you to tell me everything.' Sheila shook Tessa's shoulders roughly. Her world was shifting under her. 'But give me a little time to understand.'

'I didn't know what to think at first. He was much older than me. Mr Brown. Just an ordinary guy with an ordinary name, a bit pudgy, balding, but nice eyes, we barely spoke, then it just happened one evening not long after I'd moved in.' Tessa started nodding enthusiastically. 'He was putting up some shelves in my room. I was knackered. I just wanted to lie down on my bed. It was the day Maureen made me pack up all those boxes for the courier and hump them down to reception –'

'Someone should have helped you.' Sheila murmured, but the office was the last thing on her mind now. She was waiting to hear what Mr Brown did to little Tessa.

'I must have drifted off, because when I opened my eyes again my wrists were tied together, just like this –' she joined her hands and lifted them in the air '– and it was kind of – relaxing. Knowing I couldn't do anything. He was standing at the end of the bed, stroking my leg. Yeah, I know I should have been scared, but I soon learned it was only a game.'

'But it was a game you became addicted to?'

'Addicted?' Tessa shrugged. 'Yes, I suppose you can get addicted to games. Especially very kinky ones. And straightaway I liked it. I liked being helpless like that. Like a toy. And the first few times I just lay there, still dressed – well, maybe my skirt wrinkled up, shoes off – while he looked at me or took pictures of me. He just did what he liked, moved me about, started tying me to the furniture, undid my shirt another night, pulled down my knickers, I was so tired it was bliss not having to perform, you know, like you do with a new boyfriend. He got so hard just having me there to play with, so it was easy. He rubbed me all over with funny ointments which made my skin buzz. Even when I was bare he avoided those special bits, you know. Then it was only using his fingers at first and you can imagine what the ointments did to my – it was like being stung by nettles, but in a good way.'

Sheila swallowed. How would it be hurling yourself naked into a bed of nettles? Legs, arms, breasts, oh,

nipples, all coming up in hives, vibrating with the venom
—

'And after that, you know, not long before it all
ended, he got round to getting his prick out —'

'Tessa! I can't believe you're talking like this —'

Tessa let out a high laugh. 'His prick, Sheila. How
else can I describe it? I'm sorry to shock you. And still
he just wanted me to lie there, all smeared with his
ointments, such strong smells, some of them had chilli
in them to make the skin erupt, you know, and all this
was going on with my skin and he just wanted me to lie
totally still so he could *fuck* me.'

'He did what he liked to you. And you liked it.'
Sheila's breathing was shallow with a kind of furious
excitement. Her nails were digging into Tessa's skin
now. She tried to hide this reaction with sternness. 'So
why all the tears when you got here? I thought you'd
been attacked or something.'

'Oh, that was because I was so thrilled to see you!'
Tessa leaned back, her hair tickling Sheila's face. 'You
didn't think there was anything seriously *wrong* did
you?'

'So you were playing a game with me, too?' Sheila's
voice was hard. 'Just like you played games with this Mr
Brown?'

Tessa didn't notice Sheila's angry tone, because she
giggled. 'And because I needed somewhere to stay. His
wife came back early from some business trip, and she
found me tied up on their four-poster, and she went
berserk, so he chucked me out.'

'Just like that? So you thought you'd bring all your
problems to me?'

'Not exactly, Sheila. I advertised for a room, remember? It was just a lovely bonus that it was *you* who
answered my advert!'

But Sheila's pretend indignation was turning her on
too much to fuss over details. The sweeter Tessa was,

73

the more she wanted to scold her. And she could just see it. The wife marching up the stairs in a pinstriped suit, a hard-faced bitch with a briefcase, honey I'm home, and finding this cute little pudding stretched out on the marital bed, glistening with massage oil, arms wide in welcome, legs wide open, pussy split and spilling all its rude redness, stretched out with nowhere to hide as if on a rack, maybe the wife found her greasy husband straddling the girl's face, gripping the base of his cock while the rest of it rammed in and out of her willing red mouth, between her sharp teeth, the thick shaft glistening with wet saliva from her tongue, his cock so thick it could choke her, down into her yielding throat as her legs twitched against the ropes, her pussy wide open atop those helpless white limbs, empty for now while he rammed himself into her mouth and started to come, spurting the thick stuff into her mouth, all over her face, the tip of her tongue flicking about trying to lick it off, when he'd recovered from that, maybe gone downstairs to make a cup of tea, leaving her covered in clots of come, then he came back upstairs and that was what his wife saw, Mr Brown making himself comfortable between those open legs, maybe she saw his big white bottom pumping back and forth strong and regular as a machine as he fucked the pretty snub-nosed lodger.

'You're best out of there. Best here with me.' Sheila pushed Tessa away and went to sit down quickly by the window. 'I've undone the knot. You can take the dress off now. Get back to normal.'

A row of similar bedrooms eyed her across the scruffy gardens. Some were lit up, some still dark. That back street was much scruffier than this. It was closer to the tube line. Some people obviously couldn't afford tumble driers, because there were scraps of clothing flapping from lines in some of the gardens.

'I don't think I'll ever be truly normal again, Sheila.' Tessa came and stood beside her.

Sheila put her hands jerkily on to the radiator, then knelt and fiddled about switching it on. 'How cold it is in here –'

The white Marilyn dress slipped down to the floor like a skin, and the real, mascara-stained Tessa was back. Except of course Sheila had never seen her naked before. Her body was exactly how you would imagine a gorgeous twenty-year-old's to be. Mr Brown would have become hard just looking at her. Sheila's figure was like that a few years ago before she lost weight. Soft curves in all the right places, melding the child into the woman, traces of puppy fat giving way to jutting breasts and rounded thighs, every dip and dimple leading the eye straight into the shadow between her legs, the cleavage of her round bottom. In the shaft of light from the landing the girl looked good enough to eat.

'I like it cold, Sheila. His house was always cold, too. It makes all your hairs prickle and stand on end.' Tessa came closer. 'Are you cross with me because I let him tie me up?'

Sheila moved her eyes up to Tessa's cute breasts, the nipples shrinking to hard points in the cold air, close enough to touch. Oh yes, she knew what the cold could do to you. Her own nipples were erect now, burning under her black jumper.

'Did he hurt you?' she asked, putting a hand on Tessa's arm. Tessa grabbed her hand and moved it round her waist, so that Sheila's cheek was pressed against her tummy button.

'Of course, when he first did it!' Tessa jiggled as if she needed a wee. Sheila swallowed and removed her arm. Tessa's bare breasts were just above her head, banging together as she danced about. 'But he knew exactly what he was doing, and the funny thing is, that the tighter he ties you, the more powerless you are, the better. I was stunned, and then I liked it. It made him all masterful you know, ordering me around. But what really turned me on, Sheila, was feeling those ties round my wrists, just tight enough so that if I struggled they rubbed. The marks were like pink bracelets, reminding me the next day when I went to work. I was all stretched out in his house, and there was nothing I could do.' She bent to look into Sheila's eyes, her sweet tits dangling just out of reach. 'What do you think Maureen would say?'

Crazy laughter gasped out of Sheila. She was thrown off balance at this totally unexpected thought. 'She'd be gob-smacked. Isn't that the phrase she used?' She shook her head. 'She thought she knew it all, didn't she?'

Tessa joined in the laughter. 'So cool if she knew what the little office mouse was really like.'

Sheila nodded. So cool indeed.

Seven

Tessa giggled again and snapped on the bedside light to rummage in her small case. She bent over, her back to Sheila now, and Sheila could see pubic hair curling out of the wisp of her thong. The hair was caramel-coloured, same as on her head.

'The last full night I was there, the day before yesterday I suppose that must be, he kept me tied up all night long. He kept coming into the room, doing whatever he wanted with me, and I couldn't do anything to stop him. He was pretty rough with me. I think he'd taken Viagra or something, because usually he could only get it up once a day. But this night he was rock-hard the whole time. Just kept coming into the room with this massive stiffy and shoving it up me with no ointments this time, no talking, nothing. It was wild!' She leaned forward and added in a theatrical whisper, 'All night long, so I had to pee in the end, all over the bed.' She straightened. 'Actually it was his idea to do the Marilyn Monroe stuff, after I sang to him one time. You know, *Diamonds Are a Girl's Best Friend.* He said there was a filthy little slapper hiding underneath that timid office junior.'

'How right he was, though I'm not sure Marilyn Monroe was the answer.' Sheila's own voice shocked her, husky with desire. 'How did we miss the real you amongst the filing cabinets?'

'Not the real me. The other me. Oh, and guess what?'
Tessa was virtually dancing about with excitement now.

Sheila raised her eyebrows. What more was there? She
stood up to pace over to the bed. Her knickers felt
sticky.

'I was so good he forgot to charge me any rent!
Which reminds me, Sheila. Here's some for you.'

She turned, holding out a wad of tenners. Sheila
looked at the notes, looked at Tessa, virtually naked
apart from her white platform sandals. At that moment
she looked like a lap dancer. 'Show me what he did.
Show me how he tied you up. What he did to you.'

Tessa dropped the money on the table and put her
hand on her hip. She tilted her head coquettishly.
'You'll have to do it.'

Sheila swallowed again. 'What with?'

'How about your stockings? I know you wear stockings, Sheila. I saw you once in the ladies' at work,
fastening your suspenders under your skirt. I could see
the tops of your thighs. They're so white. You've got
such great legs, Sheila. They go all the way up to your
armpits, as the boys say.'

Tessa sank on to the bed and pressed her knees
together, wrapping her hands demurely round them.
Sheila cocked one leg in the air, reached under her skirt,
and took the top of the stocking. Her cheeks flared with
an unaccustomed flush, but Tessa wouldn't be able to
see. Her little friend watching her like this made her
want to do this more seductively. They were both
smiling at each other. Sheila hitched the tight skirt up
towards her crotch, and Tessa's eyes gleamed, but
neither of them spoke. Sheila unrolled first one stocking,
then the other, and stood up. Tessa lay down on the
bed, stretched her arms out, and opened her legs wide.

'Tie me tight, like he did,' Tessa said, licking her lips.
'I want you to hurt me.'

'I couldn't possibly –'

'Please, Sheila.' Tessa pouted like a spoilt child and kicked out one foot. 'I want you to see what it's like. What I'm like. I want you to be my mistress.'

Her firm breasts jutted upwards, the nipples already elongated and taut. Sheila knew exactly what Mr Brown had seen when he had that innocent body captive in his back bedroom. Sex on a plate, but not with a whore. Oh no. With a perfect angel. His little dolly.

Sheila wanted to be the one lying there, she wanted to be the one tied up, but not by Tessa. Briefly she wondered if John would have entered into this, but although he was addicted to sex he was always too busy for games. There would be other playmates out there, she was sure of that. She wouldn't have to go far. Just a little way down the street. Or she could stay at home. The fun was right here, at number 44, and this time she would be the master. Or the mistress. Keep her lodger captive, just for her, whenever they both wanted.

Tessa might be teaching her how it was done, but Sheila was a fast learner. She wanted to be the one in charge, at least at home, here with Tessa. Time to be like Mr Brown, the sleazy landlord. See what he saw. The fresh nubile body that was begging him to punish her. He must have thought he'd died and gone to heaven. Suddenly she knew exactly what she wanted to do with the young body stretched out before her, something she'd never wanted to do before. She grabbed Tessa's arm, wound the stocking round her wrist, and lashed it quickly to the rounded bedpost of the childish single bed. Then she did the same to the other arm.

Tessa tried to sit up, yanking at the stocking restraints. 'Oh, they're too tight, Sheila! I can't get away!' She started to toss from side to side, her breasts wobbling delightfully, the muscles in her arms straining, her bottom rolling, squashing against the blanket, lifting frantically to show the black seam between the fat butt cheeks. 'Let me out of here! He didn't do it this tightly –'

Anxiety flashed through Sheila, and she started to reach towards the knots, but then snatched her hand back. This was Tessa's game. So she must play. And Sheila was the landlady, remember, which meant she ruled whatever went on in this house. 'What kind of wimp was he, for God's sake!'

Sheila watched the struggling girl, saw the way her tongue poked out even as she whimpered, flicked back and forth with obvious pleasure. Watching her new lodger lying there like a sacrifice, trying to kick and punch her way out of the restraints, was firing her up, all the more because she knew it could easily be her there, writhing about, a prisoner on her own bed, while someone dressed in black stood over her. But just now she didn't want to be the one tied up. She wanted to do to her little Tessa whatever that landlord had done.

As she flailed about Tessa kicked her in the leg, and a burst of energy surged through Sheila. She spun around, looking for more props, picked up the white dress and wound the neck tie round one of Tessa's ankles, tied it round the leg at the foot of the bed.

'What are you going to do to me, Sheila? Are you going to keep me here all night?'

'Would you like that, Tessa? My prisoner? Here all night? But I'm not a man. I can't fuck you like Mr Brown did.' Sheila pulled the ribbon out of the neck of Tessa's cape and tied it round the other ankle, so now she was spread-eagled on the bed, legs wide open, struggling, complaining, a living, breathing dolly. 'And you call me Mrs Moss.'

'You could find a way to fuck me, Mrs Moss. You know, use something. You could be the man.' Tessa made a gasping sound of amusement. The bed head cracked against the wall as she continued to thrash about. Sheila could see Tessa gyrating and rubbing herself eagerly up and down the rough blanket on the bed. 'But I want to be the one to please you, Sheila. You're my goddess.'

Sheila's arm came up and she slapped Tessa hard on the rump. 'That's for playing games with me. All those tears on the doorstep.' The prime, tender flesh rippled under her hand. Tessa squealed. 'So stop moving, young lady, while I decide what you deserve.'

'I'm not a young lady. Mr Brown told me that. I'm a filthy little tart!'

Sheila smacked her hand down again, loving the sharp sound ringing out in the little bedroom, loving Tessa's responding yelp. Again she slapped, watched Tessa jerk off the bed, slapped again. 'Keep totally still, filthy little tart, otherwise you're in trouble.'

They were both silent for a minute. Tessa went rigid, exaggeratedly obeying orders, and Sheila stood over her, enjoying another surge of this strange new unaccustomed power. It bunched up inside her, spiking through her cunt to make it throb with wanting.

Across the dark gardens a tube train clattered over the viaduct.

'This is going to be so good, Sheila,' Tessa said into the thick silence in the wake of the train. 'You're so wonderful. I love you so much.'

'I'm Mrs Moss! Or would you prefer me to be Mr Brown?' Sheila smacked her hard her again and shoved one knee on the bed between Tessa's legs. Something tickled her. The yellow wig. Absently she picked it up, still shouting at Tessa. 'How much do you love me? Go on telling me how you'll lick the floor for me, otherwise I'll have to spank you again.'

'I worship you, I always have.' Tessa lifted her bottom off the bed, pushing her puffy little pussy at Sheila. 'I'd do anything for you. You're so beautiful, Sheila. Like the ice queen. Untie me, and I'll show you how much I love you. I'll go on my knees. I wanted to do it at the office. I wanted to show everyone, but you're like a queen. I'll lick the floor, if you like, but I'd rather lick you, suck you, stroke you – anything you want –'

The adoring words were so good Sheila could taste them. They filled the little room, dissipating all that loneliness. She stroked Tessa's legs, up her thighs towards the offered pussy. Her skin was so warm. She pushed her fingers up towards the deep crease waiting there between Tessa's legs, tangled them in the soft bush there. Her own pussy was getting wet.

'I'm not going to untie you. You're a naughty, dirty girl for trying that trick.' Sheila slapped Tessa again, felt the skin go hot. Then she shoved the wig back on to Tessa's head. 'There. And now you look like a horny slut, too.'

'It wasn't a trick –'

'Lie still, Marilyn!'

Sheila was out of breath. She unzipped her skirt and flung it to one side. Her knickers were soaking now. She whipped them off too, and there was that horny smell again, so intoxicating. In a calmer moment she must work out how best to describe it. How to bottle it.

She leaned forwards, pulled Tessa's thighs further apart, and now she could see the secret slit decorated with rusty curls, the vivid red promise as Tessa's sex lips opened, and without thinking she leaned right in and nudged with the tip of her nose, forcing the lips further open, feeling the warm wetness on her face. A ripple of delicious shock went through her to smell the other woman's female scent. This must be what animals in the jungle do – but do the females go round sniffing each other's bottoms? Never occurred to her before. Forget the jungle. The scenario right here, in this bedroom, was enough to fill her with a special kind of madness. The pale girl trussed up on the bed with the older woman half dressed in black crawling over her, exploring, snuffling into her bush.

Tessa's sex felt like silk against Sheila's nose. She was getting drunk on the smell of her. She let her tongue follow, sliding it over the slit, feeling Tessa tense and shiver as she swept her tongue once, twice up over the furls of her sex, feeling the bump of the little clit revealing itself in there. She pushed the palm of her hand against her own pussy, rubbed one finger against her own clitoris, everything contracting and squeezing urgently to come, now, straightaway. She snatched her hand away again, too soon, too soon, started lapping again at Tessa, lapping like a cat at her kitten, making the girl twitch and groan with every stroke.

'Am I your slave now, Sheila?'

Sheila jerked herself away, irritated at the interruption. 'Tell me you love me, then shut your mouth!'

She thrilled to the sharp tone in her voice, and the whimper of pleasure from Tessa as she slapped her again. 'I love you, Sheila. Slap me again.'

'Don't tell me what to do, slave! Just worship me.' Sheila knelt on Tessa's legs, forcing them open. 'For speaking you get punished. No more licking.'

'Please, Sheila. I'm creaming myself here. Lick me, please.'

'You're here for my pleasure, remember!'

But Sheila knew that their pleasure would merge, it was one and the same thing, in the end, and she herself was horribly close to coming with just a couple of flicks of her own fingers. She must hold herself back until she was ready for whatever Tessa's ultimate task would be.

She feasted her eyes again on Tessa's gaping slit, the puffy lips, the curls tight with moisture, the white thighs like columns leading eyes and hands up to her centre. She remembered Roxanne spread out on her bed across the landing, blowing hot air over herself, her silk dress ruffling, her shocked excitement and intrigue at their story of the rutting brother and sister, and now it was Roxanne's wide open cunt she was seeing all over again. The first time she'd been up close to another woman. The last time she was to be with John.

A wave of anger rolled through her. So it was still there, just beneath the surface. A very special sort of hatred. She wasn't the saintly sister any more. One more night was all John had given her. It wasn't nearly enough.

She wanted to try everything they'd shown her that night, and more. Especially what Roxanne had shown her. John had taught her nothing new in all their years together, she realised that now. Except how to break the ultimate taboo. But sod all that. Right now she needed to take that anger out on someone. And here was her perfect person.

She still held her lacy knickers. She rolled the flimsy lace between her palms until it was a thin rope. She held Tessa's legs open with her own knees and, holding each end of the knicker-rope, sliced it quickly up Tessa's slit. Tessa arched her back, pulling and tugging at the restraints, tipping herself upwards, offering herself desperately.

Sheila scraped the knickers down hard, knowing that like the curtains the other day, the unyielding fabric would be slicing right over the sensitive clit and all the flesh surrounding it, scraping at the most tender parts. She wished she could see better. In this semi-darkness she couldn't see how the pleasure would be turning Tessa's clit a brighter red. She started rubbing her makeshift prop up and down Tessa's cunt, faster and faster, thrilling to see Tessa jumping and writhing about on the bed, off the blanket, her elbows and knees flexing, her throat and back arching, her mouth open, tongue extended like a cat yawning.

Sheila was shocked to find that her own pleasure was rooted in inflicting just enough pain, that Tessa obviously wanted to be hurt, her squeals were turning into screams, but there was no fear there, just ecstasy, and Sheila was excited both by the response in her own convulsing body and by discovering in this new experiment the mad delight in inflicting such wonderful agony.

Tessa's screams were getting higher and louder. This was like being in a film, like watching someone else, another Sheila Moss, torturing a pretty sex slave in a little back bedroom on a respectable street in the middle of a pulsating city. Someone with no inhibitions whatsoever, the Sheila she secretly must be. She couldn't hold her own climax much longer.

She yanked the knickers away from Tessa, who howled in animal anger and started trying to rub herself frantically against the bed, opening and shutting her legs, to finish herself off. As she bucked off the bed Sheila swung her arm back and slapped Tessa again on her exposed buttock, then dangled the knickers over her, tickling them over her wriggling body, up towards the straining breasts, the nipples that looked like they were bursting, astonishingly big and accentuated on such a young girl.

Sheila fought the temptation to take a taut bud between her teeth and suck on it, because she wanted someone desperately to do that to her, but her own punishment to herself would be to save it, to force herself to wait for that greatest of pleasures, the sucking of her nipples. For now she would torture herself by confining them inside her austere black jumper. She would use her willing slave to bring her off some other way.

Tessa wouldn't stop wriggling. The only way to stop her was to sit on her. She settled herself astride her slave, but as Sheila's overheated pussy met Tessa's warm skin she nearly came there and then. She started rubbing her wet pussy against Tessa's legs, nearly maddened by the feeling of another woman's skin arousing her like this. Now it was Sheila who couldn't keep still. She crawled over Tessa, spread herself over her, pressed her breasts against Tessa's even though she was still wearing her jumper, fought like fury the urge to rip that off, roll every inch of her over every inch of

Tessa, so on she moved, crawling up Tessa's body until their faces were close. Tessa wasn't moaning so hard now that Sheila had stopped with the friction, but her mouth was moist and inviting and Sheila pressed her own mouth down. Tessa's mouth was open, her wet tongue flickering out to probe inside Sheila's mouth, and now Sheila knew her climax was only seconds away. Kissing another woman, a sweet girl like Tessa who loved her, was overwhelming, and with a superhuman effort she pulled back.

'Your task, Tessa slave, before I even think of letting you go.' Her voice was thick with desire as she groped for what she wanted. She looked at Tessa's mouth. Now it was her turn to groan as she crawled up until her knees were either side of Tessa's face, her pussy inches above Tessa's mouth. 'Now lick me, Tessa. Lick me until I'm screaming as loud as you were. Tell me how you worship me, and then lick me.'

She grabbed the bed head where Tessa's wrists were tied and leaned on her arms. Then she lowered herself to sit on Tessa's face. Not squashing her, but hovering as best she could, feeling Tessa's warm breath on her bottom. And then the licking started. Soft, almost feathery caresses over her pussy lips, which pulsed quietly, and here was the wet tip of Tessa's tongue flicking up the crack then smoothing itself flat over the swollen lips.

Sheila's head was spinning. She stared out of the window at the London sky, heard the sirens going about their business, another train with its row of lighted square windows rattling by. If she and Tessa were pleasuring each other in front of the window, what a sight all those commuters would see. A head of rusty curls jerking in and out between the taut white thighs of her slave mistress while the mistress struggled to compose herself, trying to stay upright, weak with the effort of not coming all over her little slave's face.

Tessa had only her mouth and lips to use. Sheila spread her legs a little further, opening herself to more intense pleasure, seeing herself as those commuters might see her if they had superhuman vision. Each carriage, rattling past, would get their eyeful of her and Tessa. They'd glance at each other, did they imagine it, did their fellow travellers see that, a woman sitting on another woman's face, framed like a still for them all to see?

She pushed herself roughly down on to Tessa's face. She could hear Tessa whispering.

'No, I'm not letting you go.'

'I was saying you taste so sweet, Sheila.'

Sheila moaned and strained, pressing down as Tessa's tongue lapped faster, like the kitten she was, and the thought of her as a little furry pet sizzled through Sheila's mind, sensations sizzling in her cunt as Tessa's mouth seemed to suck her entire pussy while her tongue probed, forcing its way further in like a mini dick, then pulling back so that Sheila ground herself harder into Tessa's face, feeling her nose pushing above her pubic bone, into her bladder and the sensation to wee started building as well.

Now it was Tessa who was torturing her because her tongue flicked mercilessly at Sheila's clitoris. Where had she learned this, who had she done this to, the little minx? That sharp little tongue started to encircle it.

Sheila couldn't help it. She started to jerk frantically. Tessa might as well have applied an electric probe when she tapped at that tiny bud and oh God now she was sucking again and again, so mercilessly. The flicking of her tongue was as regular as a tick-tock, building up the pressure. Sheila rocked back and forth, opening her legs still wider so that she was a proper feast for Miss Tessa.

She could hear Tessa's saliva as she slurped on Sheila's pussy juice. She had stopped circling and sucking the burning clit and her tongue was now pushing inside like a mini cock, flicking from side to side, sliding over the clit as it thrust in and out. Sheila rocked faster, her cunt and lips and clit rubbing against Tessa's tongue and nose and chin, her hips bucking more wildly.

An aeroplane lowered itself from the night sky as if it might land flat on its belly on the rooftops, on top of all those commuters sitting open-mouthed in their tube trains. Tessa's tongue worked her landlady to a final frenzy, her mouth and tongue lapping frantically. Here it came. Sheila gripped the bedpost, drew her hips back in a final glorious convulsion and her cunt, her whole body, drew in on itself, grew tight as she rattled the bedpost and started to come, pushing herself into Tessa's face, smearing her juices all over Tessa's face, rubbing herself on and on over her face until long after the climax had faded.

At last she eased herself away, lifted her leg stiffly and stood up. Tessa's face was smeared with Sheila's juices, the grotesque blonde wig now all askew.

'What about me, Mrs Moss?' Tessa whimpered, shivering from frustration and the cold. She pulled weakly at the ties, making the bed creak. 'It's my turn to come.'

Sheila bent to pick up her black skirt, paused. Goosebumps puckered Tessa's skin, tortured her nipples into flame-red points. Now that the basic lust was fading, Sheila's affection for the young girl was stronger than ever. She wanted to hug her close. But she didn't want the game to stop. Not yet.

'I'm going to chop ginger for our supper,' she said firmly, adjusting the knots binding Tessa's wrists. 'Then I'll come back, and I'll make you lick me out all over again. And then if you're very very good, I'll lick you, too, till you're screaming for me to stop.'

'Don't leave me here!' Tessa reared against the restraints, eyes widening with panic. 'What if your John comes home and finds me like this?'

'He'd think he'd died and gone to heaven if he found a naked girl tied up in my back bedroom. But didn't I tell you? He left me. Buggered off with his whore.'

'What's happened to you, Sheila? You don't use that sort of language.'

'Oh, I do now, honey.' Sheila laughed and tickled the messy, stained knickers between Tessa's breasts, over the mound of her crotch. 'It's just me and you now.'

Tessa closed her eyes and wriggled contentedly. 'Hurry back, Sheila.'

'Oh, we've got all night.' Sheila couldn't resist bending over and kissing Tessa's mouth, running her tongue across Tessa's teeth, tangling her tongue with hers. She pulled away, looked longingly at the curvy body lying there, just for her. 'You're going to be my new plaything, Tessa.'

Eight

Number 44 even had a different smell to it. Oh, there was still Sheila's *pot pourri* battling with the favoured French furniture wax which she liked to rub vigorously into all the wooden surfaces once a week. There was always the aroma of last night's roast or this morning's fresh coffee.

But now there was Tessa's perfume as well. Sweet, cloying, conquering the faint odour of neglect that had lingered there before. And there were other, feminine smells, mingling into the fabric of the house, so subtle sometimes that only the animal part of you could pick them up.

Sheila liked the routine they'd already adopted. She would stand on the doorstep some mornings, waving Tessa off to work like a good little wife, savouring on her tongue the taste of her little playmate's sex, stomach loosening at thoughts of the still-tentative games they might have played the night before. Tessa, admitting she was basically idle, urging her to tie her tighter. Sheila, always busy, tying her, smacking her, obeying Tessa's orders to squat over Tessa's face like a peasant pissing in the fields —

What must she look like in the cold light of day, though, to any prying eyes? A caring mother figure? Not quite old enough. A protective older sister? Maybe. Except they were chalk and cheese to look at.

A stern, watchful landlady? Definitely.

On her days off she liked to wait till she'd seen the flick of tawny curls disappear at the end of the street, give plenty of time for anyone watching to enjoy the affectionate scenario being played out. She would glance at the odd numbers for approval, the posher side of the street with their bigger gates and higher hedges, before turning to attend to her beloved house.

Annette at Smart Secs had found her a part-time position locked in a small, solitary office entering financial data somewhere in the middle of the City. There was no squawking Maureen to bother her, no cackling cronies, but nor was there a delectable Tessa with a shy blush to make her day. It was beneath her, it was dull. But when the bank statements started arriving she realised she needed the cash more than ever. Because John had stopped paying her allowance. Worse, he'd stopped paying the mortgage as well. The one email he'd eventually sent her before he went completely off the radar said, *Sorry, sis. Broke.*

But in her new state of independence that just made Sheila laugh. Broke? How would Roxanne like that?

A couple of weeks after Tessa had moved in Sheila was alone in the house, a silk scarf covering her dark hair, which was scrunched up in a ponytail. She had rubber gloves on. She was down on her knees sweeping the hearth in the seldom-used front room, which she liked to call the parlour. Tessa had produced a mini hi-fi from one of her many chaotic boxes, and put it in the bookcase beside the fireplace, but it was Sheila's music that they listened to. This morning melancholy Mahler was quietly playing.

As she polished the fender round the gas logs, Sheila noticed two of the painted Victorian tiles in the fireplace had come loose. There was a scattering of sooty brick dust behind the grate.

The rattling of the brass door knocker made Sheila

jump. Still holding the dustpan and brush, she hurried back into the hall.

'Forgotten your key, silly?' she smiled, opening the door. 'You'll get such a spanking for that!'

'Sheila! Hi. We thought we'd check up on you!'

Cherie, Flora and the white-blonde Amazon in the long white coat from the other night were on her doorstep.

'I look a sight!' Sheila put her hand over her mouth, tasting rubber. 'I wasn't expecting anyone!'

Cherie stepped forward, put her hand on Sheila's shoulder. 'We've been worried about you.'

She pushed Sheila inside, followed by the other two. The third woman was so tall that she almost blocked the fanlight above the door. The visitors stamped their feet on the precious Persian hall runner and blew on their fingers as if they'd just crossed the Antarctic.

'This really isn't a good time –' Sheila backed against the wall. In the parlour violins were still whining out of the hi-fi. 'I'm in the middle of –'

'A little light dusting, Sheila!' Flora stepped round Cherie, unzipping her white ski jacket and peering through the parlour door at the blood-red walls and Sheila's (and some of John's) gloomy ancestors hanging in ornate gold frames. 'I can recommend a really good cleaner, you know. Keeping this house spotless is obviously too much for you. You look exhausted.'

'I'm absolutely fine.'

'But it certainly is spotless. Not a thing out of place,' murmured their tall friend, walking towards the cold grate and running her finger along the mantelpiece. 'Perhaps you could come and do my place? I never seem to have the time.'

'Any chance of some tea?' Cherie meanwhile was bustling along the passage to the kitchen. 'We're parched.'

'Of course. How rude of me. It's just that I wasn't expecting such an invasion!'

'You'd like us to leave?' the tall woman queried, raising one cool eyebrow. Sheila was usually confident of her own steady gaze, but this woman was unnerving her. Sheila was sure she could see right through her skin.

'Forgive me! I meant such a charming, unexpected visit!' Still hovering in the hallway, Sheila tugged one Marigold off, finger by finger.

'Slap your wrist, madam.' Flora's fingers came down with a smack on Sheila's hand and she giggled. 'You sound like someone in a Jane Austen novel.'

She and the tall woman started prowling around the parlour, examining Sheila's knick-knacks. Sheila addressed the world in general. 'It's just that, as you see, I lead a rather quiet life.'

'We wouldn't know that if we hadn't stopped by, would we? Since we never get an invitation.' Flora came out into the hall and tossed her ski jacket over the banisters. Sheila resisted the urge to hang it on the hat stand by the door. Underneath Flora wore a tight white polo neck, punctuated by the twin thrusts of her small breasts. She wagged a finger at Sheila. 'So that's why we were getting uptight about it. I mean, there's been barely any movement from this house in days.'

'Not that we've been spying you understand,' laughed the tall woman, standing just behind Flora and slowly unbuttoning her floor-length white coat. The laughter flashed across her white face and made it beautiful. 'I'm Daphne, by the way. From number 69.'

Sheila screwed the gloves up in her hand, summoning every ounce of manners to avoid screaming at them all to get out of her house.

'But you got yourself a lodger, I gather, after you'd run the idea past me?' Cherie called out from the kitchen, flicking the kettle on and opening and shutting the cupboards. Jars rattled. Crockery clunked.

Sheila gritted her teeth. 'That's right. I've got Tessa.'

'A little ginger-haired creature, isn't she?' Daphne's coat was undone now. But she didn't take it off. Instead she spread her arms out like wings, regarding Sheila over the top of Flora's head, and waited. 'We've seen her scampering up and down your garden path.'

Flora turned to face Daphne. 'The feel of that suede,' she murmured, stroking her hands up and down the coat, over the swell of Daphne's breasts, turning the lapels inside out to finger the creamy sheepskin lining. 'I could stand here stroking it all day.'

'Just hang it up for me, could you, Flora?' Daphne demanded, shrugging the coat from her shoulders. She kept her ice-blue eyes on Sheila. 'Chilly outside, but quite cosy I suppose in these older Victorian properties.'

Sheila gaped as Flora obediently lifted the coat away, then scooped Daphne's long pale hair away from the collar and re-arranged it over her shoulders.

'Put it over there, Flora, please!' Sheila pointed at the hat stand just as Flora was about to drop it over her own ski jacket.

'Stop making such a mess, slut! You can see it bothers her,' added Daphne through perfectly painted lips, but her face was so serene Sheila wasn't sure she'd heard correctly.

Flora went to stand very close to Daphne. Her arm wound round Daphne's slim waist. Underneath the sheepskin coat she was wearing a dress version of Flora's pullover, a polo-necked dress in white jersey which clung to every amazing curve while still managing to look majestic. The two women standing side by side were a stunning contrast. Flora's sporty petite figure contrasted with Daphne's which without the coat was like a fantasy figurine, her supermodel frame altered into a cartoon by an amazing pair of breasts which jutted like boulders, high and firm and round on her slender ribcage.

'You're admiring my breasts, Sheila? I know all the girls do. You're wondering if I've had work done, aren't you?' Daphne said in a low drawl, running the palms of her hands slowly over her breasts. They didn't budge. But her nipples, previously just a suggestion, were out like acorns when her hands had finished their descent over the silky material. 'Go on. Guess. Touch them, if you like.'

Sheila caught startled amusement in Flora's baby-blue eyes, and just as she felt a blush creeping up her neck she gave herself a stern inward shake. Time to regain control here.

'I wouldn't dream of it. Touching them, I mean. But they're splendid breasts. Perfect, in fact. From a professional point of view.'

'Professional?' Flora shook her head without understanding.

Daphne's thin eyebrows went up. 'Meaning?'

'I mean,' Sheila said, folding her arms and recalling every ounce of *sang froid*, 'did you ever think of lingerie modelling?'

Daphne smiled. She had perfect white teeth. They all had perfect white teeth. 'Now there's an idea. Perhaps I might have done when I was younger and more foolish. But my husband would never let me stoop to such work now.'

'What a waste,' Sheila said, snapping off her other glove.

'Coming through!' Cherie bashed a tray into the small of Sheila's back, shoving them all into the parlour and kicking the coffee table into place to put the drinks down. She'd taken her coat off in the kitchen and was wearing another white lamb's wool sweater with a very deep V showing the wobble of her breasts. 'Christ almighty, Flora, can't you keep your hands off the boss for five seconds?'

'Won't you come and sit down?' Sheila sighed,

waving her arms at the sofas, but the three women were already perfectly at home. 'I'll just go and change –'

'You're going nowhere.' Cherie pulled her firmly into the room. She went and sat down on the biggest sofa beside the other two, so that the three of them were facing Sheila like interrogators. 'We came to see how you're coping.'

'Her husband left her, you see, Daph. You've missed a lot of gossip while you've been away.' Flora stroked Daphne's long leg, pushing the silky jersey dress up her thigh. Daphne was wearing white fishnet stockings, and very high spiky boots with a fur trim. 'Poor Sheila found him in the shower.'

'Fucking his mistress. Right there in the en suite.' Cherie leaned forward to pick up a cup, her breasts drooping from her sweater. 'Sheila confided in me and Flora, didn't you, poor love?'

On her own she had struck Sheila as quite chic. Next to the others she was positively matronly. And it wasn't Cherie that interested Sheila now. It was Daphne whom Sheila couldn't keep her eyes off.

'Told us every detail, didn't you?' Flora joined in. 'How he had his tongue stuck right inside his American girlfriend. How he was kneeling at her feet, licking at her like her little doggie. And I'm guessing he'd never done that to you, had he, Sheila?'

'So you must be horribly frustrated with no man about,' Daphne said, lifting one leg to cross it slowly over the other. 'I know I am.'

The fishnets were indeed stockings. Sheila glanced right into the dark gap as one thigh paused defiantly before resting on the other. *Basic Instinct*, right there in her living room.

'We're all horny as hell, because all the husbands are away.'

'What, together?' Sheila asked, picking up a cup that Cherie had poured out. The tea was too weak. She wondered what these perfect husbands might do. 'Playing golf, are they?'

'No, no, no. Not together, and not playing golf. They're busy making money, of course, to keep us in the style to which we're accustomed!' Cherie sipped noisily at her tea.

'Oh, they don't know how to have fun. Not like us!' Flora ran her fingers up under Daphne's dress. 'But I still miss the feel of a nice big dick when Graham's away. Don't you miss that, Sheila, now that your man's gone? Having someone to come home to with a hard on whenever you want it, taking you even when you're asleep, sucking you where you want him to suck you –'

Cherie abandoned her tea, got up and planted her wide bottom on the arm of Sheila's old-fashioned wingchair.

'That's why we went to this special spa, to cheer ourselves up. We're used to being thoroughly fucked every night. We were going cross-eyed with wanting it.' Cherie put her arm round Sheila and squeezed her shoulders.

'Special spa?' Sheila queried, tensing a little. Cherie didn't notice, kept her arm there, her fingers idly stroking Sheila's arm. 'What do they do there? I mean, that your husbands don't?'

Over on the sofa Flora hooked her own leg in its shiny ski pants over Daphne's, pulling her leg further open. Daphne didn't smile or respond, but nor did she push Flora off. 'We had all the treatments, didn't we, girls? All we did was lie around all day and be seen to. There were these guys with amazing powerful hands, pummelling, massaging you all over, they had these potions that they rub into you and make your head swim. They can make you come just by flicking a fingernail –'

'Every single treatment. For every single ailment,' yawned Daphne, stretching both arms casually along the back of the sofa. Her breasts moved upwards in perfect unison. 'Every single orifice –'

'Was this Switzerland or somewhere? You're all dressed as if you've been in the snow.' Sheila's voice felt rusty. She took a sip of tea and coughed as it burned its way down her chest.

Flora giggled. 'Knightsbridge, would you believe! And such a goodie bag they gave us, to use at home!'

Sheila felt a sharp twinge of envy at the thought of the three friends luxuriating in their scented penthouse having Thai massage and crystal therapy.

'Well, you look like a trio of ice queens, and here am I looking like a charlady.' She put her teacup down with a final clatter and stood up. 'Thanks for your concern. But as you see, I couldn't be better. And now I must get on.'

'We don't think you're fine.' Flora jumped up. 'You look pale, and too thin. Some attention, and a make-over, is what you need.'

'Not just a makeover,' remarked Daphne. 'Let's show her what we brought, girls. Let's show her what you do when there's not a real man to roger you.'

'Yes, but before we show you the goodie bag they gave us, you need to *look* like us. Which means getting you out of that awful black garb, for starters.'

Cherie and Flora heaved Sheila out of her chair. Daphne remained where she was on the sofa, her dress hooked right up round her fanny, her elegant knees still crossed, her white buttocks squashing into the sofa, visible above the stocking tops.

'You don't want to look like a charlady, do you, Sheila?' she drawled. 'You want to look like a queen. A sex queen. We'll make you look like one. And then we're going to make you *feel* like one.'

'Something white, so you look like us.' Flora's little fingers plucked the silk scarf off Sheila's hair. She hopped about in front of Sheila, unbuttoning her black cashmere. 'Come on, Sheila. Make nice. We'll beat you if you don't.'

'I never wear white.' Cherie was holding Sheila's arms, so she couldn't stop Flora taking off the cardigan to reveal the black lace bra she wore underneath. 'I could never look like you three. Please, can't you just go home now?'

'Something white, Sheila. Don't be so narrow in your outlook.' Daphne stood up, the dress ruffling slowly back into place over her body. She went out to the hall and came back with a large pink carrier bag printed with an expensive logo. 'And we're not going anywhere. Now, if you're not more hospitable we'll be making over your whole precious little house. Go and find something white for her to wear, Flora. Then we can show our new neighbour here what we've learned at our special spa.'

Flora scampered up the stairs while Cherie tossed the black cardigan away.

'Time to loosen up, Sheila.' Daphne came and stood in front of Sheila. She rested both hands on Sheila's breasts. She had big hands, like a man, but elegant and long-fingered. Sheila was so startled she couldn't move. Daphne started to push Sheila's breasts together, the lace of her bra shifting and touching at her nipples.

'I'm perfectly –' Sheila started to say, the breath knocked out of her by such unaccustomed touching. 'Now you're all getting at me.'

'You'll do it for me, won't you?' Daphne reached behind and unhooked the bra before Sheila could agree. Behind them Cherie started rifling around in the carrier bag. Sheila groaned with embarrassment as Daphne tossed the bra to one side and examined her breasts, then took them as if weighing them, lifting them upwards so that they looked huge and exposed in the wintry daylight. Sheila tried to pull away but Daphne tightened her grip and so Sheila strained a little against

99

Daphne's hands, yearning for contact. But Daphne let go of them, bending to yank off Sheila's knickers now.

'We don't do black,' she told her quietly as she straightened again. 'Just white.'

Sheila was naked now, and her nakedness removed any inhibitions one by one. The gleam of intense interest sparking in Daphne's icy blue eyes only made her feel more reckless. She returned the look, pressing against Daphne. She waited for resistance, pressed harder so that their nipples touched, their pussies touched, the slightest movement caused delicious friction.

Daphne arched her back a little so that her breasts were thrust forwards, still encased in the film of white fabric. She grabbed Sheila's hands and splayed them out on the white material. Her own hands moved on top of Sheila's, urging her to feel the big round swell of the breasts there, the way they gave under her fingers as she pushed them together, the way the nipples grew into long hard points poking side by side through the material. Sheila's stomach sparked as she fondled the other woman's breasts. Who cared if they were real or not? It was new, exhilarating, the next best thing to touching her own. How she tortured herself when she was alone, imagining lips and teeth and fingers on her nipples but often forbidding herself to touch, resisting that delicious flare of desire. She was saving that special treat. For when, she didn't know.

Well, she knew now. If Daphne wasn't going to touch her breasts, suck her nipples, today, now, she would make her little slave Tessa do it. Tonight.

She spread her fingers over Daphne's breasts. Her own were tingling, her nipples hardening, this particular, specific longing she had for her nipples to be sucked was a real, unanswered addiction. And she couldn't rest until she'd had a fix. Her stomach stirred with lust when she saw Daphne part her lips, her tongue running across her white teeth.

Keeping one hand to guide Sheila's over her breasts, Daphne pressed the other on Sheila's stomach, slid it slowly downwards. Sheila could feel its fingers walking towards her bush and as they tangled in the hair there she felt the wetness. Her thighs parted, even though her legs were shaking. Daphne's fingers paused, then traced the hidden crack, sliding down, edging right inside until she could scratch at the soft opening, then whisking up again. Sheila gasped for more. She couldn't hide her shivering response. No clothes to hide it. No point hiding it.

Her mouth opened sensuously, ready to eat or drink or suck, it felt wanton opening like that. Sheila pushed closer to the other woman and pressed her open mouth against Daphne's. Her lips opened just a little, just enough for Sheila to taste her. She flicked out her tongue and instantly it met Daphne's, tickling the corner of her mouth. Sheila wanted to suck that slippery tip but Daphne closed her mouth up again and as Sheila wondered if she'd read this wrong she felt Daphne's fingers sliding further down in her crack, probing, like a penis, in between her wet pussy lips.

Both women started to move very slightly against each other. Sheila wanted to feel Daphne's pussy but she also wanted to continue massaging the woman's strange, gorgeous breasts and Daphne pressed up closer and jammed her fingers further up, finding and circling her clit in one expert movement and driving Sheila onto a spike of excitement.

Sheila tried to open herself up wider and, as Daphne worked her fingers in harder and deeper, Sheila's cunt gave little spasms to grab her fingers, keep them up there, but everything Daphne did was done so lazily, her fingers were in no rush, they played Sheila's clit like a little instrument and the harder Sheila ground herself against Daphne's hand so you could hear the wetness, the slower Daphne's fingers played –

'Found just the right thing!'

Flora was back, totally shattering the moment. She tossed something white for Daphne to catch, then hopped across to Cherie. She seemed fizzing with energy today. A drape of white cloth fell over Sheila's face and the smell of Tessa's perfume, little Tessa who she'd nearly forgotten with all this disturbance, was suffocating. She could hear Cherie and Flora rustling the carrier bag somewhere in the room and whispering. Daphne pulled her fingers quickly out of Sheila's cunt and pushed her, now blinded and smothered with the cloth, across the room.

'See how different you look now?'

Daphne pulled the cloth down. Sheila was in front of the mirror, and the white cloth was Tessa's Marilyn dress. It was far too small.

'No, you can't use this!'

'We're your guests, remember?' Daphne tied the halter tightly at Sheila's neck. 'Have you not heard the expression *mi casa e tu casa*?'

'This is not your house. I didn't invite you here.'

'Well, I'm disappointed. Shocked, even.' Daphne's hands, the same hands that had been fondling inside her pussy a couple of minutes ago, froze claw-like on Sheila's neck. 'Cherie? Flora? You told me our new neighbour was a civilised woman with exquisite manners?'

'That's what we thought, Daphne.' In an identical movement, hunched side by side on the floor by the sofa, Cherie and Flora stuck their forefingers in their mouths like children sucking lollipops. 'Oh dear. Seems we were mistaken.'

'I am civilised. I have perfect manners. But you'll have to go. This dress doesn't suit me. It isn't even mine. Take it off!' Sheila cried, yanking at the knot.

'I think manners have to be taught, don't they? The kind of manners we expect here in Spartan Street, anyway.'

102

'Spartan Street was nothing but a row of brothels before my John rebuilt it!' Sheila shouted, twisting round. 'Yes, that's right. You'd all be living in knocking shops if it wasn't for him.'

'Er, wrong, honey.' Cherie shook her head, turning the corners of her mouth downwards. 'I think you'll find it was only *this* side of the street –'

'How dare you come into my house and tell me how to behave!'

'Well, hush my mouth!' Cherie and Flora slapped their cheeks and started to laugh. 'And this from the woman whose *well behaved* husband sticks his great greedy tongue up his mistress right under her very nose!'

'You see, you're no better than anyone else in Spartan Street, are you?'

Daphne produced the yellow wig and jammed it down to cover Sheila's dark hair. Flora rushed up brandishing a lipstick and smeared sticky red across Sheila's mouth, making it too big, like a clown. She pinched her cheeks until they were pink. Sheila shut her mouth, feeling the lipstick gluing her lips together. The painted stranger in the mirror looked like a doll.

'Oh my God, how sexy is that look! Now you're just like us!' Flora squealed, turning Sheila round and round till she was dizzy. 'Not scary Sheila any more!'

'We can call you sexy Sheila, now.' Cherie pulled her trousers over her hips and kicked them off, leaving her white boots on. Then she sat astride the arm of the sofa, her hands shoved deep inside her big white knickers. She started to stroke herself. 'That white dress and yellow hair – it makes you look so much younger, Sheila!'

Flora was wiggling about as if she needed to piss, pulling down the zip of her trousers and putting on a little whiny voice. 'Oh, I'm so ready now. I'm getting so wet, Daphne. I want to play. Can we do it now?'

'For being greedy, you'll have to wear the

contraption.' Daphne reached into the carrier bag and chucked what looked like a heavy leather belt at Flora.

'I thought you were going to make Sheila do it!' Flora plucked at Daphne's sleeve. 'You said you were going to teach her a lesson!'

'Stop whining, Flora.' Daphne knocked her out of the way so she could recline against the cushions with her legs splayed open and bent at the knee, her spiky heels digging into the worn brocade of the sofa. She closed her eyes. 'Show our hostess the presents we brought from the spa, Cherie.'

'This will show that rotten husband of yours that you don't need him, Sheila.' Cherie obediently scrabbled on the floor picking everything up. Her big bosoms dangled out of the white sweater she still wore. Her bare buttocks and thighs seemed enormous in the daylight. 'See what we do when we're missing our men.'

Sheila turned from staring at herself in the mirror. Her breasts were squashed tight by the stitching of Tessa's dress, making it hard to breathe. The cleavage was dark and pronounced, the breasts bulging where the halter hoisted them upwards. The skirt of the dress was letting all the cold air in, so short on her that she felt like a schoolgirl. She could remember playing hockey in the winter until her knees went purple, but still she'd bend over the stick and ball and relish the cold air creeping up under her skirt, kissing her tight young pussy.

'Oh, I know what you do at home, Cherie,' she said, walking towards the sofa, experimenting with a deliberate Marilyn sway in her step. She put her hands on her hips. The three women all looked at her from their various places in the room, appreciation flashing across their faces. 'I've seen you in your kitchen window. I've seen Flora's hands round your neck. I've seen you touching each other up. I've been outside, looking in. Cherie likes to be strangled.'

'And look at you! You're *jealous*!' Cherie pulled down her knickers to show the bleached white hairs curling over her sex. Her fingers started to part the lips, show the red slash between. 'How about that!'

'Groping in the kitchen? So? That's just a normal coffee morning,' Flora mocked, staring at Cherie's crotch. 'Just a bit of entertainment to stop us getting bored.'

'Show her the new toy, Flora,' Cherie whooped, tossing her curly head back. One hand held her pussy lips open while the other hand rubbed frantically up and down the crack. 'Can she, Daph?'

Flora turned her back without waiting for Daphne's permission. She kicked her ski pants off to show the moons of her neat bottom and the tiny white thong slicing up the crack between them like dental floss. As she made a show of dancing about her butt cheeks opened and closed, showing a glimpse of the lilac-coloured crease and the puckered little hole in the centre. Sheila was transfixed at the rude sight, but Flora was upright again now, buckling something round her waist. She swung dramatically round. 'Feast your eyes, Mrs Moss, on this stupendous gift from the spa.'

Flora was transformed into a girl-man. Round her waist was a thick belt off which ran various other straps, bolted and buckled, straps running round the tops of her legs, up the crack of her backside, one particularly thin strap slicing between her pussy lips, and then poking out in front was a great thick penis made of leather rearing at an angle to her body as if growing out of her pussy. She jerked her hips obscenely so that the leather cock jumped at Sheila.

Sheila's mouth dropped open in horrified wonder, excitement fizzing in her cunt just where Daphne's fingers had pinched and tickled moments earlier. Flora started marching around the room with a mock masculine swagger, still wearing a tight white vest, her sporty arms and legs not much bigger than the phallus bolted on to her.

Cherie gave a yelp of fury, fumbling with her own belt. 'I can't do mine – it's too small! Help me, Daphne!'

Daphne sat up lazily, slapped Cherie's big white buttocks as if she was a cow in a stall to make her turn round. 'All that money your Jamie makes, and you're still just a lazy peasant, aren't you?'

Cherie backed on to the sofa, her rump in the air as Daphne started to buckle her up. Cherie's body jerked back and forth, her pink lips parting in a euphoric smile as Daphne pulled and tugged the sharp buckles into place. The leather straps criss-crossed Cherie's stomach and thighs and buttocks, digging in so that Cherie's doughy flesh bulged out either side of each strap. Sheila thought of Tessa, trussed up on her little bed upstairs, her wrists all tied, her ankles kicking joyously against the restraints as Sheila started her nightly torment.

Her pussy was crawling now with frustration.

When she was strapped in, Cherie pulled her sweater and her bra off in awkward, clumsy movements, then turned on all fours and crouched over Daphne like a big white dog. Her huge white breasts hung down over Daphne's face. She leaned her weight on one hand, bending closer so that her nipples grazed Daphne's mouth. Daphne didn't move. Sheila's stomach kicked with excitement. Her own breasts swelled against the white dress every time Cherie tried to interest Daphne in her tits and Daphne turned her face away, pursing her lips. The game was tantalising. Sheila snaked one hand under her dress and pressed it against her aching pussy. She wanted to push Cherie off Daphne and straddle the woman herself, rip Tessa's white dress off and feed her nipples into the cool, closed mouth. Her pussy was tightening now with desire, contracting frantically under her hand, and she couldn't help rubbing at herself as she stood right there beside the sofa.

'So it's fucking you want?' Cherie changed the tempo. She shifted back a little, took the big leather penis, and used it to push Daphne's dress up round her waist. Sheila gasped. Daphne wore no knickers, and her fanny was hairless. Her sex lips were primly closed as if over a secret, the smooth flesh so white it was almost blue. It was as if she really was made of ice.

Cherie spread her legs a little to get the angle right, and pushed Daphne's slim white legs in their white stockings further open. Sheila watched, waiting for those bare lips to open, but still they remained shut. Cherie was breathing heavily, holding the great leather prick. The sight of the obscene male member had certainly flicked Daphne's switch. She stretched her throat and lay back again, suddenly all demure. Her hands clutched Cherie's bottom, her nails digging and scratching where the flesh puffed out between the strangling straps. But she didn't look at Cherie. She turned her head sideways across the cushion and looked calmly at Sheila, who stared back at her, shaking with the effort to breathe normally.

Cherie was pink in the face, her thighs shaking to keep her up on her knees. She stroked Daphne's white thigh where it bulged slightly over the fishnet stockings. Flora stopped her prancing and barged on to the sofa, her buckled phallus swinging between her legs, trying to get between Cherie and Daphne.

'You bitch!' screeched Flora, taking hold of Cherie's arms to shake her, trying to heave her off Daphne's legs. 'I want Daphne!'

They both flailed about on the sofa, kicking at the teacups on the table, punching and scratching like a couple of cats.

Flora had one knee up between Cherie's legs, banging it into her pussy, and was shoving her friend awkwardly about on the sofa. 'You can wait your turn. You're a greedy fat pig!' she screeched.

'Teacher's pet! I haven't had a go!' shouted Cherie. She grabbed Flora's fake penis and yanked her violently back and forth with it. 'You always get what you want.'

'Get in line, Flora!' Daphne may have been supine beneath her furious friends, but she could still bark orders. 'We're here to show our hostess what we've brought to the party, remember? Now behave.'

Flora glared at Sheila, and something in Sheila flared up at the sight of the sulky girl stamping her foot. Flora was like a petulant version of her sweet Tessa. Small, just like Tessa, but so fiery. And unlike Tessa, who only played at it for other people's pleasure as well as her own, Flora really *did* need some serious taming.

Cherie grunted with satisfaction as Flora flounced off the sofa. Still keeping near, though, she started to gyrate her hips, running her hands up and down her own phallus as if masturbating it, and the excitement in Sheila rose to fever pitch. Cherie settled down to business, planting her knees to coax the dildo up Daphne's primly closed crack. Daphne's eyelids merely fluttered.

'What, no foreplay, Cherie?' Flora asked, strutting round behind Cherie, getting one knee up on the arm of the sofa and rubbing her dildo against Cherie's fat buttock. 'Poor Daph.'

Cherie poked her fingertips into Daphne's slit and peeled open the lips. Sheila realised she'd been waiting for this moment, waiting for that flash of pink to break up the white ice of Daphne's skin.

'She's ready, don't you worry. Nice and damp. She's been playing with Mrs Moss, hasn't she?' Cherie was bold now that she was playing the man. She winked at Sheila. 'She teased out your inner blonde, didn't she, Mrs Moss?'

Flora giggled. Sheila nodded weakly and sat on the coffee table. Her thighs were sticky as she rocked back and forth on the hard surface, sliding her hands up and down her aching pussy. Cherie braced herself and then without warning thrust her hips forwards so that the dildo thudded into Daphne's vulva, splitting her redness open. Daphne's knees jerked upwards and locked behind Cherie's waist, pulling her closer, and the dildo edged itself further inside. It looked so big it could do damage. But it slid further and further in, the dark leather inches swallowed up as Daphne arched her back, the white dress still covering her torso, her long white legs winding round Cherie, muscles tensing as she dragged Cherie back and forth.

Seeing that the action was hotting up, Flora got up close behind Cherie. She had a spare leather strap in her hand and was winding it round her knuckles. The other hand held her dildo and she started to push it between Cherie's fat buttocks, which parted with a damp sucking sound. While Cherie concentrated on sliding her phallus in and out of Daphne, who was biting her lips with her sharp teeth as Cherie slammed back and forth, Flora had ideas of her own.

She suddenly brought the leather strap down on one of the wedges of Cherie's flesh, and Cherie screamed out loud, giving a mighty thrust into Daphne.

Even though the scene before her was like something in her head rather than real, Sheila still glanced out of the window as her guests started screaming and the whip-crack of the strap coming down on Cherie's wobbling buttocks got louder. Anyone could walk past and see.

But they were all past caring, and why should they care? It wasn't their house. Their houses were all mini castles with their moats and drawbridges – Daphne's even had a little in and out gravel drive – so no one would be able to look in.

Sheila's house was wide open to all callers.

The three of them were moving as one now. Cherie was screaming with pleasure at Flora's whipping. Every time the strap came down, she crashed backwards on to Flora's phallus. Flora was like a cowgirl, flicking her hips back and forth, waving the strap like a lasso, her phallus buried deep inside Cherie's anus. Cherie was like her overfed mount.

Sheila could only imagine how tight the fit of that dildo up the backside would be. But both her cunt and her own anus seemed to know perfectly well, because they squeezed hard as she watched both false cocks thrusting into the willing holes. Cherie had Flora's dildo right up her now, because every time her dildo fucked Daphne, she shoved Flora forwards with her.

Daphne was right up the end of the sofa so her head was jammed against the other arm, and suddenly she pulled herself half up, tensed her knees hard round Cherie's waist, rode up and down the dildo fast until she gave a rising whoop of ecstasy and threw herself backwards in a balletic climax.

Flora accelerated her rhythm, ramming into Cherie's bottom, whipping her all the while and leaving red lines all over her white flesh until Cherie came too, falling heavily on to Daphne, gasping for breath as Flora pulled the dildo back out, glistening with all sorts of Cherie's juices, and swung round to face Sheila.

'Well, that's finished them off,' she cackled, giving the dildo a wipe with a cloth and still making it look as if she was masturbating. 'What do you think, Mrs Moss?'

Sheila realised she had been rocking herself over the smooth wooden surface of the coffee table until she was sore as she watched the rutting threesome, but all she was achieving with the friction was a rising sense of desperate frustration as she saw and imagined but couldn't feel.

'It's cold in here,' Daphne said in an astonishingly composed voice. 'Do you think you could light the fire? You've obviously been scrubbing that lovely Victorian fireplace all morning.'

She punched at Cherie to get her off. Cherie heaved herself backwards, still panting, and her dildo sucked out of Daphne, wet with her cunt juice. The soaked new leather on both dildos gave off an enhanced smell of female sex mixed with another, harsher aroma.

Daphne crossed her long legs. The nude sex lips kissed and closed again, but Sheila could see that they were swollen now after their battering by the dildo, and tinged with lustful pink.

'Lay the fire? Of course, Daphne.'

Now she was talking like the others. Obeying orders. Sheila shifted to the end of the coffee table, her skin squeaking on the wood. She was leaving a trail of wetness on the surface. She dropped to her knees to crawl over the rug. Her thighs stuck together as she knelt down on the hard marble slab of the hearth and she jammed them together to try to stop her body's endless fidgeting. But still her bottom was in the air, and Tessa's white dress barely covered it, and that in itself, watched by her bizarre audience, excited her.

The bizarre audience had gone quiet. Part of her wished they would just go, so she could ponder all this on her own. Tell Tessa about it later.

'Now, girls, Mrs Moss – sorry, sexy Sheila – has welcomed us into her home, given us tea.' Daphne's voice was low, and just behind her. She was like a teacher calming her unruly class. 'The least we can do is thank her properly!'

Nine

The gas flames leapt up from the dead coals. Sheila felt the warmth on her face. She noticed another tile had come loose inside the chimney breast. Keeping hold of the little brass lever, she turned to look back over her shoulder.

Cherie and Flora were kneeling on all fours behind her, their dildos jutting forwards like weapons. Cherie was still red in the face. Flora looked like a whippet waiting for the starting gun. Daphne was standing above them, the ice queen restored, with her head cocked on one side, her fingers tangled in their hair as if she had them both on leads.

'Which one would you like, Sheila?' she demanded, yanking Cherie and Flora up on to their haunches. 'Which one of these little bitches would you like to fuck you?'

The clock ticked on the mantelpiece as the gas flames hissed. 'You decide, Daphne.'

Daphne nodded slowly and slapped both Cherie and Flora on their bottoms so they strained forwards. 'Go, girls.'

Flora got to Sheila first, her false penis aimed like a javelin straight between Sheila's legs. 'I'm good at this!' she crowed, pushing Sheila roughly down on to her hands and flicking the white Marilyn dress up over her bottom. 'But I want my reward!'

'Making our hostess come all over the hearth rug will be reward enough, Flora.' Daphne went and sat on the sofa again, pulling her dress down over her legs. Somehow the fact that she was fully clothed made the scenario all the more fantastic. Her tight white lips were once more hidden, but Sheila remembered how they had opened like petals a few minutes ago to show the livid gash of sex inside.

But now she was at Flora's mercy and the thick blunt end of that imitation knob was banging at her bottom, forcing its way inside, forcing its way down the crack, under her one hole, seeking out the other. But it wasn't Flora who was jabbing at her backside, because Flora was wriggling round to lie beneath her, slipping like an eel in between Sheila's legs. From behind, Cherie tipped Sheila forwards just as Flora forced her legs apart so that as she struggled for balance she landed on the waiting tip of Flora's massive prick, felt its blunt end poking inside her swollen lips.

A little scream bunched up in her throat. As it did so a pair of ice-cold hands stroked her face. She arched her neck like a cat, enjoying the contact, but then suddenly her eyes were blindfolded.

'Another free gift from the spa,' murmured Daphne.

Sheila could see nothing but silky darkness. Her heart started to beat faster. She wasn't afraid, but she was vulnerable. But more than this she realised, as the invisible Flora pushed the phallus further inside, pushing her swollen sex lips open, that not being able to see raised every hair on her body to high alert. Every sense was magnified. The warmth of the fire on her breasts, still heaving out of the tight dress. The colder air behind, and the bulky warmth of Cherie's body.

'So wet it's like you've pissed yourself, Mrs Moss,' Cherie crooned, running her fingers up and down Sheila's buttock crack, probing and groping her sex lips which were nibbling their way down Flora's false knob, everything starting to open up so wide. 'This should go in nice and easy, then.'

Cherie was running her dildo up and down between Sheila's buttocks as Flora's entered her and with a sudden rush pushed her upwards, so fast and hard that Sheila was lifted slightly by it, every muscle flexed to grip and engulf it, and as it went in she shuddered with delight. She tilted forwards, impaled by the huge shaft, and Cherie tilted with her, jabbing her dildo now at Sheila's raised, offered butt hole.

Sheila's black world was like a blank screen. If she wanted she could superimpose faces and people into this scene. Fantasise about someone else doing this to her. But there was no one. There was only her, and her three neighbours, and their props.

The hardness of the dildo was almost visual, sparks coming off it, off of her, as she slid up and down the false cock, opening her legs wider to accommodate it, stopping to feel it standing rock-hard up inside her. Flora lay still. But fingers were tugging at her dress, and someone was undoing it so her breasts could fall free. She imagined that Flora was lying back, arms behind her head, watching Mrs Moss losing control, sliding up and down and groaning, and she reckoned those little teeth would be bared in a grin. So who was undoing her dress?

As her breasts were indeed laid bare and her nipples shrank up into points, someone's fingers started to pinch them.

'Suck them,' she whispered. Her voice came out as a kind of gruff bark. 'Please suck them.'

'Demanding, isn't she? Aren't we doing enough for her?' Someone sniggered.

From beneath her Flora mocked, 'Oh, but we haven't used all the toys yet. Here's one we used earlier. On our Cherie at the spa when *she* got above herself.'

The fingers went away and her nipples shrivelled tighter, burning for more. Sheila tried not to care.

Everything was going on inside her cunt, anyway. Her nipples were bare, and that felt good. The more she thought about them, the harder they got.

Suddenly they were pinched again, but not by fingers. It was as if they'd been bitten by something very sharp, or stung by a venomous insect. And then the sting eased into a deep, red-hot throbbing.

'See that?' Flora said. 'Nipple clamps. Marvellous.'

'Course I can't see,' Cherie grunted into Sheila's ear. 'I'm taking her from behind.'

She pulled open Sheila's buttocks. Sheila could feel her flesh there wobbling as Cherie pulled and pushed and then wedged her dildo forcefully up between the cheeks, shoving at Sheila's bottom hole. On the other side of that fine membrane of skin, Flora's dildo was pumping Sheila so hard she didn't think she had room in her head or body for any other sensations, but here it came. Cherie's dick was pushing at her butt hole. At first the hole closed like a fist against the shame of it. Sheila bit her lips, dreading that she would let out wind or worse. She tried to pull away, but she couldn't stop her own manic rhythm and she was grunting out loud now, letting herself go, safe behind her blindfold.

The nipple clamps were like terrier's teeth, worrying at her in her world of blackness with the exquisite pain which radiated through her breasts growing duller but no less insistent the further into her body it reached. It only added to the stack of sensations making her lift herself and plunge harder on to Flora, so hard she must be driving the girl right down into the floor.

Cherie held her like a limpet, the phallus pushing further, further at the little dry hole but just as it started to loosen, it contracted again as if to expel the intruder, then loosened again, and each time it loosened the dildo went up more easily, lubricated by her juices. She didn't understand what juices they might be, but she loved them anyway.

As she rocked forwards she was penetrated up her cunt, as she rocked backwards it was up her arse, so that now her insides were melting too, she was opening her legs and buttocks as wide as she could and both girls were opening her as wide as they could, and so her muscles were being trained, slackening to accommodate both big poles just pinning her there, and now she had two thick cocks wedged up her and how perverted she must look, as if she was on some kind of medieval torture rack, and that made her arch her neck with pleasure and now her body was gripping everything tight and the climax was coming.

Through her own ecstatic moaning and Cherie's soft laughter she thought she heard the doorbell ring. But Cherie's breath was hot on her neck as she fucked her harder, and she didn't hear it again, and now Cherie was fanning her hand out on Sheila's stomach to keep her in position as she thrashed wildly. Cherie pressed on Sheila's full bladder and the searing sensation was instant, building with her climax and as her anus clenched she rode it, feeling it storming through both cunt and arse. She tasted the dirty words in her head, she was one big pleasure zone, and she shuddered as if she had a fever and let her body grip and slacken, grip and slacken, until everything was spent and she was coming.

She hung there, shivering, on all fours, coming. Her nipples pulsated in time with her heartbeat. Without a word Flora and Cherie, who had worked like, well, like dogs to pleasure her, yanked their tools out of her so that she staggered forwards, and almost immediately there was an uncontrollable downwards rush from her bladder and she started to piss in convulsive spurts, relief flooding through her like another orgasm as the hot liquid ran down her stiff legs.

Mortified at the fact that she was urinating, and in such an abandoned way, Sheila tugged at the white dress, trying to cover her wet legs and mop at them before the others noticed. She couldn't see, she couldn't tell if they'd noticed. They weren't speaking. She thought she could hear them moving or walking about the room, whispering.

But then she heard the dripping on the rug. She sat back on her haunches, every movement stiff and laboured. She lifted her arms to do up her dress, and her tortured nipples shrank at the movement, the clamps scraping so agonisingly against the dress as she tried to knot it round her neck that she had to stop, hold it away from her. She couldn't see to undo the clamps. Now that she'd come the game was over. She wanted them off. She was weak, almost delirious with the pain from her nipples, the throbbing in her battered cunt, the stinging of the piss on her thighs.

'Get this off me,' she demanded, trying to rip the blindfold off. 'Get it all off. This has gone far enough.'

The floorboard in the doorway to the living room creaked. She blinked as she got the blindfold up to see three white figures moving round the furniture like weird angels, and a fourth, dark, figure standing at the door.

'Well, I came about the room,' a deep voice drawled, blowing a stream of cigarette smoke into the warm, scented room. 'But it looks like you've a houseful already.'

Ten

'How marvellous to meet the neighbourhood – and all in one room!' The woman laughed, lighting up a long black cigarette. 'I am Olga, by the way. I didn't know you English were so sociable.'

'We're not.'

Sheila sank back in the sofa. Her skin gave a ghostly shiver as her thighs brushed each other.

Her visitor was a black silhouette against the lowering afternoon light. How long had those witches been here? But thank God they'd gone – for now. A jet of smoke dissipated into grey wisps.

'I don't allow smoking in my house.' Sheila stretched feebly for an oversized crystal tumbler squatting on today's unopened bank statement. 'I don't recognise this?' She lifted the glass to the light.

'Mine. Czech crystal with best Czech vodka, a dash of cranberry. Ice for the bruising.' Olga twisted the burning end off the cigarette and tossed it into the fireplace.

'Bruising?'

'All over, believe me! Those toys! Enough to scare a horse!' Olga laughed. 'But still you look confused, Mrs –?'

'Moss. Sheila Moss. I recognise you from the Smart Secs office, but I don't understand what you're doing here.'

'I need a place to live.' Olga glanced at the house opposite. 'In this street. And I understand you let rooms.'

'Please, make yourself at home – would you mind? I have to wash first.'

Upstairs she kicked the white dress into a puddle on Tessa's bedroom floor. Wearing it was both bewitching and a betrayal. She glared at Tessa's bleach-framed mirror studded with seashells. She didn't recognise the black-eyed woman with the electrified yellow hair and the smeared red mouth glaring wildly back. She tossed the offending wig on top of the dress, trying to direct her anger. Those women had barged in here and dragged her into their sordid game, humiliating her. No. She'd allowed it, hadn't she? She'd let them strip her, play with her, watch unsurprised as she abandoned herself to it all, the brutal thrust of those leather cocks going up her arse. The word Maureen would use.

But now Sheila Moss would use the word "arse", because she was no better than Maureen. Her stomach shifted. How could she purse her lips when her backside had been invaded like that, driving her demented with dark pleasure?

What pride was left when the blindfold was the best part of it? Not seeing, only feeling. Sensation without the distraction of sight.

She twisted on the shower, spraying the snail-trails of pee already drying down her legs. She whimpered as the water jetted over her nipples, eased bubbles of soap very gently across the red raw points. She could see the piercings like vampire's teeth left by the clamps.

Even when she was dry and arrayed once more in black, descending the stairs stiffly in her widow's weeds, she couldn't shake it off. She suspected, as she stepped over a collection of very expensive luggage, that not only would she never forget the experience – before long she would be wanting more.

119

'I'm between lovers, you know? And that means I'm between houses.' Olga continued as if there'd been no break in the conversation. She was tapping her finger-nails against her crystal glass. 'So you see I need the room.'

'The room?'

Olga pressed her big lips together apologetically. 'I memorised the number from that newspaper. The working girl, looking for a room. You wondered could she be a hooker?'

'Tessa.' Another wave of shame crawled through Sheila. 'She's not a hooker. She's a lovely girl.'

'I can tell. I spoke with her. I asked if she'd found a room, and she said yes and you had empty bedrooms, and you would be pleased for another lodger.' Olga's knuckles were white around her glass. 'I have plenty money.'

'Working for Smart Secs?'

Olga shook her head. 'I'm hostess in a jazz club. Much better than sitting at a desk. Great music. Very rich men. Tips, you know. But I can't sleep at my work, and my last lover had a wife. So I need somewhere to stay. Immediately.'

'You're not put off by – what you saw?' Sheila asked, shifting about on the sofa. 'Because I can assure you, that's not what happens –!'

'This is your house. You must do as you please!' Olga grinned. 'And I hope you do. Girl on girl? Not really my thing, but my friend would enjoy to see it.'

'Your friend?' Sheila took another gulp of vodka and felt her strength returning.

'I bump into him just now, in the street. Client. From the club. That's why I can't take a room with him. Must keep business and pleasure apart. For now.' Olga raked her thick red hair with her nails. Outside the street lamp glowed pale pink, turning slowly to orange. A single light from number 43 shone through the stark trees.

120

'You know him? He lives over there. Says he wants this house, but another man got it. Your husband, perhaps, Mrs Moss?'

Sheila felt hot. She felt like she knew him. If Olga knew him, that brought him even closer. It was daily now, her habit. After Tessa went to work she'd go to her window, jumpy with desire. She'd open her legs, stroke a scarf up her crack, push something from the fruit bowl, a banana perhaps, in, out, into her wet, hungry cunt.

She would fantasise about her neighbour's cock getting hard if he could see Tessa tying her up. If he could see little Tessa swinging her leg over Sheila's upturned face, opening her pussy lips, rubbing her little clit against Sheila's teeth, grinding down until Sheila could hardly breathe, spots jumping in front of her eyes and her head light from lack of air.

How his big hand would pump, milking his erect penis, if he could see Sheila come into the bedroom, hair in bunches, dressed in Tessa's baby-doll nightie, taking a hairbrush to Tessa's cute bottom, see those peachy buttocks bounce, driving Sheila on to deliver sharper slaps. He wouldn't be able to hear those little mewing cries for mercy, but he'd see Sheila thrusting her free fingers between her own legs, turned on by Tessa's cries, see her frigging herself while Tessa's girlie tears and entreaties made her want to punish her more.

'My husband has gone,' she said shakily.

'He says once there was a brothel here.' Olga clapped her hands. 'He says it has fascinating history, but the walls are rotten.'

'You mean the foundations? Nonsense. All these houses are perfectly sound now. My brother rebuilt this street.'

'So it's your brother lives here, not husband?' Olga looked around the room, crossing her legs slowly. 'There was a man here. And big woman.'

121

'It's just me. And my lodger, Tessa.'

'I'll tell him mistake.' Olga wagged her finger at the fig tree. 'He said he saw the man and the big woman in the bedroom with you. Through the window.'

Sheila was going hot again. 'You must introduce us. As you say, it's a friendly neighbourhood.'

'You haven't said I have the room.' Olga took the glass and flounced towards the door. 'Maybe I live with him.'

'Oh no. You can live here. Then introduce us.' Sheila sat forward, trying not to look too eager. 'But tell me one thing, Olga? If you're not into sex with women, why were you staring at me like that the other day at the agency?'

Olga sat down beside her. 'Because all attractive women are competition, you see. I have to watch them, in my work. You always wear black and tight? Good choice.' She twitched Sheila's skirt. 'And stockings. I knew it.'

'I'm proud of my underwear. I used to model it,' Sheila said, enjoying the feel of Olga's hand on her leg. 'You can see it, if you like.' She started to roll her skirt up.

'Save it for the neighbours! But the man over there? He's mine.' Olga winked sexily. 'Now, I have to get ready for work. I have the room?'

'Yes. OK.' Sheila stood up, knocking a frame on the coffee table. Funny. Her photographs were always arranged on the shelves. She turned it face up. John and little Toby at the vineyard in France, linking arms and striped with shadow.

'Marvellous.' Olga spread open her arms and embraced her. Her breasts pressed into Sheila's. Her perfume was rich, almost headache-inducing. 'We are going to be friends!'

Whoever said life was too short to stuff a mushroom was wrong, Sheila decided as she hummed along to her

Enya album and crumbled feta cheese and basil into a buffalo tomato. If she took in one more lodger she could afford to give up her dreary part-time job and live a life of leisure, cooking and keeping house. Which reminded her. She licked tomato juice off her fingers and went to find that bank statement. It was on the coffee table, beside the photograph of John.

'I am flying to work!' Olga called. 'I'm too late!'

Sheila darted out. 'Are you going to your friend across the road?'

'He's my moonshining. I work for him in the day.'

'Moonlighting? You'll break your neck jumping like that!'

Olga leapt from the top of the stairs. She had changed into a very short, mint-green dress. Sheila glimpsed a triangle of spangled thong. 'Where on earth did you learn to leap like that?'

'Ballet school. Didn't I tell you? I'm a dancer.' Olga held out a handful of hairpins and shook her head about. 'It's a mess. Can you help me?'

'You told me you were a jazz club hostess.' Sheila licked tomato juice off her fingers and twisted the thick red strands into one coil.

'Did I? Oh, it all happens in our club! I'll bring you some CDs back, instead of that awful music!' A key scratched in the lock. 'Now remember, I'm working on finding my next man. And then I'll be out of your hair!'

'I don't want you to be out of my hair.'

Olga laughed and bent to kiss one cheek. Sheila turned her face awkwardly, so that their lips bumped together.

The front door creaked open, and there was Tessa, her cheeks red with cold. 'Sheila? What's going on?'

Eleven

Sheila pulled away. Olga's saliva was on her mouth.

'Darling? This is Olga, who you spoke to about the room! She's going to be our lodger!'

Tessa stepped inside the door, her mouth distorted into a pout. 'I never said she could come here today. I said I'd arrange a meeting.'

'Don't wait up, girls! I won't be back until dawn.' Olga flung her big coat round her. 'Now you two? Behave.'

'Cocky bitch! What does she know?' Tessa snapped as Olga swept up the garden path.

'Olga, I apologise!' Sheila called from the doorstep. 'She's a little possessive –'

Olga waved as she disappeared through the gate into the night. Sheila turned, embarrassed, to come back inside and Tessa slapped her on the face.

'How dare you talk about me as if I'm an idiot!'

'Tessa! What's come over you!' Sheila banged the front door shut. She took hold of Tessa and tried to draw her into a hug. She could feel the girl's heart knocking against her chest. 'I've never seen you like this!'

'What were you two doing, cosying up like that in the hall? You've been screwing each other all afternoon, haven't you? I can tell by your face!'

Tessa knocked her elbow sharply into Sheila's stom-

124

ach, winding her. Sheila grabbed her arms and started to shake her, breath jerking out of her.

'Don't you speak to me like that, young lady! Who the hell do you think you are?'

'Your favourite dolly, that's who! At least I was this morning!' Tessa went limp, allowed Sheila to shake her even harder. Her voice shook as she went on, 'Looks like our Russian mud-wrestler is going to be your pet now.'

Sheila lifted her hand to slap Tessa's pink face, but Tessa caught her wrist and bit into Sheila's arm. Sheila snatched her arm away. 'And so what if she is? This is my house! I can do whatever I like!'

'So you *do* fancy her! All our games, all our lovely nights! I've turned you into a two-timing dyke!' Tessa screamed, breaking away to race up the stairs. 'I'll never forgive you, Sheila!'

Sheila felt desperate laughter careering in her throat at the turn the day had taken. She was perfectly happy to leave Tessa to her tantrum. But then the laughter switched off, and her stomach plummeted. She tore up after her and into the little bedroom, but she was too late. Tessa was standing over the crumpled, stained white dress and the fuzzy yellow wig. Then she started to grind her feet into them, kicking and stamping until the dress ripped and the wig flew across the floor.

'Stop, darling, stop, I can explain!' Sheila grabbed at Tessa and again Tessa slapped her. The smack resounded in the room and as the two women stared in horror at each other a tube train rattled across the distant viaduct. Sheila wished that the train was long enough to drown out their argument until she could think of something to say.

'You've been making fun of me with your new pet, haven't you?' Tessa screeched, bunching her little hands into fists and stepping closer to Sheila. 'Dressing up, were you? Having a laugh? Getting out of those horrible black boring clothes for once, pretending to be young and pretty like me?'

'That's it, Tess. Go on, be angry!' Sheila's breath was coming thick and fast. That manic laughter was back, this time pulling at the corner of her mouth. 'I'm evil, Tessa. Wicked. I did some terrible things today. I'll show you the things we used. Come with me, and I'll show you, and then you can punish me.'

Tessa's mouth hung open, a little trail of saliva dangling down. 'What things? What are you talking about, you silly, stupid bitch?'

Sheila stumbled along to her room. Olga had left her bedroom door wide open, and the place was a tip. But Tessa couldn't see her sneaking a peak at Olga's possessions, could she? Sheila went to the chest of drawers and pulled out the blindfold and the nipple clamps that the neighbours, in their excitement at meeting the glamorous Olga, had left behind and which Olga had thoughtfully left on the chair in the hall. Nothing apparently kinky about them. Anyone coming through the front door would think it was a silk scarf and a pair of earrings.

Tessa's coat was thrown across the chair and she was kicking her shoes off. Sheila put the toys down on the bed and came towards her. 'You must be so tired after your day. Let me help you undress.'

'Undress?' Tessa stepped backwards and stumbled over the chair. 'I'm not letting you near me.'

'Let me do it for you,' Sheila crooned, starting to undo the little buttons running down the front of Tessa's dress. 'I'll do anything for you, Tessa. You can punish me for hurting you.'

Tessa stuck her chin in the air, refusing to look at Sheila as the demure dress peeled away and her perky breasts pushed out from her chest. Sheila sat meekly down on the bed so that Tessa towered over her and she could feel really small. She undid the last buttons and pulled Tessa's dress off. The fabric was warm with Tessa's body, and she held it against her nose to sniff it. Then she pulled Tessa's knickers down.

'Give me your sweater,' Tessa said suddenly, kicking the knickers into Sheila's face. 'You take all that black stuff off.'

'I like to keep something on, Tess –'

'Every stitch.'

Sheila caught Tessa's knickers and held them against her nose. The gusset was damp. She inhaled the sharp aroma of Tessa's pussy coming off it, indicating Tessa's day, all her toilet visits, her obvious sexual reaction to their argument. There was an answering kick inside her as she laid them down beside her and undressed, still sitting, finally removing her own French knickers.

Tessa snatched her clothes out of her hands. 'I'll be back in a minute.'

Sheila's body was shaking with exhaustion now. Her groin screamed with the effort of keeping her legs spread open earlier, each tight hole aching from being pushed and penetrated and stretched not only to take in those inhuman inches of thick leather cock but to take all the thrusting and pumping. She pushed her hand against her crotch. It was warm, throbbing as soon as she touched it. It was almost too sensitive to touch. She wanted to cover it, protect it.

Tessa was coming back along the landing. Quickly Sheila wriggled into Tessa's cream pants. Her swollen sex lips tingled as the fabric slid over them. The pants were too small. In her rush she pulled them awkwardly so that the hem of one leg edged inside her sore crack.

The cold air brought her skin up in goosebumps. As her bra fell to the floor her nipples shrank into hard wrinkled nuts, still burning with the bite of those clamps. As she touched each tip it burned slowly redder with renewed excitement and she closed her eyes, her head falling back slightly as she recalled the scary blankness of the blindfold. She crossed her legs slowly, pressing her cold thighs over her fidgeting pussy.

'What are you smiling about? Look at me. Have you been misbehaving while I've been out?'

Sheila opened her eyes. She gasped. Tessa was dressed in her clothes. She glanced at herself in the mirror and yanked her red curls back into a tight ponytail, glowering when she spotted Sheila staring at her. 'Well?'

'Yes, Tessa. I've been very bad. Revolting, in fact.'

'You've been drinking with that woman, haven't you? In the middle of the afternoon, for God's sake!'

Sheila nodded. 'Two large vodkas. She brought her own glasses.'

'Then you must drink this.'

She held out a pint glass.

Sheila swallowed. 'I can't drink any more vodka!'

'Then that should be your punishment. But no. This is water. To wash your filthy lying mouth out.'

Sheila took a sip.

'Every drop.'

Tessa bent down in front of her. Her eyes were glittering. She looked years older. Sheila was tired of the game. She shook her head. 'I can't. I'll piss myself again – I mean, I need to go to the loo.'

'You're going nowhere. Now. Every drop!' Tessa took the glass and held it against Sheila's mouth. Sheila closed her lips firmly.

'You don't want me to break your nice white teeth, do you?' Tessa demanded, shoving one knee between Sheila's legs to pin her back on the bed. She pushed the rim of the glass hard and Sheila opened her lips. Would Tessa really go so far as to chip her landlady's teeth? Tessa tipped the glass almost upright so that Sheila had to drop her jaw, opening her mouth to catch the water and it swilled over her tongue, down her throat, and she swallowed and coughed down half, but half spilled down her chin, dripping on to her breasts, a few cold drops touching her sore nipples with a hint of relief, the rest gushing down her chest and stomach.

Sheila tried to wipe it off, but Tessa grabbed her wrists and twined one of Sheila's stockings round both of them so that she was handcuffed.

'You want me to lie down?' Sheila was glad of the excuse to rest.

'On your front. Bottom in the air. You are going to get such a spanking.'

Sheila started to sit up again. 'No, Tessa, that's not what I meant. I've been bad, sure, but I don't deserve a spanking. I'm bruised and aching all over as it is –'

'Whose fault is that? On your front! You have no say in what I do to you.'

Tessa took Sheila's shoulders and pushed her face down into the pillow, sitting on her shoulder blades while she wrenched Sheila's arms out to tie her cuffed wrists to the bed head. Sheila was heavy with exhaustion now. Tessa was only small, but she was strong, pushing her face into the pillow so she could hardly breathe.

'The blindfold's good. Please –' she choked. 'I wanted to show you the clamps –'

'You want to play with those cheap little gifts from your sordid friend do you? You know she's nothing but a lap dancer, don't you?'

'She did ballet –'

'She told me what she does on the phone! You're so stupid, Sheila.' Tessa yanked at Sheila's hair. 'Aren't you?'

'Yes, I'm stupid.' Sheila felt her eyelids fluttering as she gasped for air. The pillow was pushing into her mouth. 'But Olga didn't bring those things. The neighbours did.'

'The neighbours? There was a crowd of you? This just gets better and better. In that case I will have to get rid of their little toys, won't I?' Tessa shuffled downwards, coming to rest on her thighs. No need for ties. Sheila was trapped under the girl's weight. 'I can't let you have a reward for their sneaky little visit, can I?'

'Please, Tessa! Let me go!' Sheila struggled wildly. 'I'll let you try them later. You'll see what fun they are!'

The stockings were pulled tight. Tessa was no slouch. There was no way Sheila could get away. The excitement stirred as the stockings bit into her flesh. This was obviously the way to do it. When she tied Tessa up she always made sure she could get away if she wanted. Well, she wasn't going to be so slack next time.

'Quiet! The only thing I want you to say is sorry!'

Sheila twisted about, trying to get her nose sideways out of the pillow, but she could still barely breathe. Briefly out of the corner of her eye she saw Tessa raise her arm, palm flat, above her head. She couldn't have made a sound even if she'd wanted to. She opened her mouth, but her breath was hot against the pillow. And then Tessa's hand came down smack on her bottom, the sting instant and sharp. Sheila jumped with shock. She tried to lift herself away in protest. Tessa was supposed to love her, even in their private games. Especially in their private games.

'Tessa! Stop it at once! This is ridiculous. I'm your goddess! I won't have it. I forbid you to treat me like this –'

Her horror and shame was intensified by the awful thought of how this must look, tied up, smothered face down on the bed, her white bottom wobbling in aftershock.

'A bit late for that, bitch. Look at you. You're not my goddess. You're my pathetic little prisoner. What did I ask you to say, Sheila?'

'Sorry. You asked me to say sorry, Tessa.'

Sheila twisted about frantically as she spoke. She needed to breathe. The sting of the smack was fading. She was getting light-headed with the lack of air, the vodka, and now she was distracted by something else. Her stomach was pressed against the duvet where Tessa sat on her. Without wanting to think about it she thought of the pint glass of water, and instantly her bladder swelled like a balloon.

'What are you sorry for, Sheila?'

Tessa stroked the spot where she had slapped Sheila, lightly with her fingertips as if tracing her own hand-print. Her voice was soft, hissing almost. Sheila relaxed, allowing herself to sink back into the bed, but as she did so the urge to pee grew.

'For letting those women into my house –'

'Those women? Witches, you mean. Bitches, trying to make friends with you. What was that you said? *Your* house?' Tessa's stroking continued, so gentle Sheila could barely feel it. The sting of the slap had gone. Tessa would let her get up now.

'Our house, Tessa. I should never have let them in.'

'No, you shouldn't. And you shouldn't have let them play with you. What did they do to you?'

Tessa lifted her arm again, and there was a second slap, harder, on the same spot. The stinging went deeper this time, radiated further, on the already tender spot. Sheila twitched, unable to control her own reflexes now. This was like being another person, in another body, watching herself in a muffled dream, but beating like a drum over everything now was the nagging of her bladder, far worse than when Cherie had pressed on it and made her piss herself because there was also a slicing sensation just where Tessa's tiny knickers were hooked inside her red-raw sex, trapped there by Tessa pressing her into the bed.

Tessa stroked that buttock again, very lightly, and as she did so she started to rub herself up and down Sheila's leg, her crotch in Sheila's own knickers getting wet against Sheila's thigh. 'I'm waiting for you to tell me, Sheila.'

Soothed by the stroking, Sheila said, 'They had leather cocks on straps, and Cherie was on top of Daphne, fucking her with it.'

131

Tessa slapped Sheila's other buttock, and the shock and pain prodded at Sheila's cunt. She could feel it opening, twitching, and her bladder pushing down too, opening her up there, the first drops waiting to rain. Tessa smacked her again, riding up and down Sheila's leg as she did so. Sheila writhed against the duvet, the hem of Tessa's tiny knickers scraping her clitoris like a match at a flint, her bladder bursting for release, all of it filling her with a mad desire for more. Tessa smacked hard again and now the pain didn't get a chance to fade or radiate because there were only a few seconds before she was striking the red, sore patch again, offering no hope of stroking or soothing.

That little hand. Like a quick, vicious whip. In her light-headed confusion Sheila could see herself, clear as day, lying on the single bed, her white body stretched like a sacrifice and the girl bouncing on her like a dervish, smacking her again and again because she'd been so naughty.

She'd heard of people who liked to be smacked. Men, mostly. Judges, politicians. She'd sneered. What pleasure could there possibly be in prostrating oneself and begging to be punished for some made-up crime, to feed a fantasy? What pleasure could there possibly be in wanting to be hurt so it would make you come? What was so sexy about smacking and being subjected to that kind of humiliation?

Well, now she knew. And how dark it was. She wanted everyone to see. Straining on the stockings that were bound so tight round her wrists, she understood. Being helpless, out of control like this was liberating. Being a little scared, enduring a particular kind of stinging pain, was exhilarating. Being ordered about and struck and told what to do and what to say and what to be, was a cheap, nasty thrill. And all the excitement wasn't even in her mind, not really, her mind was a kind of numb screen where pictures flickered occasionally. No, the excitement was all right here, between her legs, under Tessa's hand, jerking and rising every time Tessa shouted and smacked her.

'You sat and watched them, did you? Too shy, too pathetic to join in. You always like to watch?' Tessa's voice was harsh with her own excitement. She rocked faster, riding Sheila's leg and leaning close to pant into Sheila's ear.

Sheila tilted her pelvis just enough to snag the knickers hard against her clitoris, the rest of her rubbing against the bed. Her pussy opened, her bladder started to open, more warm drops going into the duvet, a warm patch soaking through. Everything was pushing down, waiting to flood out of her.

'They fucked me too,' she grunted into the pillow, her breath wheezing in her chest. Tessa put more pressure on her as she started to buck, rubbing herself in Sheila's knickers against their owner's leg, her pussy getting wetter, and now she started slapping again as if she was a cowgirl whipping her mount.

'Where did they fuck you? Which bit of you?'

'Front and back.'

As her clitoris caught the hem of the knickers once more, Sheila came in a short violent burst. It shivered through her as her breath became shallow.

'Where did they fuck you? Where did they put their great big dicks? Say the words, Sheila. Not front and back. Say the fucking words!'

Tessa's buttocks bounced on Sheila and now she was coming too, slapping and smacking the flats of each hand on each sore buttock.

'Cunt!' gasped Sheila, for the second time that day letting the piss flow hot, spreading all over the bed under her so that she was lying in her own piss and her pussy squeezed like a strong fist until she was emptied out.

'Arse,' she gasped out, as if it was her last breath.

Tessa cackled with laughter, snaking herself up and down, smearing her knickers up and down her prisoner, faster, bucking and writhing until she shuddered with her climax and fell sideways onto the bed and at last Sheila could let out a long, slow breath.

'Are you OK, Sheila?'

Tessa's voice was a mewing in the dark. Sheila's head jerked up from the pillow where she was drifting. 'Yes. But you were so angry with me, Tess.'

Tessa unhooked the stockings from the bedhead, but left Sheila's hands tied. She rolled Sheila on to her back and kissed her hard on the mouth.

'I'm an actress, Sheila. Remember?'

Sheila drew her knees up in an effort to relieve the throbbing all over her body and to escape the wetness on the bed.

'I need to get on with the supper.'

'So you'll never really know what's real, will you?' Tessa snapped the light on beside the bed and stood over her. Sheila blinked. Tessa was still dressed in all her black clothes. She still looked different. Older. 'But you're not an actress, Sheila. Are you?'

Sheila shook her head then nodded it. 'I thought I was good at hiding things.'

'And although we've had a lovely time – *are* having a lovely time together, there's something missing. There's only so many false dicks a girl can take.'

Sheila snuffled weakly. Tessa put her hands on her hips and tipped her head to one side. 'We need a man about this house.'

Twelve

Halloween was past. It was nearly Christmas and she'd done nothing about it. Even the dreary bank was hung with tinsel and gold stars.

'So you can't elaborate on who made this payment into my account?' she demanded for the tenth time. 'It definitely wasn't a Mr John Moss?'

The spindly cashier shook his head for the tenth time. 'We only have the name Spartan Street. It was a wired payment. But it's certainly intended for you. He, they, had all your security details. Right down to your mother's maiden name.'

Sheila stared at the bank statement. Not only had they paid off the mortgage. They'd paid all the utility bills as well. How curious was that?

'I should rejoice and be glad,' said the cashier, flushing slightly at his own seasonal merriment. 'The house is yours now. No debts. No loans. Go crazy.'

Sheila sucked at the cold air as if it was a double vodka. Spartan Street was hers. Well, number 44, anyway. She crossed to the odd numbers side so she could have a good long look at it. Her little empire. The little garret room at the top was like the watchtower of her castle. And she'd never noticed before how much higher her roof was than the other houses. How uneven the roofline was on the even side of the street. The house two doors down seemed to have shrunk. The one on the corner, opposite Daphne's, had erected scaffolding.

She didn't remember John planning such a quirky outline. She'd never be able to ask him, now. She'd tried his mobile when she left the bank, but it was out of service. His conscience must finally have got the better of him. He'd delivered this final gift, before vanishing off the radar. And what a gift. Because she was finally rid of him. She gave a little skip on the pavement, feeling as light as Olga's leopard-skin coat would allow her. A single fleshy leaf from the fig tree caressed her shoulder.

She'd buttoned Tessa into her own black coat this morning because she was off for a week of soap workshops, auditioning as the prissy girl next door. The coat was too big, but in Sheila's clothes and with her hair up, Tessa looked ten years older. She was going to base her character, she said, on Sheila. The producers needn't know that she was even wearing Sheila's knickers. Unwashed and smelling of Sheila's dirty fanny.

How ironic would that be if she got the part? The British public watching little Miss Innocent on the telly, what would they think to see her, still dressed in her character's tweed and pearls, kissing her landlady on the mouth before tying her to the banisters, leaving the front door open for the passers-by to see, bending her over, lifting her skirt, slapping her with her leather gloves until she left red prints over her white bottom?

A cold wind knocked the fig leaf against her again. Sheila shivered and shoved her hand into the holey lining of Olga's pockets. Something metallic nipped at her fingertips. She took out the tiny object. The nipple clamps. She smiled to herself, opened the coat, let in the freezing night air, slid her fingers under Tessa's cropped pink T-shirt to find her cold nipples, opened the little jaws.

'Olga? You're moonshining tonight?'

The deep male voice was somewhere near her elbow. The powder-blue car had glided up beside her, and the electric window was whirring down.

Sheila jumped, and the clamps snapped on to her nipples. She let out a shivering squeak and shook her head wildly.

'I'll pay double. I could really do with it tonight after the shit day I've had.'

Sheila shook her head again. She couldn't move, not until she'd acclimatised to the fresh pain. Mingled with the cold night air, the pain was exquisite. She leaned heavily against the car door.

'So let me eat your pussy.'

Sheila gasped again. The man in the Aston Martin was pulling her hips, getting her closer to the low-slung car. Her coat was already open. Her crotch was on a perfect level with his face. She didn't need to speak. His breath was hot on her crack through the silk gusset. He dug his nose in between the lips and started to lick, a big long tongue sliding up and making the flimsy fabric all wet. She parted her legs, pushed her hips forwards, into his face, through the car window. Her burning nipples grated against the car roof and she started to push at him more urgently. His tongue touched on her clitoris, right through the thin silk, and his fingers moved off her hips to stroke her bottom in little circles but she barely noticed because the knickers were sticking to her now, sticking up inside her pussy lips, tangled with his tongue, silk grating against her so she was pushing more urgently, what a day *she'd* had, she wanted to come, she could come rubbing against her knickers and his tongue and pretending to be Olga, no time to take the knickers off right here in the street, she was ready to come –

'Turn round. Want to kiss your pretty arse.'

She pushed herself harder into his face, but he shoved her away. 'I said turn around. You can play the silent

137

game if you like. I prefer it, frankly. But you do what I want, OK?'

He grabbed her hips. She could easily get away, but she wasn't done yet. She bent over, pulled her soaking knickers down. Hanging down like that her nipples throbbed madly. She pushed her bottom in through the car window – miraculous no one had come along the street yet – and he paused. Didn't kiss, or lick. Just stroked her left buttock, stroking over the birthmark that Tessa always made fun of. That John always made fun of.

'Having fun over there in number 44, Olga?' he asked softly, stroking the birthmark. Sheila bent further over, nodding frantically. His breath was warm on her crack. She slid her hands up her thighs, got one finger into her pussy. It was twitching and wet. 'What has he done to her, though? The bastard.'

Sheila half straightened, half turned her face. Spread one hand as if asking a question. Kept the other hand quietly busy, working at her pussy, waiting for him to start again, wanting him to lick her arse if that's what he wanted so she could make herself come at the same time.

'Your landlady? What's Moss done to Sheila? All thin and pinched like a widow.'

Sheila's heart started to thump. He knew her name? He knew about John? Who the hell was he? She tried to straighten, get away, but her legs were aching and he was holding her fast by the hips. She rested against the car. The smooth metal door handle dug under the crease of her cheeks. The desire was ebbing away, leaving her shaking.

'Those black clothes, that vicious hairstyle. She was so gorgeous. Did you know she was a model? You'd be good at that, Olga. You have the same big breasts as Sheila. I choose all my women to look like her. But what's that bastard Moss done to her? And who's the other lodger?'

A set of headlights swung round the corner past Daphne's house. Sheila pushed herself away from the car, her knickers halfway down her thighs and staggered across the road.

'Who is she?' called the man softly after her. 'The woman behind the curtain?'

Thirteen

Behind its wintry fig tree, number 43 this morning was turning a blind eye. But the window was open. A curtain, in a sudden glorious red, flipped under the sash like its owner's silky tongue. *Are you there?*

Inside number 44 the floorboards, the walls, the landlady, were creaking with frustration. Olga's bedroom door was banging in a draught. Just when Sheila needed to corner her, get some answers, she'd vanished for days without a word and without paying next month's rent.

Appropriately for someone who "moonshined" as a hooker, it was like a Madame's boudoir in there. Olga's dresses and shirts and wraps hung from curtain and picture rails, wardrobes, the door, even the ceiling lights.

A black basque was splayed on the bed, unlaced. Sheila fingered it as if it might bite. It looked hard and shiny like the breastplate of a suit of armour, but to the touch it was softest leather. She held it against herself, brushed aside a Spanish shawl to peer at the mirror. The house was silent. She whipped her blouse off, then her bra. Her white breasts fell heavily forwards, nipples shrinking sharply in the December cold. She shivered with pleasure. She liked the cold, how it made her super-sensitive. Liked the way her skin puckered in acute response to its discomfort. Every touch was like a scratch, every lick of air like a blast. The promise of warmth was held away, a blanket or a hot bath, at arm's length.

She fitted the two cups over her breasts, hooking the corset tightly round her ribs to keep it in place. She could hardly breathe now. Her breasts oozed over the rigid whalebone top, puffing in an effort to gain oxygen. If it was tight on her, it must squeeze the life out of the voluptuous Olga. No wonder the girl rushed through life in a permanent state of over-excitement.

Olga. Desire uncoiled inside Sheila. She'd tasted Tessa, been tasted by her neighbours, she wanted to taste everyone. And Olga was next on her list. If the man at number 43 wanted her so badly he'd lick her clitoris in the street, then Sheila wanted her too.

And then she wanted him.

Olga still had a kind of scented wall around her. Standing in the other woman's bedroom, Sheila sniffed the air and wanted to know what Olga would look like having sex. What she would do to seduce her men. The man across the road. How she would look before he fucked her, her thick red lips sucking his mouth first, his cock, how her cunt would look when she lay down for him, the thick damp hairs curling over it, her back arching to give him her hard red nipples to suck, he'd said her breasts were like Sheila's, he must have seen those advertising hoardings all those years ago.

Olga's cunt splitting red and hot between her spreading thighs –

Sheila bit her lip, excitement stabbing at her. As her breasts heaved, her nipples flipped over the tight seam of the corset. She watched them stiffen in the cold air. She licked her finger, made them wet and cold with her saliva, started to pinch them hard. Her pussy started to throb. The corset squeezed her body, squeezed the breath out of her until her ears sang and she felt tipsy.

Tessa was away. She hadn't expected to be alone again so soon. She wanted Olga to be here, touching her. But Olga was the exotic ship that came and went in the house, adding her own *frisson* of sex, mystery and cash to the already electrified household. Occasionally she cooked them Czech meals, mostly knuckles of bony meat and heavy, sticky pastries, but Tessa was always rude, ordering Sheila about or dragging her upstairs. Olga never commented on the moaning and thumping, oh God, the smacking and slapping and female cries. She never told, even if she did catch a glimpse through Tessa's door (always wide open to the landing) of Sheila's splayed legs, hands and ankles tied to the bed, her smarting pink bottom quivering under Tessa's slaps.

Sheila turned about in front of the mirror, making herself even dizzier. To the outside world of Spartan Street they could pass for a jolly household of three women going about their business. Respectable housemates. No scandal at all.

Except that Olga might look fascinating, but you couldn't describe her as respectable. And certain neighbours had wasted no time in bringing the beast out of Sheila herself.

She struck a pose. They wouldn't recognise her now, though. The corset made her look almost debauched. Her pussy twitched as she admired herself. She was allowed to admire herself brazenly, because she was Olga now. Her breasts were huge, her waist pulled unnaturally tiny. Her face was deathly pale.

Suddenly Sheila thought about old mocking Maureen in the office. What would she say? 'Going to a tarts and vicars party are we, Mrs Moss?'

Sheila pouted at her reflection in the floor-length mirror. *No, Maureen. This is no party, no play-acting. I am a tart.* She bent with difficulty to pull off her sensible skirt, then her knickers. The corset dug in under her ribs as she straightened. The body parading there was someone else's body. Her own clothes were gone, leaving her standing naked in Olga's room, her pussy stark black and furry in the daylight, her nipples dark red and sparking with the cold, her white thighs pressed

142

together in fake modesty like she'd seen in John's collection of old Parisian dirty postcards.

The corset squeezed until she wanted to squeal with pleasure, like someone else's fingers. Tessa liked to button her into her girlie bras and dresses. They giggled as the garments strained over Sheila's bigger breasts, ripped and tore around her taller frame, an overgrown schoolgirl. She had only to take a few steps, make a few baby faces, and Tessa would be pouncing on her, lifting up the broderie anglaise petticoats to spank her hard, wait for her to beg for mercy before squashing her sweet, opening pussy impatiently down on Sheila's face, cheeks painted with rouge dots like a doll.

But these clothes were designed to squeeze, make the body throb and burst. This was no schoolgirl fantasy. This was the uniform of a professional whore, a couple of steps off the street corner.

She gasped with laughter, tried to take a deep breath, couldn't, wondered if she should loosen the corset, felt hornier when she decided not to. She straightened. Black corset. The rest of her was naked now. Her bush, left luxuriant and furry, on Tessa's orders, curled over her primly shut sex.

Breathing hoarsely, she prowled about the room looking for more garments to put on. She had to move differently, swinging her hips stiffly, all the natural suppleness reined in.

Sheila glanced out of the window, hoping wildly that someone, the poor old postman perhaps, might be up a ladder looking in. But this room was on the side of the house, and all she could see was the blank brick wall of the house next door.

In her own room she saw the dim reflection of herself crossing the carpet. She pushed the curtains as far back as they would go to let in the stark morning light. The red curtain was still lapping at number 43. He must be in. Waiting for Olga. Well, he couldn't have Olga.

143

She pulled what felt like a very long rubber glove from the random pile she'd snatched from Olga's bed. It was a pair of black rubber leggings.

She had to roll these on like stockings, still in front of the window. They were so tight she nearly gave up. But she couldn't get them off now. They were stuck fast, sucking on to her. Her own sweat made a kind of glue. The rubber squeaked and snatched viciously at every little hair on her legs, making her wince. The corset dug into her ribs as she twisted and pulled.

The rubber was on. Painted on, like that stuff that solidifies to a membrane after you apply it. Instead of shedding her skin, acquiring a new one. What did that make her? A chameleon? A butterfly regressing into its weird chrysalis? Whatever, she wasn't Sheila Moss any more. If she walked into that office now, Maureen and her cronies wouldn't recognise her. Olga wouldn't recognise her. Tessa would take the scissors to her. John would sneer. Roxanne? She'd applaud.

Sheila laughed, a dirty laugh, spreading her thighs and thrusting her hips. She was a mannequin in a fetish magazine. Where the crotch of the "trousers" should be, was an oval hole. At the back, her buttocks were totally exposed. *Like wearing skin-tight riding chaps. No wonder the cowboys got down to it in Brokeback Mountain.* She stuck her bottom out, breasts dangling down, waggled her bum at the window. This was like the debauched Hollywood party Rupert Everett described once, heaven for gays like him, where the gorgeous waiters were dressed in leather trousers, cut away at the back for easy access.

Sheila pictured it. Cute men, gay or straight, anyway chosen for their looks, loping round with oiled chests carrying trays, taking orders, pouring drinks, then being bent across the table or the leather banquettes by lecherous studio magnates, quickly massaging their cocks, getting them sucked to readiness by another willing waiter, maybe even another guest, male or female, before thrusting between the buttocks, shafting quickly, brutally, coming up the guy's arse, and out before the second course is served –

In her case the front and back openings were joined only by a string-thin rubber thong which ran like chicken wire between the two. Her sex lips were pinched shut by the front oval opening, enfolding the string, trapping it up between them where it instantly started to chafe. Her pussy was a thick, bearded mouth, pouting through a mask.

She touched the sulky lips and nearly jumped because they were sensitive as if they'd been burned, already throbbing, trying to push through their rubber trap. They were turning dark pink. Her stomach tightened. Her fingernail scratched between the squeezed lips, knowing it would hurt, feeling the wet slick springing up there. She flinched. Oh, she was so hot already. Why not just finger fuck herself, file away at those fragile lips, let it all spill out? But not yet, not yet. She ruffled the pubic hair and nearly screeched as the greedy rubber twanged and yanked. Now it didn't look right. She should be sleek, like cat woman. There was too much hair sprouting and poking, like an old lady's perm sticking out of a swimming cap. Not streamlined enough.

Once she'd applied the finishing touch of a pair of spiky thighboots, pulled on over the tortuous leggings, walking to the bathroom was virtually a sex act in itself. She tried tripping along like a geisha, then loping mannishly with splayed legs like those cowboys. Whichever way she walked the tight thong shaved away at the tender perineum separating her two holes. She'd barely even thought it existed before. Now it was burning like a sheet of flame. There was no slack. Each time it cut, the string sliced a little bit tighter into the groove.

The window rattled. She never turned the heating on in the day. She liked to deny herself. It made hot drinks, duvets, baths, embraces, all the more pleasurable. She liked to deny her lodgers, too. But she was rarely bare like this. Now the cold air on her breasts and shoulders, touching through to her bones, was a mean contrast with the salty sweat steaming up inside the rubber.

In the bathroom she smothered her exposed, swollen labia in soap, and razed off the hair. The blade was like salt in a wound. Tessa would be furious. She preferred Sheila hairy and gauche. The kick of rebellion was exhilarating as Sheila scraped clumsily at the foam. Her pussy was pulsing urgently. She tugged the labia through the slit as far as they could go. They bulged out painfully, reddening like a complaining mouth, a line of saliva and itchy soap bubbling up between. There was hair left inside the trousers, prickling and itching. Every individual hair was being tugged by the root. But she couldn't prise the rubber off to get at it.

She glanced up at the bathroom mirror. Black corset, bulging, red, nude pussy. Pale, staring, shocked, un-made-up face. All wrong. Back in Olga's room she rooted through the lipsticks scattered all over the dressing table and chose a dark-purple one, the colour of a bruise. She twisted back the black lid, the lipstick's head emerging like a penis.

She smeared this over her mouth, opening it wide, breath clouding the mirror. Her hand was shaking so much she went over the edges, making her mouth big and uneven as if she'd been punched. She touched some stripes of colour on to her bare pussy lips. It felt so good, the cool stickiness over her like an animal's tongue. The make-up was going to make such a mess. She probed and pushed, rubbing the lipstick in, over the lips, easier than a finger to push it into the tightly closed crack, poking at the lining, wetting the end of the lipstick with the juice it found there, mixing it, painting that on as well.

She was just angling the lipstick further into her pussy, nudging the blunt end between, letting it wiggle inside, pressing it harder like a tiny dick, her hips giving little involuntary jerks, she was just biting her lip to think of Olga coming home, unaware, bending over the dressing table to tart herself up, Sheila's come smeared all over her favourite lipstick, Olga opening her big fellatio lips, smearing her purple lipstick on first the top, then the bottom, lipstick unusually wet because of Sheila's pussy juice, would she be able to smell it, would she know Sheila's juices were smeared wet now all over her purple mouth too, her juices on her tongue when she licked at it, wondering at the taste, would Sheila creep up behind her and tell her, show her where she put the lipstick, how far in it had been – when the doorbell rang.

'Alan Smith? Come about the room.'

Sheila tried to open the front door, but the cold weather must have warped it, because it would only open a crack. She stuck her painted face round. It was gloriously freezing out there. 'You're early.'

A tall, thin young man with lanky black hair stamped his feet on the doorstep. He had the spindly body of a featherweight, but the sharp cheekbones, sunken eyes and full mouth of a Russian ballet dancer. The breeze snatched at Sheila's sore pussy, no hair there now to protect it. She clutched at the door. She was faint now with lack of breath.

'Er, it's freezing out here?' Alan Smith pushed the door, trapping her against the wall. 'And I'm bursting for a – I really need to go!'

She had no choice. He was in now, barging up her hallway, searching for the loo. He and his bulging rucksack. On the doorstep he'd left what looked like a couple of milk crates. She couldn't lurk about forever, leave the door swinging open. *Come on. What would Olga do?*

She stood on the welcome mat in the only way you could stand in fetish gear so tight it was threatening to cut off your circulation, with her legs apart and her hands on her hips.

'Looks like you caught me dressing up, Alan Smith. My secret side. But that's fine. Just make yourself at home.'

Alan turned, glanced absently towards the kitchen, his hand hovering over his crotch.

Sorry?' He backed up against the broom cupboard. 'Oh my God. I've come to the wrong house! I thought the lady said number 44 –'

'Not what you were expecting? Don't worry. This is most definitely the right place.' Sheila walked slowly towards him, the front door banging open, the air rushing in, anyone from the street could see. This was how Tessa did it. This is how Olga would walk towards a cute, untried young victim. Olga would relish the way he was gaping like a rabbit in headlights, big hands dangling, mouth drooling. As she moved, the rubber encased her, outlined her like a mould. So Sheila slotted into her new self. 'I've been waiting for you.'

Every inch of her was being squeezed or frozen or overheated, but now she had someone to see her in this state. Maybe even share the sensations. Her pussy lips throbbed in time to her heartbeat, thrusting rudely with every pulse through the oval hole. All her organs were being throttled by the corset and rubber trousers. And now that he'd mentioned needing to go, her bladder was aching as well.

'Don't be shy. You're free to run away if you like. But I think you'll like it here.'

She was aware – who wouldn't be? – of her nipples poking out at him over the top of the corset. He clutched his rucksack in front of his trousers, eyes darting about under his lank fringe of hair. He looked at the floor, the ceiling, her eyes, her knees, anything to avoid the tits, oh Christ, he couldn't help it, she could hear his mind running, his eyes just went wide and stared. Sheila felt a tug of triumph.

'No need to look so nervous, Alan. Do I look as if I'll bite?'

He nodded his head, long tongue running over dry lips. The more nervous he looked, the stronger the triumph, the more physical. Her body, dressed and squeezed like this, felt like a weapon. His nostrils flared like a wild animal's. Cornered.

'Does this scare you? Have you never seen a woman dressed like this before? Want to see my little toys?'

He shrugged cluelessly, eyes moving down to her swollen labia, back up to her long, stiff nipples, bony fingers clutching at his rucksack.

Sheila smiled at him. The lipstick felt wet on her mouth. She licked it slowly. She felt so sexy in Olga's mask. 'We'll talk about the room, if you like. Of course we will. Once you've adjusted to the place. A little dark in this hallway, isn't it?' She could hear the lilt of laughter in her voice, even as it rasped deeper with seduction.

He was still gaping at her stiff nipples like a kid in a sweetshop. Best just to wait a little, go slow. Sweets are treats, not threats. She looked down, too. They were ridged and dark red, and the sight of them, with Alan Smith also staring at them, made her knees weak. The hard red nubs showed how horny she was.

'Good enough to eat, aren't they?' she murmured, flicking one stiff nipple with her fingernail. 'You know, if I could reach, I'd suck them myself.'

She looked straight at him, tweaking her nipples, enjoying the sharp tingle of excitement, smiling a wide, purple smile. 'Would you like a suck, Alan? You'd love it. Tessa never sucks them.'

'A piss,' he croaked desperately, holding his crotch through his loose jeans, 'is what I need.'

'The flush is a little dodgy downstairs,' she said calmly, lifting one knee to step on to the stairs. *Plenty of time, now he was here.* Her pelvis tilted up, showing her red slit. The sight of him, so lanky, young and clueless, made her want to rip herself open in front of him. She knew she was going to do it. The thing that had stirred in her was uncoiled now, ready to pounce. She was going to shock him. And then she was going to have him. She was sore all over now, with wanting. 'Come up.'

He dropped his rucksack with a thump and started to follow her. She swayed exaggeratedly, her buttocks opening and closing right in front of his nose. Suddenly she stopped, pretending to fiddle with her boot, stuck her bum right in the air. The air from the open door rushed right up her crack. She felt her anus squeeze shut, her cunt twitch. She waited.

The door slammed shut. Was he gone? She waited. He was on the stairs, creaking up behind her. Up to where she was bent over like a doggie, her big bare bottom wide and open, the garments pulling tight round her waist and ribs so she couldn't breathe, only pant as if she was permanently coming. Now she could feel puffs of warm breath on the back of her legs. His face was nearly on a level with her big bare bottom. She bent further over, felt her buttocks bulge as they pushed out of the rubber trousers, sticking to each other before parting with a fleshy popping sound. Just by bending she could spread herself open, all the way round to her pussy. She knelt on the top step, spread herself further open. Waited.

'Oh, man, this is so gross. Your arse in my face.' She could feel his breath on her skin. 'What do I do now?'

'That's good, honey. Just take a look.' A bubble of excitement rose in her throat. 'See? Just look at your new landlady. And her cunt.'

'Your arse, you mean. That's all I can see from here. You like it up the arse?'

'How would that feel, I wonder?' Sheila paused. She wondered if John stuck it up Roxanne's arse these days. Or was that still too dirty for him? Did Roxanne have to use other things if she wanted it up there? Her hair dryer for instance? Sheila started to smile. 'You know, I've only ever had a big fat leather dildo up there.'

She reached very slowly backwards through her legs, fanned out her fingers to open her pussy for him. Her fingers fumbled to prize it open, but the bloated lips felt glued shut, pinched in the rubber hole. She tickled her nail in between, tried to force it inside, moaned with the sudden pain as her nail scratched in there. The labia were bulging out like obscene lips, almost repulsing her finger from the sealed crack. Her fingers hovered for a moment, stroking the soft surface again. She felt ready to wet herself with pleasure. She was shivering.

'Want to touch?'

She waggled her fingers as if choosing a chocolate from a selection box, squirming from the filthiness of what she was doing. The house seemed to be reeling back in shock.

She tipped her face sideways so he could see her face, bit her tongue and slipped her longest finger further back and into the dark crack of her bottom. Her stomach tightened with disgust at herself. It was hairy and warm in there. Damp. She forced herself to keep her finger there, draw it up and down to show him, because showing him was so sexy. Like lifting your skirt in the playground. Or in front of the window. And now touching herself was sexy, too, touching her own dirty bottom.

She bunched her hand into a fist and knuckled her buttocks apart and a totally new sensation kicked in, right there in her butt, her anus hole squeezing with sheer pleasure, wanting more touching, more force.

'Want to look?'

Fight or flight. Those were his choices, but from the croakiness of his voice he could do neither just now. But that was fine. She was getting her kick out of showing herself to him, thrusting in his face like she was in a zoo. The baboon. As she wondered what he would do, Sheila's bladder started to join in, to ache again, a deep, descending ache, straining against the rubber trousers. Urging her to do more, be more outrageous, feel the kick. She waggled her fingers again as if beckoning him, moved them up the warm crack, still hesitating because she'd never touched herself there before. She kept her touch light, aware of those black eyes of his, darting nervously about behind her, keeping still and silent on the stairs behind her. He hadn't touched her. Any second she expected to hear the creak of the stairs under his fleeing feet, and the slam of the door.

But he was still there, breath wheezing through his nostrils, saliva sliding in his mouth as he swallowed. 'You're putting your finger up there?'

'Want me to?'

Encouraged by the husky drawl she'd assumed to go with her outfit, her forefinger poked experimentally at the hole and immediately it squeezed tighter shut. Her cunt squeezed in echo. Her bladder gave a twinge. She groaned, and tipped her head back, pushing her finger back in. The little hole seemed to suck at it. There was a sharp kick high up inside her. Now every orifice, pinched and trapped, wanted to suck at something, was screaming to be poked and filled. Or fucked. Where? But now she wanted to pee. How?

'Want to touch?' She reached backwards, fumbling for one of his hands, grabbed nothing but air.

'OK. Let me just show you round the house,' she said casually after a long pause. She pulled herself upright slowly, her head spinning with this new game. Her voice was soft, but inside she was taut as steel, tight with the excitement of being in her house, showing her bottom to a gauche lad she'd never met before.

The tight rubber was her disguise. Dressed in this she could go even further, wanted to go much further than the dirty games she had started with Tessa. And better still, here was a man she could play with. They had all morning in her silent, empty house, while she played behind her mask. She might never dress like this again. He need never see her again. He need never see the real Sheila Moss at all. Whoever that was. Her buttocks wobbled, her muscles strained as she stood. 'I'm rather proud of my house, you see.'

She walked slowly across the landing in front of him. Slowly was the only way she could walk, stuck inside this hot, pinching rubber. 'The master bedroom. Or perhaps I should say the mistress bedroom.'

Still he was silent. She walked over to the window. In the glass she could see her stark outline, waist pinched right in by the corset, legs apart, an exaggerated cartoon figure, black mouth, jutting breasts. Shadowy figure, scruffy lodger, lurking behind her. She was about to turn to Alan when for the first time she saw movement in the house opposite. The window was still open. Open wider, in fact, despite this cold. She could see a figure standing, the torso in shadow, only visible from the waist down. How funny. He was visible in his window, for the first time. He didn't know it, but he'd already tasted her. His mouth, lips, tongue, had licked her pussy through his car window. All the while he'd thought she was his little whore, Olga.

Sheila's mouth spread into a black lipsticked grin. She pressed herself against the window. *Look at me, honey.* Her breasts rose over the corset, squeezed together, catching her breath.

Behind the curtain she noticed a crack had opened up beside the wooden sash, making a jagged rip in the wallpaper. She followed it up the wall and halfway across the ceiling.

'Do you have a whip?' Alan's voice was hoarse. He'd

put down his rucksack and was by the bed. 'You look like one of those headmistress types who like to whip.'

Sheila glanced away from him to hide her smile, looked at the house opposite. The man was still there, just the trousers visible. She had to keep him there. 'Oh, I'm a pussycat really, Alan. Just after some loving. Come here.'

He shuffled closer, looking from side to side then again straight at her breasts, at the swollen cushions of her pussy, back to her big breasts. Down in his trousers there was an enormous bulge. She kept right up against the window, so the guy across the road could see, so anyone coming along the road could see. She just stood there with one hand on her hip, the other stretched up the window frame, an exaggerated figure, whore in the window, and let her new young lodger come right up to her, lift his hands, reach to touch her.

They landed on her aching breasts. She put one hand on his shoulder and arched her back, pushed her breasts at him. His hands gripped harder, closing on to them. She was sideways on to the window. Across the road a hand came down to cover the crotch of the watcher's trousers.

'What do I do?' Alan groaned, his tongue swiping back and forth like a dog's across his full lower lip, hands twitching over her breasts, one hand grabbing at his crotch, rubbing up the hard outline of his cock.

'Lick my nipples.' Sheila was breathing hard now. Her nipples were burning, extended with pain. Down inside the rubber leggings her cunt was on fire. She studied her young playmate. His baggy street clothes, the long thick bulge visible through the material of his trousers, a young meaty erection reaching right up to his waistband, the awkward hands with the big wrists and long fingers running first through his long hair, flitting back to hitch at his trousers.

Sheila stayed very still. This was a first for her, but she wasn't going to let on to him, was she? Instead she wanted to see what he would do, what urge would take him over. Her nipples were sore, hard points, inviting him. Her body was pure comic-book fantasy. She wasn't Sheila. She wasn't Olga even. She was a silhouette in a window. Across the road the hand was pulling a thick pale shape out of the trousers, balancing it briefly on the palm, and just as she saw the length of her neighbour's penis, resting, waiting for what was going to happen, her new lodger started massaging her breasts roughly, pushing her back against the wall so he could mould and squash them in those big hands of his. She thrust them at him, the pain of the corset round her back and his awkward handling singing through her. He started wobbling and flipping at them, side to side, seeing how they bounced and then he pushed them hard together, squeezed them together so the nipples were side by side, twin nuggets of exquisite wanting, Sheila's pussy so numb now that all sensation was centred on those nipples.

'Put these on me.'

She gave him the nipple clamps from her bedside table. He knocked her hand away at first, pushed her breasts tight together so that the nipples were positioned tight side by side, bent his head to suck them. Instant hints of approaching ecstasy, she could let him suck all day, but she wanted the pain more. He bit hard, first one nipple, then the other. She pushed his head away.

'The clamps.'

He fiddled with the tiny little vices, then snap, they were on. No niceties. Sharp teeth, nipping tight. Hot pain cinching her tight. She wrapped her arms round his head so he couldn't move, lowered herself stiffly to balance her bottom on the wide window sill, spread her legs on either side of his head, pushed him down to the floor so that he was kneeling between her legs.

Her outfit kept her so rigid in this position that her limbs felt almost wooden now, her nipples the only part

155

of her with any feeling, so that feeling was triply intensified. Across the road, past the bare fig tree, the circle of her neighbour's finger and thumb was running up and down the thick, pale penis. He was right up against his own window. Anyone could see what he was doing if they only stopped shuffling along staring at the ground and looked above their own noses. Anyone could see the man at number 43 starting to jerk off, right there in the window.

He knew something about her. John must have sold that house to him, mentioned something. Mentioned far too much, actually. But maybe it was John's way of asking the guy to watch out for her. But now she knew something about him, too. He was rich and glamorous and drove a class car. He liked to tongue tarts in the street. He liked to watch landladies pleasuring themselves in their bedroom windows. He liked to get his cock out, also in full view, and masturbate while he watched her.

Alan was trying to stand up again, fiddling with the laces of her corset now, trying to get it off her. She longed for her breasts to be able to flop out freely, wanted to rip everything off so she could breathe, but she didn't want to lose this haughty pose, she wanted to hold it until her man behind the fig tree had ejaculated, his white creamy come landing with a slow splash to slide down his window pane.

'Leave it,' she hissed. Alan tried to kiss her, slobbering over her mouth and chin. She didn't want the man in the window to see her kissing. Whores didn't. She was sure Olga wouldn't kiss.

'Slut.' Suddenly Alan raised his voice. 'Look what you've done. Christ, what a slut. You've given me the horn. Always wanted to see a woman's arse up close. I need to fuck you now,' he grunted, tugging now at the rubber trousers. But they were welded on. The body heat had made superglue of her sweat. He couldn't get a grip. His fingers just slipped out of the waistband again. Sheila ignored the flicker of panic at the thought of being drowned in her own sweat, trapped forever in these evil trousers.

She grabbed at his ears, but Alan tossed his head sideways and was standing up again now, towering above her. This wasn't right, a dominatrix was supposed to stay on top. Alan was getting his prick out of his trousers, and there it was with his fingers gripping it, huge and red and juddering out of the tangle of thick black hair all around it. It wasn't pale and hovering like the one opposite. Alan's prick was waving and jutting like a pole in front of her face.

'Gonna fuck you!' Alan's voice was rough like a man's now, not a boy's. 'Bitch. Get on the bed. Look what you've done to me!'

He started to lift her, to get her on to the bed, but the bed wasn't close enough to the window, the neighbour wouldn't be able to see if the action moved to the bed. There was no time to push it closer, she would do that another time. Alan was stronger than he looked, he had her round the ribs and was lifting her. Across the road the hand had slowed on the big white penis, seemed to be waiting for what would happen next. She noticed a signet ring on the little finger.

Toxic desire stirred again. She wanted the man at number 43 to see what was happening. He could watch her young lodger taking her by force. He could imagine doing that to her, coming across the street and fucking her. Her big horny neighbour could have a free x-rated version of *Rear Window*.

Her body was swollen inside its vicious rubber trap, blood thumping as it struggled to circulate. Her nipples burned in the clamps' teeth. Her cunt was also throbbing with the violent urge to come. It was like she'd rubbed stinging nettles all over herself, drank some kind of yew tree poison. And now her bladder! She imagined

157

it puffing in and out like a bellows, swelling taut, deflating like a balloon inside its rubber prison, and now the jagged urge to urinate was slicing through her as well, making her rock frantically, hopelessly, no hope of the pain and the urge to piss ever fading.

Alan's cock was enormous, just there in front of her face. She was powerless to move. Somehow he had taken over. So much the better. What would a dominatrix whore in the window do? She glanced across the street. She didn't want to do anything. She wanted to be used and abused and she wanted him to see it. She was feeling deranged with lack of oxygen. Every laboured breath made the corset tighter. The trousers were slowly suffocating her.

Across the road the thick white penis had grown longer and fatter. Harder. It seemed suspended in thin air. Her trapped ribs were a cage round the expanding excitement inside her. Her neighbour's cock was like a telescope, watching her. Maybe he had one. Then he could see her, she'd open her legs for him, show him her newly waxed cunt. Like she wanted the postman to look up at her finger fucking herself in the window, rubbing the curtain into her cunt, sad old woman in the window, now she wanted the man across the street to watch, get a close-up if he wanted, see her bend over to finger her little tight arsehole another time, but right now he would see the boss lady at number 44 clear as day in the window with a great cock bludgeoning in her face. He might even catch the gleam of lust in her eyes.

The blackness of the room behind her neighbour, the superimposed reflections of her own window all confused her. But the neighbour would see it clearly. Her pale face turned up like some kind of saint praying in front of Alan Smith, with his trousers dropping off him. Alan Smith taking handfuls of her hair to hold her still, drawing back his hips, standing over her like he was now the boss, his big prick jabbing through his flies, into

158

her face, into her mouth open in a frantic effort to breathe.

What would Olga do?

There was the smell of sweat and the hint of spunk in her nostrils and now Alan's cock was prodding its blunt end into her cheekbone. She glanced across the street, dug her nails into Alan's buttocks, straightened her spine so the neighbour would be sure to see, then opened her mouth wider, a great wet tunnel so that the plum-round knob end slipped stickily inside.

Alan tensed backwards. Remember he's young, Sheila told herself. He doesn't have to know this is my first time sucking cock. *But I want him to bang it into my mouth until it hurts. Show the man across the road what I look like with my jaws clamped open, a cock thrusting down my throat fit to choke me.*

She followed the jerking of his body with her mouth so as not to lose track of him, so he could teach her without knowing it. Now Alan's hands were closed over her ears. She could only hear the frantic rushing of her own blood. She gripped the tops of his legs and kept the moist tip of his cock in her mouth. His cock jumped over her tongue, probing between her teeth. She opened her jaw wider, hoped the guy across the street would see how wide her mouth could go. How wide would Olga's go? She would probably be famous for her blow jobs.

Alan's cock was engorged now and huge. Maureen would say hung like a donkey. It was shoving and pushing down her throat, no attempt at control, going on until it gagged her. She pushed the thick shaft back with her tongue. That closed her lips round his length, and she automatically sucked it back into the warm wetness of her mouth.

Gripping his buttocks the better to grind her face into his groin, Sheila could also rub her own sore nipples against his legs, rub her bloated pussy lips against his knees for some relief, but all this did was stack up the agony.

He didn't care. His penis stiffened and swelled even more inside her mouth and she sucked on it, the feel of a stiff male cock and his obvious, thrusting pleasure both turning her on and flaying her with frustration. She could taste as well as smell the salty droplets oozing through the slit. He was thrusting against the roof of her mouth. His hands dragged her head up and down the length of his shaft, more roughly now, yanking at her hair. She was his sex toy now, just like she'd been everyone's sex toy when the neighbours came round for parlour games. She wondered if the guy across the road could see that clearly enough, whether his hand was now driving up and down his stiff cock.

Sheila felt like a kind of robot now, her mouth the only part working, her cunt and bladder stuck together inside the rubber muzzle, one dragging ball of hot liquid. Black spots were popping in front of her eyes. Her mouth felt loose, sliding up and down Alan's cock, her lips losing their grip. She started to bite instead, her jaw quivering with exhaustion, nipped the taut surface of his cock, no idea how hard she was biting, because she was losing her strength.

'Cut it out, you old bitch!' he yelped, yanking at her hair, his voice high with excitement, nervous lad transformed into plain male brute who needed to shoot his load. He shoved it in more roughly, spreading his thighs to get a better angle.

Sheila lost her balance, fell off the window sill, banged hard down onto her knees as he laced his fingers behind her neck to keep her in position, mouth clamped on to his cock. How would that look from over the street? Mrs Moss down on her black rubber knees in front of a bloke, her dark-purple mouth open and smudged and gushing wet with saliva and spunk as her latest lodger shafted her.

Sheila tried to get up. The circulation was completely blocked there behind her bent knees so that pins and needles were pricking her legs. If Alan moved she would fall flat on her face like a doll. But he wasn't moving. He had hold of her head and was thrusting harder inside her mouth, narrow hips whipping back faster into her face, using her face like a cunt, so she was kneeling there before him as if he was her master, sucking him, pleasuring him, her own bursting pleasure locked out of reach, and then suddenly his cock stiffened, seemed to extend another couple of inches right down her throat. Sheila started to choke, tried to loosen her throat to let him in, how come she was the one on her knees, how come she'd gone from dominatrix landlady to supplicating orifice coated in rubber?

She actually heard him laugh quietly. How come the weedy Alan had gone from spindly kid to masterful brute impaling her on his dick?

As his cock rammed down her throat, Sheila remembered the game her neighbours wanted to play. Vet the lodgers. An hour after he'd stepped through her door, and look at him! He was the one. Vetting the landlady.

Angry now, Sheila balanced herself against him, her bladder and cunt screaming and bulging in agonised pissing coming frenzy, trying to get her mouth off him, push him away, but her mouth was locked in that position now, locked around his thrusting, pumping cock.

'Not till I'm done with you!'

He yanked at her ears so that her head fell back sharply. Now the man opposite would see Alan change his angle again, thrust into her wide open mouth, jaws hinged open to take him in. He whipped his hips back then pumped once, twice, straining so hard down her throat that he knocked her head back against the window. She bit hard on him as hot spunk shot down her throat and he yelped, pulled out, and kicked her violently onto her back.

161

As he staggered against the curtain, holding his spurting cock with disbelief, she pulled herself up with a superhuman effort, her head throbbing, breath coming in tiny gasps. She stood as upright as she could there in the window, her legs splayed wide for her audience, her hands pressing hard on her bloated sex lips, the edges of the crotchless crotch biting like red hot pincers.

Sheila clawed at the murderous rubber trousers like a madwoman. Across the street the man's fingers dragged up, then rapidly down to the base of the big white cock. She glanced at the pointed arch over his window, gothic like a church, the ornate gabled roof, at the houses on either side, all far more flamboyant in design than her sturdy Victorian villa. And unlike her rather haphazard side, all exactly equal in height until they reached Daphne's mansion, whose spread wings almost doubled its flanks. Had John never shown her the plans? She'd forgotten that the two sides of the street were so different.

Her eyes slid back to watch her peeping Tom. He aimed his cock straight at her. It jumped, and spunk shot star-shaped against the glass.

Fourteen

Alan was crashing about in the room behind her. The man in the window stepped away, cock melting into the shadows. He left his mark where it was, splattered all over the window like a sign.

Sheila was in agony. All she could do was dance about on the spot. Her bladder was desperate to rip slowly open even if it meant drowning in a rubber bath of piss.

'Alan. Get these things off me!' she shrieked.

He was in the bathroom, leaving the door open. She came after him, tugged at his arm. But he was over by the loo, scrabbling about with his trousers. His cock was slippery with her saliva and still so erect that the length of it seemed welded to his stomach. He tried to angle it down, hold it over the loo.

'Excuse me? Can't do anything till I've had a piss.'

Sheila was shaking as if she had some kind of fever. 'No locks in this house, Alan,' she tittered. She was twitching frantically inside the rubber, the jagged build-up of piss threatening to wet everything in sight. 'You'll have to get used to that if you come to live here. Now help me out of this outfit.'

He shook his face. He was red. He turned his back and mumbled something. He stood there. She watched. Nothing happened.

Outside she heard the powder-blue car rev and pull away.

'It's not going to work, is it?' She pushed in front of him and yanked his hands from his cock. It flipped upwards, banging back into his stomach. 'I've heard you can't pee with a hard on.'

'Whose fault is that?'

'Fine when it's tucked away in my mouth, hmm?' She stroked him a moment, feeling the ridges of muscle under the surprisingly soft skin. 'Maybe we should start this again.'

Alan gulped and swallowed as if she was hurting him, and tried to pull his still thumping erection away from her. His face flushed redder as he stumbled against the basin. How young he was. Twenty or so. Young enough for Tessa.

But she couldn't concentrate on that right now. Sheila hopped about, trying to relieve the pressure in her own bladder. Already she felt the sting of the first trickle, her muscles gripping vainly to keep it in.

'No! I can't hold it! I'm going first!' It came out as a screech. She pushed him out of the way, struggling and stumbling. The rubber leggings were stuck on, her sweat like glue. She tried hooking one finger under the string to pull it aside. It was taut to breaking point, and instead of loosening it just twanged back, hard as catgut, slicing right up into her vagina almost cutting her in two. She was practically dancing with desperation now. She'd have to pee over it, through the hole. She started to lower herself over the seat, but the trousers were so tight they wouldn't let her bend further than a ballerina's *demi plié*.

Alan smirked and then groaned faintly, leaning against the basin. He held his cock loosely, but it wasn't going to subside while he watched her. *Young enough to do it all over again.*

A couple of drops seeped out, elongating as they dribbled from her crushed pussy lips and hung there, waiting to fall. She shivered violently as it started. Her insides were caving in. Once she started, she wouldn't be able to stop. The feel of her bladder loosening, weakening, was intoxicating. The stinging inside and out made her moan with shameful pleasure. She knew how good it felt secretly to wet herself when Tessa was slapping her, how it felt just like an orgasm when the relief flooded through her, the humiliation when it first happened, now growing into an awful mixture of shame and excitement each time, because it happened nearly every time now, wetting herself because she was being punished, being punished because she was wetting herself, wanting to show Tessa but Tessa telling her she was a dirty little girl, nice girls pissed in private, the hot, yellow liquid soaking into her skin, pricking acid as it dried on her skin, on Tessa's sheets – did Olga ever wonder why there was always so much washing? – but this was different, she was standing blatantly over the loo like a man, her shaved pussy bare, her bottom bare, her bladder hot and explosive.

She should be crouching behind a bush somewhere, locking the door, not about to wet herself in her nicely tiled bathroom in her quiet house, in front of a stranger –

'Can't hold it,' she gasped, opening her legs further to straddle the bowl. A scrap of useless modesty. 'Some privacy please?'

'Privacy? You're the one who barged in here and started laughing at me. Bit late for privacy. You just sucked my cock, remember?' Alan laughed. His insolence was like a signal. The drops turned to a hot thin trickle, dribbling over the G-string splitting her in half, urine finding its way everywhere, along the string, up between her pussy lips, burning like salt in an open wound, running down her rubber legs.

Alan stared, still holding his cock. 'Christ. My landlady, wetting herself! We used to spy on the girls at school when they came in from games – we called it golden shower hour! We thought we'd just watch them changing, but then they used to hitch their little netball skirts up, pull those big white panties down round their knees –'

'Golden shower hour in the girls' changing rooms. All smelling of adolescent unwashed pussy and piss. It must have made them horny to know you grubby schoolboys were spying on them, having an eyeful.'

She let out a loud moan as the piss came. How low could you go, for God's sake? Humiliation crawled through Sheila with the urine dripping out of her, down her legs. Oh, she wanted to go lower.

'Which makes you a dirty little schoolgirl who needs potty training. Look at you, wetting yourself.' He came closer. Sheila tried to hide her fanny, tried to cross her legs. 'All wet. All down your legs. Wetting your knickers. Let me see.'

'Stop looking at me –'

He grabbed her legs and pulled her so that she was away from the loo, then he got down on his knees and nudged his head between her knees so that she was standing right over him. He let go of his cock, let it bounce there in his lap, took hold of Sheila's thighs right at the sinewy top of her legs, dug his thumbs into the tender triangular spaces just behind the trapped pussy lips, where bone turned to aching flesh, pushed his thumbs in, pulled her legs open, tilted his face upwards.

Sheila gasped. Instinctive horror warped into hysterics. Here was the rush of urine jostling down her bladder, the little valve opening like a floodgate, then the messy trickle started, spraying up and sideways before it focused into a neat yellow jet, a hot wet jet of piss arcing straight into Alan's face, into his hair, over his closed eyes, then his mouth was opening, she couldn't believe it, her instincts were to stop the stream, but she had no control even if she'd wanted to, and it was too good, so dirty, pissing on the young red face,

166

watching the mouth open up and her piss shooting in, dribbling down his chin, his lips wet with her urine, he was actually swallowing it, she could see his Adam's apple jumping, and it was her turn to make it pump and laugh out loud with the release of it as it went on and on splashing into his face, his thumbs digging hard, his face so close to her cunt, always digging. It kept spurting out of her. His thumbs dug harder and deeper, milking every last drop but still she wanted it to go on and she pushed her soaking crotch into his face, the oval trap of rubber and those tortured pussy lips rigid now, so swollen that they were curling apart like overblown petals.

As it slowed to a dribble, Sheila realised she was still shivering. Her knees knocked. 'Look what you've made me do.' Her voice shook, too. 'You naughty, dirty boy. Puddles all over the floor. What a mess, Alan. We need to clean this up. Tessa is going to be disgusted with us.'

'Us? You're the one who pissed everywhere –'

She kept her hands on his shoulders. She'd fall over if she didn't. She was mad with frustration. 'Whatever. Just lick me clean.'

He shook his head at her, wiping slicks of piddle off his mouth.

'Fine. You can go then, Alan, if you don't like what I'm asking.' She pushed her face nearer. He smelt of her cunt. Salty, like the sea. 'So, do you want the room, or not?'

Now he was nodding, looking again at her breasts. Her nipples were numb from the clamps.

'Of course you want the room. You liked what we did here, in private. You liked the way I tasted, didn't you?' she said softly, before pushing him down on to his knees. 'So come on, baby. Lick me.'

He paused. She braced herself for some lip. It was a very long time since she'd dealt with anyone his age. Since she'd called anyone baby. Except Tessa. She hadn't been near a guy as young as this since *she* was this age. And that was very different, two young kids fifteen years ago, shagging the summer away in rural France which seemed like the innocent frolics of a yoghurt advert compared with what she was doing now. John, older than her, ordering her about, his little sister, taking her when he wanted her. Now little Tessa, making up the sexy games that Sheila loved to play, transforming herself into the master, Sheila the slave –

But just now, just this minute, Mrs Moss wanted to play at being in charge ...

She grabbed handfuls of Alan's surprisingly silky hair and ground his face against her stomach. She started jerking her hips, rubbing frantically against his face. He didn't have to move. She couldn't stop herself. She could bring herself off with her hands, with Olga's lipstick, with a toothbrush for God's sake. Or she could make it ten times hornier and use his face, his mouth.

Her puffed-up pussy lips bumped his wet mouth and hard chin, touching open a little on contact, making her scream with pleasure. 'I'm all wet and dirty, remember. Normally I get slapped for that. Tessa thinks it's disgusting when I wet myself, all over the bed. You have to lick me clean, before she gets home!'

He stuck his tongue out, tapped her sex lips with it, started to lap at her, still kneeling under her. His tongue slid over all the exposed sore, stinging parts of her, adding his saliva to all the other wetness. He made slurping noises as his tongue swiped over her. Sheila spread her legs wider, again tried to hook the string aside, but the only way he could get to the stinging, burning centre of her was with his tongue. She pushed herself harder against his mouth, letting his teeth bang and bite. His tongue ran up between her labia and the thickened lips closed over it like a trap. The tip of his tongue flicked over her bulging, burning clit and she rammed herself hard into his face, yanking his head up

168

and down to make his nose and mouth rub harder, make him lap harder and faster, and at last she came, furiously, the pleasure jerking her about against his face like a rag doll.

Her legs shook so that she fell forwards but the rubber held her so tight that she could only land stiffly on all fours, half in and half out of the bathroom, panting hard like a dog.

'So what about the mess?' he said, sitting back on his haunches. 'You said it needs to be cleaned up.'

Sheila thought of Tessa. She couldn't begin to imagine what Tessa would say about her playing games with someone else. Let alone wetting herself, all over him, all over the floor.

'She'll kill me,' she murmured, still dizzy, still breathless.

'So clean it,' he said, running his tongue over his mouth. 'I've done what you said, I've licked you. But that's because I want the room. Now it's your turn. You have to lick the floor.'

'Why?'

'Because you want a lodger.'

'I can advertise –'

'Lick the floor!'

Sheila raised her voice to match his. 'Don't be disgusting!'

Alan pulled a towel off the rail, flicked it in the air. Sheila winced as it flicked against her rump. 'Lick it, Mrs Moss. Or I'll tell this Tessa of yours what you've been doing.'

Her bottom was in the air. He had hold of the towel. He brought it down with a sharp smack. Sheila's head snapped back. The smack seemed to punch a shocked groan out of her. She could feel the weal coming up, burning on her white skin. He smacked her again with the towel. Her breath whistled through her nose, through her mouth, she was dribbling, and she started to crawl about in front of him, feebly pretending to avoid the slaps.

'Lick the floor clean, Mrs Moss!'

She bent her head down to the floor, raising her bottom for more smacks, breathless from the tortuous corset, feeling the jolt powering through the towel as he smacked her, through her rump, down to the answering smack in her cunt. She stuck her tongue out, made it as long as she could, and licked the first cold puddle on the tiled floor.

Under the sink she could see that the grouting had crumbled and the edging tiles had come right away from the wall. Bloody John. What was happening to her house?

'How kinky is this?' He whistled softly, trailing the towel over her bottom, tickling between her cheeks with it. 'Just wait till I tell the boys about this!'

'The *boys* won't believe you. Because you're not going to tell them. Look at me. Out there everyone thinks I'm Mrs Respectable. In here, in my own house –'

'You can grovel about on the floor being as cringing and perverted as you like!'

He raised his arm, and smacked her hard on the other buttock. It sang through her, fingers of fire clawing at her cunt so that she clenched against the pain, but as soon as the hot glow had spread through her, as soon as the towel's mark sprang up red and sore, she wanted more. She dipped her head to the floor, waited for the next blow, stuck her tongue out, lapped at the salty wetness, even slurped at it to draw it up into her mouth and taste it. How low could she go? She crawled about, licking at the puddles and splashes of her own pee. But the smacking had stopped.

'Better than any website, this. They'll never believe me.'

He was talking to himself. Sheila glanced over her shoulder. He was standing up in front of the loo again,

170

towel draped over his shoulder, holding his cock, swinging it slowly from side to side. There was a golden drop dangling off the end of it.

He aimed his still-stiff prick at the bowl. She watched his knees sagging, his head falling back slightly as the piss prepared to come. She couldn't understand why she was still edgy with desire. The tight clothes and not being able to draw a proper breath had her in a permanent state of arousal. The excitement and the corset and the wetting and her position on all fours licking the floor had finally reduced her to an animal, a bitch dog growling and pissing herself and barking.

He went red again. He still had her come and her pee all over his face. He looked down at her and tried some bravado. 'Your turn to taste my piss.'

His cock jerked in his hand like some kind of rocket moving of its own accord.

She wanted to. Badly. Wanted to feel hot liquid bursting down her throat from his cock, hard jet so different from the creamy dollops of come. But it was time to regain some kind of ground, or dignity, or something. Surely?

'Don't be disgusting!' she snapped, injecting her voice with all the hauteur she could manage while still on her hands and knees. 'I'm not a human toilet.'

'Oh yes, you are. So I'll just have to make you.'

'Look at you. You're a little boy. Not a man. A mouse. Can't even pee properly.'

Sheila tried again to stand up, but her cramped limbs refused to let her move. She couldn't even turn round to face him properly. She felt like a dog wagging its tail. It was the only movement she could make.

'And you're just an incontinent old lady who's all mouth and who pees everywhere then has to lick it up and doesn't know whether she's mistress or monkey!'

He came up behind her and pushed her down again. Of course she struggled, even as she bit her lips to stop herself screaming with mad delight at his crude, clumsy insults.

'I'm your monkey!' she squealed, drawing in great gulps of air. 'So fuck me like I'm your dirty little monkey!'

'Shut up, you old bag.'

He pushed her head down, held tight to her hips behind her, then he groaned and she felt the hot piss splashing on her, bouncing off the rubber trousers as if she was wearing an umbrella.

'You're disgusting!' she hissed, jerking her head about helplessly as he sprayed his piss all over her. 'You're making me all dirty again.'

'Shut up!' he ordered.

He shoved her roughly back to the floor. She pushed her buttocks nearer, tipped herself up at him, ah, now she felt the warm jet on her bottom, going straight at her arse as if he was firing a water pistol, felt the hole opening, not closing, both holes opening hungrily to be filled up.

'Fuck me up there, piss up me, fuck me!' she screamed, reaching back to get at his cock, feeling the piss spraying on her fingers, his cock slipping about, his knees squeaking on the bathroom floor. He spread her cheeks open, his nails digging into the flesh. She chewed her mouth with pleasure at the needle-sharp pain in her already sore flesh. He stretched her cheeks open until the skin felt ready to tear.

'You're the one who's disgusting, Mrs Moss. I was a good boy when I came to this house. You're the one who waved your bottom about on the stairs like a bitch on heat. Wait till I tell the lads you like it up the arse because your cunt's too tight. That's what baboons do,' he grunted, the tip of his cock jabbing at her, the piss still shooting over her, showering her aching, stretched backside and cunt in salty, stinging piss. 'Now who's the boss?'

'Stop bragging. You're not in the pub now,' she grunted back, arching her back as the hot piss dribbled down her crack. The image of Maureen with her metallic-purple mouth, her baboon's arsehole mouth, came to her. Tessa said it was unkind to baboons to compare them. Sheila tried to imagine that shiny mouth with Alan's oversized cock thrusting into it, forcing those sagging sarky lips open, thrusting between those crooked teeth.

Sheila shook with pleasure, like a cat now more than a dog. A favourite turn-on for her and Tessa was to plan evil sexual tortures for Maureen, involving various items of office equipment, a willing messenger boy or two, and an appalled, gaping audience consisting of everyone from the manager downwards. The more wriggling and screaming and wobbling of jelly-like fat flesh this involved, the more pleas for mercy and apologies as they tied her up and impaled her, maybe left her out in the rain, the better.

She started to crawl away from Alan, shivering with the delicious cruelty of it. Wishing someone would do all that to her.

'I'm going to get out of these things. I think I'm coming up in some kind of rash here. You can clean up now, and then we'll talk about the room.'

But Alan's hands were on her hips, pinning her down on the floor. They were both halfway across her bedroom now, but too far from the window. A car engine fired up in the street below.

Alan pushed her head down so that her bottom was in the air again, her cheek scraping the carpet.

'Sorry, haven't finished, can't stop now, still pissing. You told me to fuck you up there, Mrs Moss. You're the mistress, ' he said, his voice thick and deadly with arousal. His hands were too strong to struggle against, even if she'd wanted to. 'So that's what I'm going to do.'

Her bottom was open and exposed, fat cheeks open and the little hole tucked inside, waiting, cringing open and shut. The rest of her was paralysed. She pretended to struggle, still thinking of a watching Maureen, a giggling Tessa. She was tugged by rising excitement as he stretched her cheeks so wide apart that it was like he was going to examine her. The skin that was open to the air felt dry and salty from her wetting herself, patches still wet from his piss, all anyone would see of her was her great baboon arse, up in the air, because his cock was unscrewing it, the tip easing it open and drilling inside, she'd unleashed the beast in both of them, she was spread-eagled on her bedroom carpet, and her shy new lodger was screwing her up the arse, making it open for him, making it soften and loosen to let him in, and this time there was no clenching and resistance, just opening and gripping, there was a hot ball of pleasure up there, this was better than any sex toy, this dildo had tight balls which banged against her as he fucked her up the arse, prostrate there on the floor.

'Let's just keep this our dirty little secret,' she grunted as he whipped his narrow hips back and forth, thrusting her across the piss-damp carpet, thrusting hard till it hurt into her tight bottom until it opened, welcoming him. 'Tessa will kill me if she finds out.'

'Whatever. All I wanted was a room.' And Alan gave a curious, polite whimper as he came.

Fifteen

They were in the kitchen when Tessa came home two days later. Sheila was wearing her own clothes for a change. Black trousers and a V-neck cashmere sweater. Tessa would be annoyed. She preferred it when Sheila greeted her dressed in one of her too-short dresses or gym shorts. To make up for it, Sheila was ironing Tessa's blouses. Alan was wearing his chef's snowy tunic and breaking egg whites into a big bowl.

'Very cosy this looks. Settled in then?' asked Tessa, handing Sheila her coat and sticking her finger into Alan's mixing bowl without even introducing herself. 'What's this going to be? Soufflé?'

'If you don't mind.' He moved the bowl along the counter away from her and started to whisk petulantly. His lank hair fell down over his face with the effort. Sheila noticed the muscles flexing in his arms – the arms that lifted the towel, or her bra, or today, shockingly, one of his belts, and smacked her across her sore, smarting bottom.

He looked manly, bent over his task. 'Meringues for the restaurant.'

Behind his back Tessa mouthed at Sheila, flapping her wrist. 'Is he gay or what?'

Sheila was about to shake her head but instead she just smiled and laid a hand on Alan's shoulder. 'Oh, he's a genius. You should taste his *coquilles saint Jacques*.'

175

Tessa frowned and took off her pinstriped jacket. She stalked towards the door on Sheila's borrowed heels. 'Did you run my bath, Moss?'

'Not yet.' Sheila handed Tessa her ironed blouses. 'I've been a bit busy today what with showing Alan round the neighbourhood –'

'Well, come and do it now, will you?'

'So that's Tessa, is it? From everything you said I thought she'd be a diesel dyke. But she's like some snotty kid who's raided the dressing up box.' Alan swung round when Tessa had gone up the stairs, the whisk still whirring in his hands. 'How come you let the little bitch speak to you like that?'

'She's been for a tricky audition up north.'

'Audition for what? Uptight prison governor in *Bad Girls*? I can just see her rattling a bunch of keys –'

'She's bound to be tense after being scrutinised by a panel like that.' Sheila swiped a flurry of meringue mixture off her breast. 'But the way she treats me? It's only a game.'

'Funny sort of game where she's allowed to walk around being fucking rude. I thought you were the boss around here?'

'That's what I thought.' Sheila sidled closer to him. 'Until you got me on all fours like a doggie –'

'She's the one who deserves a proper slapping, not you.' He grinned and turned the bowl upside down. The meringue mixture didn't budge. He rattled about in the cutlery drawer to get out a spoon. 'Redheads always have evil tempers.'

'Oh, she's a pussycat really. Now, not a word –'

The pussycat was clattering down the stairs again.

'Sheila, there's a leak upstairs. Your carpet's soaking. And it smells of something. I don't know. Rusty water?'

Alan bent to fiddle with the dials on the oven. Sheila went bright red and pretended to help him.

Tessa yanked Sheila away from him. 'We might need a plumber, Sheila!'

176

Alan looked at his watch. 'I've got to get to the restaurant.' He pushed the tray of meringue whirls into the oven, removed the batch that had just finished browning, then danced over to the fridge to get out a bright berry *coulis* and some clotted cream.

'It could bring the ceiling down!' Tessa went on. 'You have to phone the plumber, Sheila. And another thing, just what the fuck's this?' Strips of black rubber dangled from her fist. 'Been changing a bicycle tyre or something? This was in the bin in the bathroom.'

'Those sexy trousers, Mrs Moss. You looked so hot when you answered the door wearing them. I mean, they fitted you like a glove, didn't they? A rubber glove!' Alan joked, and Sheila smirked. He waved a tiny knife the air. 'Shame I had to cut them off you.'

'You were wearing rubber trousers?'

'Olga's rubber trousers. She has fetish gear, Tess –'

Tessa jabbed her finger at Alan. 'Sheila may look like Mrs Danvers but she couldn't dominate a pack of cards. Who could she possibly want to dominate, anyway? You?' She dipped her finger in the bright red *coulis*, held it up, then ran it slowly down Alan's pure white tunic, following the trail of his buttons. 'Mmm. Cherry, is it?'

'Redcurrant.' Alan started dabbing at the bright stain. 'I can't go to work with this mess on me. And where's my piping bag?'

The steam from the iron was making Sheila sweat. 'Why are you so fierce today, darling?' she asked Tessa. 'Where's that cutesie who used to gaze at me all day at that horrible office?'

'The same cutesie who likes to whack you on your big fat bottom, Moss?'

Alan swallowed.

Sheila set the iron down. 'The same cutesie who shows me what her fat ugly landlord Mr Brown used to do to her. The cutesie who gives me new pleasures every day, you have no idea how it turns me on, each new pleasure growing in the dark till I can't wait for the first slap of the night.'

Tessa snapped the handful of rubber strips in the air and the sound they made was exactly like a cat o'nine tails. Sheila winced, imagining the sting on her skin. Her cunt clenched. Tessa's eyes gleamed, too. Her little pink tongue ran across her lips.

'What were you doing with these bloody trousers?'

Alan picked up a J-cloth and dabbed uselessly at his stained tunic. 'Yeah.' He moved the glass bowl of fruity goo out of Tessa's reach. 'The only way was to cut. They were stuck to her like glue.'

'Did you use one of these, Alan?' Tessa ran her fingers over a leather pouch lying open beside the hob, where knives were laid out like surgical instruments. She took a long one out of its sheath.

'They were hurting her. They were pinching her, you know?' Alan tried to grab the knife, but Tessa whisked it behind her back. 'And she couldn't breathe in that corset thing.'

'She was wearing a corset thing, too?' Tessa had the knife at his throat. 'What was going *on* here?'

'Hey! These knives are for food, not for fighting, and they cost a fortune. A present from my parents, when I graduated from catering college this summer.' Alan waggled the smaller knife in her face. 'Could do some damage.'

'So tell me what was going on,' Tessa said, pressed up close. 'Olga will do some damage when she comes home and finds her clothes in shreds.'

'Christ almighty!' Alan wiped angrily at his sleeve and tried to push past. 'What are you three, the bloody Witches of Eastwick?'

Tessa laughed. Alan sighed. 'We had to get her out of the trousers, OK, because they were all wet.'

Sheila held the folded ironing board in front of her like a shield.

'All wet?' Tessa sniffed what remained of the rubber trousers. 'You peed in these stupid trousers?' She took the ironing board, propped it against the wall and wrapped her arm round Sheila's waist. 'Does all wet mean you've peed on the floor?'

'Let's drop this, shall we?' Sheila squeezed Tessa, stroked her hair. 'Poor Alan. He'll think he's come to a mad house –'

'Will you tell me, Alan? Or do I cut up this beautiful white jacket of yours? Make you so late for work?' Tessa flicked the knife across the top button on Alan's jacket, worrying the sharp tip at the thread. Alan undid the button before she could do any more harm, but still she flicked the knife at each button in turn until they were all undone.

'It's too embarrassing. Let her tell you. She made me do it,' he mumbled, stretching cling film over the glass bowl. 'And now I'm late.'

'She made you do it? So you're only a little boy, hm?' Tessa tossed the knife down and pulled his jacket off him. Underneath he was bare. His nipples went hard in the cold. 'Oh, let's forget the bloody trousers. I've had a very bad day. Very stressed. How about we get to play with our new housemate?'

'How about that lovely hot bath now?' Sheila tugged at Tessa, trying to pull her out of the room. 'Did you get the job?'

'Yes, I got the job.' Tessa twisted away from her. 'But it's not me who needs to get clean, is it, Sheila? Who'd have thought it? Mrs Moss, posher than thou, pissing all over the floor?'

'We both did it.' Alan packed the meringues carefully into a Tupperware box. 'I never knew these posh women could be so dirty. She pissed all over my face.'

For once Tessa was speechless. 'And did you drink it, Alan?'

'Why not? I'm a chef. I have to taste everything.' He grinned, tapped another of the knives on the lid of the box. 'Then I got my cock out and fucked her up the arse. How about that?'

'You drank Sheila's pee!' Tessa gave a great dragging gasp. 'Oh my God, it's even worse than I thought! I'm on my own with two perverts.'

'Hey, that's a bit tough –' Alan started to say, half laughing.

'I mean, how base can you get!' Tessa flicked the rubber whip in the air, then before Sheila knew what was happening one rubber strip was round her wrists. 'Moss? You wetted all over our new lodger, all over yourself, all over the carpet?'

Sheila nodded stiffly.

'Did you drink his piddle?' Tessa jerked at the binding. Humiliation and excitement popped alternately inside Sheila like bubbles. She didn't recognise herself. She'd wet herself. She was in the corner in disgrace, a naughty girl with no shame. She kept her eyes on Tessa, saw the light glinting there hard as stone. Harder. That meant punishment was on the way. Something Sheila hadn't seen before. Something else Tessa had learned from her fat, sweating landlord.

She knew how to make the punishment better. 'So?' she whispered, leaning forwards, flicking her tongue at Tessa's mouth. 'You forget, Tessa. It's my carpet. I can urinate on it. I can even shit all over it if I like!'

'And you used to be so cool. So dignified, Sheila.' Tessa clicked her tongue. 'Look at the state of you.'

'So leave, if you don't like it!' Even with her hands tied behind her back, Sheila could still look imperious. 'You can get out of my kitchen. Out of my house.'

Tessa pressed her hand over Sheila's mouth. Her hand was warm, and tasted of salt and soap. Sheila closed her eyes, hoping for some comfort, some soothing. Some apology, even. Her heart was hammering with fury.

'What nonsense are you talking now? You invited us

to stay, Sheila. No, sorry, it's more than that. You *advertised*.'

Sheila tried to shake Tessa's hand off, but Tessa was using her grip on Sheila's face to drag her across the room and push her to lie face down on the heavy old refectory table John found last year in a reclamation yard. Sheila's cheek hit the hard oak surface she had scrubbed so lovingly while she waited for him to come home.

'And actually, it's *our* house now.' Tessa spoke softly, but a spray of spittle settled on Sheila's cheek. 'We all pay rent to walk about on that carpet. But perhaps we should stop paying good money to live in a shit hole like this.'

'This house is my pride and joy!' Sheila struggled furiously. She knew Tessa was snapping deliberately at her Achilles heel to get a rise. Clever. After their nightly games Tessa had quickly learned that when Sheila was roused to anger she was wide open. To anything. That it was only a very short step to turning her on.

'It's a hovel. It's falling apart at the seams. Haven't you noticed the damp crawling up that back wall?' Tessa spread Sheila's legs open so that she had no way of standing up or getting away. Quickly she dragged Sheila's skirt down her legs and off.

'What damp?'

'We expect our landlady to be proper clean. So that gives us the right to be very, very annoyed about all this.'

'You can leave me out of it,' breathed Alan, trying to edge round the table to get to the door.

'I don't think so.' Tessa pulled Sheila's arm and tied it to one table leg. 'You let her urinate all over you. Goodness. What would chef say?'

'Tessa! This has gone far enough! Stop being such a little bitch!' Sheila found her voice. She struggled against the belt tying her down. She twisted, her hip digging into the table's hard surface.

Tessa's eyes filled with tears. 'Did you hear what she just called me?'

Sheila pulled at the tie biting into her wrist. 'Stop acting.'

Tessa ran out of the room, sobbing like a baby.

Sheila was still pulling ineffectually at her bonds, pride preventing her from asking for help, when she heard a discreet cough behind her.

'I let myself in. Your front door was wide open?' A stocky man with a raincoat and a clipboard was standing in the kitchen doorway. He looked from Alan, who was trying not to laugh, to Sheila, who was trying to stand up straight with her arm tied to the kitchen table.

'Party games,' she cried, waggling her wrist. 'Ready for Christmas.'

'Quite an impressive knot. You'll not get out of that in a hurry. By the way, your garden path is beginning to sink. Bad enough outside, but I'm here to report on the inside of the house,' the man said, walking past her to peer at the damp seeping through the wall. 'The entire street, actually. Is your husband here?'

'I have no husband,' Sheila said, twisting round. He was holding up a damp meter and sucking his teeth. She could see moisture running down the wall.

'No point protecting him, Mrs Moss. Mr Tanner knows all about what's been going on here.'

'Mr Tanner?'

'Of Spartan Street Estates. He lives opposite, when he's in the country. Mr Moss has been seen here quite recently.' He craned forwards and jabbed his thumb through the French windows. He had surprisingly nice eyes, deep and brown. 'There are cameras, you see.'

Sheila followed his thumb. Sure enough, mounted on the side of the house and pointing straight into the kitchen, was a neat surveillance camera.

'Cool,' said Alan. 'Can he do that?'

'He owns the street. Of course he can. Those little beauties can film every nook and cranny, believe me. And not a moment too soon.' The man seemed to be growing in stature as Sheila and Alan hung on his every word. 'I've never seen anything like it. Subsidence, zero underpinning, shoddy masonry – did you know this side of the street was condemned? It was built on a kind of rack system over a plague swamp. That's why those knocking shops mushroomed in the last century. It should never have been built in the first place, let alone got past planning last year for redevelopment.'

Spartan Street Estates. The bank statement. 'He owns all these houses? He's paid for them all?'

Upstairs they could hear Tessa stamping about, still in a sulk.

'Some sort of leasehold arrangement. You should be relieved, Mrs Moss. All pretty irregular, but I'm not a lawyer. I should have said,' the man went on comfortably, holding out a business card. 'The name's Brown. County surveyor. Heads are rolling in the planning department.'

'Oh, I can imagine it only too well. Not a pretty sight. I was temping there, not long ago. A horrible woman called Maureen works there. So did my lodger, actually. Tessa.'

Mr Brown shrugged. 'And your husband, who developed the slum – sorry, site – is wanted for corruption and fraud and whatever's in the book they're going to throw at him.'

'He's not my husband. He's my brother. I don't know where he is.' Alan folded his arms, trying not to laugh. Sheila flushed. 'But he did the other side of the street, too. The odd numbers. So he didn't do a botched job with all of them. I mean, *they're* not falling down, are they?'

Alan spluttered with laughter.

'No. But that's Mr Tanner's half of the site. They were business partners. Or rather, business enemies. Mr

183

Tanner is out for blood. This half,' Mr Brown dabbed his finger in the green slime on the wall and glanced up at the orange fuzzed sky, 'is unfit for human habitation.'

When he had left, having failed to get the door closed behind him, Tessa came running down the stairs.

'Christ!' she said, staring down the pitted garden path. 'What was my old landlord doing here?'

Sixteen

Sheila's cheekbone was pressed against the table, the voices swimming above her head.

'Seeing that little pervert again, all respectable with his briefcase, has made me even more mad. She needs cleaning up, Alan. Take them off her. I want that dirty slut's bottom bare.'

Alan pulled Sheila's knickers down. Now her buttocks were bare, the skin pricking up in pimples of cold. The knickers were tight, hemming round the crease under her cheeks, so that she could feel them bulging. She was hot with creeping, delicious shame. Her pussy was rubbing over the same spot where this morning she was calmly eating muesli.

Tessa dug her fingers in hard, spreading Sheila's legs so that she was wide open. The puckered nub of her anus hole must be visible now. It squeezed frantically, sending up spasms. Who knows what this kind of excitement could make her do?

'You didn't think you'd escape your punishment, did you? I should have kept Mr Brown to show you how it's really done. But what's even worse is he pretended not to recognise me.' Tessa snatched the knickers and had a sniff. 'Smell how dirty you are.'

Tessa pulled the knickers over Sheila's face. She could smell her own damp crotch and breathed the sharp smell of arousal.

'Smells of fish and piss!' Tessa giggled. 'A new recipe, Alan?'

There was a shivering in the air, and then the slap and sting of the rubber tails flapped down on Sheila's rump. Compared with Tessa's hand, the whip seemed almost to tickle at first, until the impact struck home and the skin rippled across her plump buttock, the warmth of the slap seeping inwards. Sheila groaned as the sensation drove straight at her cunt.

'Now you, Alan. Do it, or we'll ask chef over to watch what his *commis* or whatever you are likes to get up to.'

Sheila had given up struggling. She couldn't see anything as her knickers clung to her face when she breathed in, suffocating her, clogging her nostrils with her own smell.

There was another shivering pause, then the whip came down again, each rubber tail slapping its mark on her before sliding off.

'Harder!' screamed Tessa. 'You wimp! She's dirty! She needs it harder than that!'

Sheila was arching her back now, flinching so her red sore bottom was exposed for more, legs pressing closed then kicking frantically open again, fat cheeks split wide open to show her dark purple crack, studded with the closed promise of her arsehole.

'Want more.' It came out as a croak. Saliva was dribbling from her mouth because she couldn't take a full breath through her nose. The dribble soaked her cheeks, made them prickle and itch.

Sheila plucked at her aching pussy, all shaved, the fringe of unshaved hair still there, every sensitive fold pulled open, sore in the open air.

She waited for another strike. Another word from Tessa. The front door slammed, and there was an answering splintering on the wall where Mr Brown had been poking at the damp. Feet shuffled in the hall, coming into the kitchen, but no one was speaking. She could see nothing except dim shapes moving through the fabric of her knickers.

'Good evening, everyone.' It was Olga's voice, throaty with amusement. 'Meet your new neighbour.'

'My God, Mr Brown said it was bad,' said a deep voice. 'But I never realised it would be this bad!'

'I'm a dirty little girl,' Sheila murmured out of the corner of her mouth, dribbling again. They all stopped talking. 'I need teaching a lesson. So naughty and dirty.'

'Excuse me, Mr –?'

'Tanner. From number 43.'

'But as you see you're interrupting us, Tanner. Can it wait?' Tessa's voice was icy. Just as Sheila's would have been, if she'd been her other self.

There was a low laugh. 'I've waited this long to speak to Mrs Moss. Be my guest.'

'It won't be pretty –'

'Nothing shocks him. He likes to watch.' Olga's throaty voice was back. 'What's going on here, anyway? What are you doing to Sheila?'

Sheila choked out, 'Let me go!' but the knickers were in her mouth. She tried to spit them out, but the more she spat and struggled, the more they stuck inside her teeth. She started to kick frantically. She didn't want him seeing her like this.

'That's Sheila Moss?'

'We're punishing her, Tanner.' Tessa slapped her, just to show him. 'She's been dirty, haven't you, Moss? You weed all over the floor. Into Alan's mouth, too, didn't she, Alan? Now, you're going to wash this little untrained bitch, splashing yellow smelly piss all over the lovely clean carpets.'

Tessa pulled Sheila's legs apart and tied her ankles to the table legs as well. 'This will make you very, very cross. Would you like to do the honours, Tanner? You can leave if this is going to shock you.'

'Allow me.'

Something cold and slimy dropped on to Sheila's spine.

'It looks just like spunk!' Olga screeched, clapping her hands.

'Give her a good washing, Alan. She's so dirty! Right up inside her dirty little cunt, where she weed.'

'Those are organic bantam eggs!'

Someone's hands rubbed the slimy stuff over Sheila's bottom. It felt like cream over the soreness, and dragged her nearer to the pricking climax. But she didn't want gorgeous or soothing. She didn't want Tanner seeing her in this disgusting, humiliating position. She wanted more whipping and pain.

'All the eggs, Alan. All your precious eggs. Call it lubrication!'

Tessa cackled and yanked Sheila's thighs wide apart.

'No, no!' Sheila's words were a gagged muffle, and they all laughed. She went hotter with shame, knowing her pussy was on blatant display now at the base of the dark violet crack, the dark pucker of her purple arsehole trying to stay primly closed as Tessa spread her bottom open. Alan, or someone, smeared the eggs up the crack between her legs. He was being rough, cursing as Tessa and Olga kept breaking the eggs. Sheila shivered as the slime started oozing into all the stretched snippets of flesh. The slime felt good all over her, it felt dirty and messy. She was liking how it smeared on to the table so that when she moved it slithered on her legs and stomach as well.

'Push it in there, too, push all this mess into that tight little arse. Looks like Sheila's tight little mouth, doesn't it, Olga? What do you think, Tanner?'

'It's *Mr* Tanner, actually,' said Olga.

'I've seen Mrs Moss before, you know.' Mr Tanner was still there. 'I'd know that bottom anywhere.'

Sheila struggled feebly.

Olga leaned down. 'I warned you I was keeping him for myself, Sheila. How has he seen your bottom?'

'Hungry, Mrs Moss? I've something nice for you to eat.'

Someone briefly pulled the knickers away and pushed something against Sheila's mouth, forcing it right in until it crumbled. It was delicious, but dry with sugar, and the crumbs filled her mouth, making her cough. When she'd got half of it down, another one was pushed in.

'How about a strawberry, too? You deserve it, darling.' Tessa was all sweet and loving as she rammed the strawberry, leaf and all, between Sheila's teeth. Juice spurted down her chin. 'And now those other holes need filling, don't you think, Alan?'

Someone was rubbing meringue crumbs up the hot dark divide of her arse, which was now wet with egg and sweat. The crumbs were prickling into her crack, all round her hole. The girls were whispering as the egg stuck the crumbs to her, making it squeeze and pucker in response. They were scratching at her so that the sensation was like being sandpapered on that velvety strip of skin. Excitement kicked deep in her groin. She ground herself against the table, craving movement to relieve herself, but an order was barked and someone, must have been Alan, untied her legs and heaved her violently up on to her knees so that her buttocks waved in the air.

'Do you think this went on when this was a brothel?' Mr Tanner wondered, somewhere in the room. 'Perhaps their spirits live on. Everyone on this side of the street seems totally debauched.'

Crumbs scraped inside her swollen pussy lips, throbbing and glistening with the eggs and bright berry *coulis*, but it was when the crumbs scraped like gravel over her clit that she choked and kicked and slithered on the table. But the more she struggled the wider apart her legs and her buttocks were held open and the more exquisite the splintered pain of dry crumbs being rubbed into an already sore, wet, aching pussy ripped through her.

'You fucking bitches. I can't believe you've made me do this.' Alan was half growling, half laughing. He rubbed even harder, rough crumbs up and down Sheila's pussy and the first tight waves of her climax, fighting through all that searing pain, started up.

'Because you've behaved like a grubby little boy, that's why. Do you think anyone would eat your desserts if they knew what you did with them? What you're doing now, with those lovely big hands, smearing eggs and cream and meringues all over your landlady's arse? What you're about to do?'

'Do you know how tough it is to be taken on as pastry chef?'

Olga and Tessa burst out laughing. They were both close to her face. Sheila twisted with helpless jealousy. They'd never laughed together before. They hated each other.

'There's one more. What do you think, Olga? Shall we pop it in that little shitting hole? I think it needs feeding,' Tessa said, scrabbling around in Alan's chill box. 'What have we in here?' She ran her nails down Sheila's stretched butt cheek, scratching streaks in the sore flesh. Sheila could only moan, and try to press her legs together to keep herself from coming. 'I think this will fit nicely right up there –'

'For God's sake!' Alan shouted from further away in the room. 'That's the last one I've got. Don't use that. Let me use this.'

Tessa's voice was low and deadly. 'Let's see how much that dirty little bottom can take.'

'Don't be so stupid!' yelled Alan. 'It'll break!'

'I've never seen anything so fucking horny in my life!' Mr Tanner's voice rose with excitement. 'God, wouldn't John go mad?'

'She's not his business any more!' chortled Tessa. 'He left her to our tender care, didn't he, Moss?'

'And isn't Sheila getting her revenge on him for doing the dirty? Who could have imagined she could go so low?' Tanner mused. He sounded far away. 'Pity about the house, though. I did warn him.'

'Look!' Olga interrupted, stuffing another strawberry into Sheila's mouth so that the crumbs and sticky juice fell all over her chin and on to the table under her head and tickled and messed her cheeks and her ears and her hair. She had to take a tiny breath otherwise she would breathe crumbs down her windpipe, but the light-headedness was sensational, making everything seem drunk and dreamlike. 'Sheila's laying an egg!'

Sheila whimpered, shaking her head and trying to pull her buttocks closed. What did Tanner mean about the house?

'Alan, give her a whack to shut her up! Christ, this looks like a prize winner from the village fete! Obviously from one of your organic vegetable patches!'

Something long and blunt thwacked down on Sheila's bottom, so hard that it must have left a dent. Sheila felt her flesh wobbling as she instinctively lifted herself for more. She whimpered to hide her delight, then instantly started coughing again.

'I thought you made puddings?' Olga said. 'Why a vegetable?'

'I wanted to have a go at stuffing it,' Alan said, as if this was a serious conversation. They all shrieked with laughter again.

'Prize winning cucumber,' spluttered Tessa. 'How about being rogered by that, Sheila?'

'You know, she still looks majestic even kneeling there with her bottom wriggling about in the air like a filthy doggie!'

'You don't think it's enough?'

'Don't be a wimp, Tanner! She loves nothing more

than being punished. Tessa's just going a bit further tonight, aren't you?'

'How did you know she likes being punished?' Tessa's voice was harder. 'She been talking to you?'

'I've got ears, Tess. Christ, she shrieks like a stuck pig.'

'Over-dramatic Russian!'

'You both shriek. I have eyes. I saw when the neighbours had a go at her, remember? Where were you?'

Sheila wriggled feebly, delighted as they started to argue and earning herself another thwack. She bit down hard, chewing a mouthful of pantie as she relished the radiating pain. Her climax crawled closer, her clit swollen with urgent desire, her pussy soaking now.

'Turn her over, quick. She won't be able to have a drink, will she, all down on her face like that.'

'And she needs something to wash down all those lovely meringues.'

Sheila was untied and slammed down on to her back. Through the thin material of her knickers she could see the glare of the spotlights, the others moving about. But they didn't remove the blindfold.

'Stop now, Tessa,' she pleaded, finally clearing her throat of meringue so she could speak. They bent her knees up. The eggy mess was congealing under her, drying up her crack, stuck inside the lining of her sex lips, up her cunt. Alan's meringue crumbs pricked and nagged at her tender flesh. She wondered if they could see the urgent squeezing of her cunt, desperate for something solid to rub over it or ram into it.

'Be quiet!' shouted Tessa, and with that a hail of blows rained on her bottom and her thighs, so that she was squealing and thrashing about, bucking on the hard table, her legs opening and closing with delight, then kicking and waving in the air, twisting so that they would smack it harder.

192

Then the blows stopped and someone – it must have been two of them – grabbed her knees and tied them together so that she was forced to keep her legs bent up to her stomach.

'This'll stop you piddling again, Moss.'

'And this is for the dirty little slut who likes it up the arse. Say it. Dirty little slut.'

'I'm a dirty little slut.' The words spewed easily out of her mouth now, along with the meringue crumbs and dribbles of red *coulis*. She wished she could see herself, splayed and trussed on the table, her cunt and her anus spread wide open, on show in front of people who were essentially, in another life, guests in her house.

Sheila started to shiver. She felt weak now with shame, humiliation, confusion, a ferocious frustration at the climax that might never come. Something nudged at her aching pussy, crunched through the crumbs stuck to all the sauce and her own juice smeared everywhere.

The very mention of piddling made her want to go. Her bladder started to ache. But it was her cunt that was shrinking and squeezing with frantic excitement, and she knew they could see, because first her cunt was forced open, the blunt, cold object pushing in, pushing the walls of her tunnel outwards. She pressed her knees together to hold it there, actually manoeuvred it further in as if she was on her own with it.

'What would you call that, Alan?' came Tessa's voice from somewhere above her head. 'How would you name this recipe?'

'That's easy,' laughed Olga, also from just above. 'Cucumber à la cunt!'

The two girls fell about laughing. Friends again. Shit. So it must be Alan shoving the cucumber up her cunt as far as it would go, pulling it out just a little, then pushing it further in while her juices sprang out of her to lubricate its passage and the tiny muscles gripped at the new object.

193

'It won't be safe here for much longer. The subsidence is far worse than I thought.'

Tanner was behind her now. He must be standing by the far wall, the one with the French windows opening into the garden. The one, now she thought about it, with yet another crack fizzing through it.

'Don't fuck her with it,' Tessa shouted. 'She's not supposed to be having fun, is she? We're just seeing how much we can shove up her.'

Alan didn't reply. Now he was prising open her anus with something hard like steel, Christ, not a knife, surely, he had plenty of those in his arsenal, hah, arsenal, he was sliding something into her anus hole. At first it was easy, she was sticky with egg and mess, but then it pinged inside, bumped over the rim, and the sensation nearly took the top of her head off. It didn't go very far up, but the very way it hovered at the entrance was worse, making her anus cringe with the effort of trying to close so that she wouldn't embarrass herself, but the implement was keeping it open, stretching the tender edges of the hole until it sang with pain.

'Please, Tessa, stop this, you're hurting me!' Sheila cried out. She was shaking violently now, her thighs aching with the effort of holding her knees flexed over her stomach. Because they were tied together she couldn't just lie back and let them flop open.

'I'll be back,' Mr Tanner said suddenly, walking smartly past her. She felt his sleeve brush her face. 'The bloody place is falling down.'

'I see you later?' Olga's voice went high.

'Try keeping me away.'

The front door slammed again. It was the only way to shut it now, as it was so warped. There was a pattering of dust from the ceiling, dropping onto Sheila's face.

'They train well at English chef school,' Olga murmured vaguely. 'He has tied her just like we tie pigs at home, to go over the spit.'

'I don't want to be your piggie any more!' Sheila was trying to make a feeble comeback. 'I'm sorry for pissing on the carpet. I want my little Tessa back. My sweet Tessa, who loves me.'

'Don't look so disgusted, Alan,' Tessa interrupted, ignoring Sheila. 'After all, you're the one who let her piss all over the place and put your dirty cock up her arse.'

'But this is my grandmother's silver spoon, the one I always use for –'

'Of course it's a spoon. How else do you eat your eggs?'

'What is that you're putting in? Tessa! Who gave you these ideas?'

But weirdly even the sound of her own quavering voice, and the way nobody answered her, excited her, the rising fear had warped into greedy desire, the fiery agony in every orifice which she should hate but was actually loving, her cunt with Alan's cucumber sticking out of it, the utter degradation of all this, it all just nudged, pushed, shoved at her waiting climax, dragged it downwards, down to where her clit rubbed against the stiff ridged green surface of the cucumber, pulled it closer so that any minute she would end up shuddering and jerking and coming in front of all of them.

Alan sighed harshly as he pushed something over the spoon.

'Sheila looks like – what is it – the turkey on the table for Christmas dinner!' Olga clapped her hands, danced her heels on the floor. 'And now she's going to lay an egg!'

The smooth oval shape sat in the spoon for a moment before Alan pushed it half inside. He removed the spoon, its hard edge bumping over the little muscular ring. Sheila's knees banged together. Now the egg was sitting just inside Sheila's ring, holding it open, it must look so bizarre, an egg in there too big for the hole to close round and swallow it, too big for her to expel it no matter how hard her muscles instinctively tried to. The sensation of it holding her open, her backside bulging, all bloated like that up her anus made her panic at first, stirred her insides and she was terrified it would encourage her bowels, everything, to plunge downwards, down that hot dark passage and out into the open, but the egg was a fat plug. Her muscles gripped in spasms, trying to get a purchase on this foreign object, trying to find a hook of pleasure to ride on.

Sheila was swinging her head to and fro, moaning with frustration.

'How's that for a butt plug?' Tessa chuckled, slowly peeling Sheila's knickers off her face. Sheila blinked at the light, the laughing faces, the sudden distraction from her focus on her most secret parts, the sudden glaring realisation of them all standing over her, doing this to her.

'My little Tessa. Enough now.'

Tessa leaned over her, and kissed her on the mouth. 'You're right. I bet you could do with a drink, couldn't you?' Her voice was totally back to normal.

'Please untie me, Tessa. Please let me off now.'

'Hmm. You must be so hungry.' She flicked her tongue out, scooped up some crumbs off Sheila's chin, then pushed her tongue, with the crumbs, into Sheila's mouth. 'I thought you could stay here, all night, stuffed up every orifice like a turkey. Maybe you'll crap yourself. Then I'll know you're sorry.'

'And you have to lie very still, Sheila,' Olga warned from behind her, 'otherwise Alan's egg will break. Can you imagine how sharp, jagged eggshell would feel like up your arse?'

'Clever you, Olga! Come here and give me a kiss.' Tessa said softly, putting her arms round Olga. She brushed her lips over Olga's mouth before Olga had time to turn away. Sheila's stomach twisted with jealousy. 'I didn't think of that.'

'Don't be so stupid! Enough's enough!' Sheila tried to twist round, but when she opened her mouth as wide as she could no words came out because Olga quickly stuffed one last meringue to the back of her throat to join the remainder of the huge, crumbling meringues and strawberries she had only just managed to swallow.

'You think you can act like the Queen? Have you seen yourself slipping about on this table making it too dirty to eat off and with bits of food stuck up you by the master chef himself? Don't be so ridiculous!' Tessa taunted, letting her hands wander close to Olga's big breasts. 'But we'll untie your hands while I get you a drink.'

As Olga untied her wrists, Tessa climbed up on to the table and knelt astride her. Sheila's arms were so weak after being pinned over the side of the table that she could do no more than let them flop by her sides as pins and needles filled them. Tessa lay down on Sheila's chest for a moment, her cheek pressed softly against Sheila's face.

The knocker banged on the door. Alan went to tug it open.

'In a minute, Mossy, I'm going to take Alan upstairs and get him to fuck me, on his little bed in the little garret. I told you to keep him till I got back. I've still not forgiven you for having him first.'

'How does Mr Tanner know you, Sheila?' Olga pushed Tessa out of the way. 'What did he mean, *I'd know that bottom anywhere*?'

'From the birthmark, of course.' The deep voice was back.

Sheila struggled to sit up and see his face, but now Olga had clambered up on to the table as well, blocking out the light.

'That stupid thing?' Tessa shoved her hand between Olga's legs. 'Looks like she hasn't washed.'

'Ever noticed it's shaped like England?'

Had he felt that in the dark, through the car window?

'Whatever. Ignore him, Olga,' Tessa commanded. 'Oh, yes. You're wet and horny, aren't you? Show Sheila how wet you are.'

Olga slapped Tessa's hand away and started to climb off the table. 'I don't do that with women.'

'Now who's being a wimp, Olga?' Tanner said. 'Come on, I'll give you fifty extra to sit on Sheila's face. Then you can come back to mine and do it all over again.'

'Bravo! So rub your cunt in Sheila's face.' Tessa held her still. 'You're wearing knickers. If you're that fussy, it doesn't count.'

'So I keep them on!' Olga scowled.

Tessa pushed her. Olga wriggled forwards and waved her crotch over Sheila's face. The fabric of her knickers was stuck to the mound of her sex, a wet line down the centre. Tessa pushed Olga again so that she stumbled slightly on her knees, falling on to Sheila's face, enveloping her with a new sex smell, smearing across her face. Sure enough she was sopping wet.

'There, not so bad, was it? You're enjoying it!' Tessa was crooning in Olga's ear as Olga started to rub herself faster over Sheila's nose and mouth. 'But you'll have to pull away a little, sexy. Sheila needs a drink.'

'Yes please,' Sheila croaked. 'Water. Wine. Anything.'

'How about your favourite? Some lovely, delicious wee?'

'No! Please!' Sheila tried to struggle, pinned as she was by Olga's thighs. 'Can't drink that! Need water!'

'If Alan can drink piss, you can. Where is he, anyway?'

Sheila lifted her arms and tried to bat Tessa away but Tessa lifted the black skirt she was still wearing –

Sheila's skirt – and pulled her knickers down, showing the wet slit cutting under the neat ginger curls. She kicked the knickers away, then knelt beside Sheila's face. Sheila turned, and nuzzled at Tessa's warm thigh. But Tessa nudged her away and turned to Olga, who was wiggling her hips in a little mocking dance.

'You happy there, squatting on Sheila's table?'

'Sure. I'm a dancer, remember. We always use props.'

'Talking of props. Tanner. Would you mind? Give that cucumber another shove.'

The cucumber jerked aggressively upwards then, like a gigantic cock, taking Sheila by surprise. It grated right past her burning crumb-covered clitoris, making it tingle and flame so that she jerked her bottom up off the table.

Tessa slapped Sheila hard on the top of her leg. 'Don't move, Moss. You'll break the egg!'

'Have to move! Want to come!'

Sheila sounded like a halfwit but her whole body was aching to come now. She wanted to jerk up and down, drag herself along the length of the cucumber until she reached the peak. She felt it rub past her burning clitoris and she wanted to feel it again, but now she had to keep absolutely still, her stomach twisting with helpless fear that it would ram too far.

Tessa ripped off Olga's red knickers.

'Hey!' Olga yelped and put her hand uselessly down to try to cover herself, but now both Sheila and Tessa could clearly see the stark nakedness of her slender white sex lips, waxed clean and bare, the skin almost see-through from the lack of light, flimsy like paper, not plumped up like Tessa's. Sheila could see from the way Olga was squatting with her thighs spread that the lips were half open, the edges sticking together here and there with Olga's juices, but still showing the red twists of hidden flesh.

'That's what you look like, Moss, since you went mad with the razor. You should have asked me first. I prefer

199

you all hairy. But what a feast! Two bare pussies! Want to see, Tanner, before we make everything wet? Show him your pussy, Olga!'

Tessa pulled Olga right round so that they had their backs to Sheila now, their bottoms inches from her face, their butt cheeks spread and resting on their thighs as they squatted there, little licks of wet ginger hair streaking up Tessa's purple crack, absolutely no hair up Olga's paler one. Sheila couldn't take her eyes off the sight of those twin butt holes in her face like – what? Like Maureen's baboon face.

Sheila's instinctive disgust at two bottoms squatting over her face, so close she could smell them, was ebbing. Something about their baseness, the bottoms of those two beautiful girls, fascinated her. She wanted to touch. As she thought this, her own anus opened a little more around the egg. Her cunt closed over the cucumber. She wanted to touch.

'Making you horny, I hope, Tanner? Maybe you should pay us all!' Tessa was saying, bouncing a little on her haunches so that her fat butt cheeks squashed and spread with each bounce.

'No need. I'm getting all the payback I want just watching this.'

'Ooh, I do need to piss,' Tessa crooned, gyrating. 'Ooh, I can feel the piss coming, rushing down me. Can't you feel that, Olga? Don't think I've time to get to the loo.'

Olga shook her head. She clutched at her pussy in an effort to hide it or stop the pee coming. Sheila could see Olga's fingers reaching right round to her crack. But she could also see Olga staring straight down at Tessa's crotch. Again Sheila twisted with jealousy, unable to move to clasp Tessa, or Olga for that matter, or push them apart, tormented by the stiff wedge rammed up her cunt tormenting her but keeping her from coming, the egg balanced in the entrance to her anus, holding it open, keeping her insides in perpetual, teasing motion, her knees still up in the air as if she was ready for roasting –

'Let me go, Tessa, please,' she croaked, her voice coming from miles away. 'Can't do this. Just want to hold you.'

Tessa bounced round, opened her legs a little wider, yanked Olga round again. Pussies over Sheila's face now. Tessa leaned forwards on her hands so that she could get a little lower. Olga held an almost balletic posture, her slim white sex lips hanging open, inches from Sheila's face so that the aroma from both women was overpowering.

'Cheers, Mrs Moss. Bottoms up! Wash away all those crumbs!'

Tessa gave a kind of hitch of her legs, and then started to pee. A couple of drops dripped onto Sheila's lips, so that she licked automatically at the salty liquid trickling into her mouth then tried to spit it out. Then Tessa grunted again, held her own thighs open, and let it all out this time, the stream gushing and pouring out of her, between her curly-haired pussy lips, into Sheila's face, filling her mouth so quickly that she had no choice but to drink it, not even tasting it at first, feeling the hot liquid gushing straight to the back of her throat so that she coughed and spluttered, the piss coming back up, running up her nose, into her eyes, into her ears as she lay back on the table and for a moment she let it happen to her, let it splash all over her, her mouth gulping like a fish to try to catch the yellow fountain.

She squinted through her wet eyelashes and saw that Olga was still squatting there beside Tessa, but that her fingers were poking in and out of her cunt as she watched her landlady's degradation. The sight of Sheila being pissed on obviously turned her on, and as Sheila lapped obediently at the pee flooding her mouth, stinging her cheeks, and as she watched Olga's fingers working hard into her cunt, she felt the humiliation gnawing at first like the worm she had become, but then the full reality of what was happening started to make glorious sense, especially how it must look to Mr Tanner. Was he holding his long cock right now, standing in the doorway watching, as he always liked to watch?

And what would baboon Maureen think, licking her own fat purple lips with dirty curiosity, what would the neighbours think, seeing how low she'd sunk even since their fun and games with her the other day?

'Your turn, Olga. Show your Mr Tanner. Maybe he should be paying all of us for the floor show.'

Sheila kept her mouth open, wet and still dribbling. Olga wanted to show off, like they all wanted to show off. She hunched herself eagerly over Sheila's face, right down low so that her arsehole was bumping against Sheila's chin, my God, Olga was going to be even more filthy than Tessa, her own little competition, because she wasn't just pissing, she was masturbating all over Sheila as well. With her fingers still rammed up her cunt she started to piss, jerking her hips back and forth, fingers in between those curious flimsy sex lips, yellow piss streaming out. Sheila could hardly breathe but she was fully alive now, tossing her head from side to side inside Olga's river of piss, jaws hinged open like a baby bird's to catch it, cough and choke, yes, now she was swallowing it, her throat contracted to drink it, how disgusting was that, open to catch some more. She stuck her tongue out, wallowing in the lasciviousness of her own tongue sticking out rudely to suck and lick this other woman's piss, and when her tongue bumped on the peanut-sized clit Olga was pinching, Sheila started to lick frantically, her nose buried inside those soft lips, her arms pinned under Olga but her hands able to reach greedily down to grab the cucumber, pushing it in and out of her. Even the cucumber was wet from all the pissing.

Closer and closer, challenging herself to keep her bottom still even as she pumped the phallus in and out. She started to come at last, nipping Olga's clitoris with her teeth and Olga shrieked, arched her back as she came. Somewhere, Tanner groaned.

Olga bucked into Sheila's face, smeared piss and juice all over her as she writhed about and Sheila took the cucumber, pushed it further in, her knees banging together as she fucked herself with it until she jerked so hard that the egg broke, jabbing her with its fragments.

Tomorrow, after she'd cleaned and cooked for them, her lodgers would eat off that same table, their food seasoned with her juices and her piss and that was, for her, the pinnacle of her degradation.

The urge to empty her own bladder overtook her and she was just in time to see their visitor's long fingers grasp the edge of the table before he took the full force of her pee all over his straining erection.

Seventeen

She wondered if it showed, the life she was living behind the curtain. Maybe it showed in the way she walked, or could barely walk. Surely there was a lustful glint in her eyes, reflecting the incessant, nagging urge that gripped her day and night. In the first few days after that night in the kitchen she had been hopping up and down on the doormat by the time Tessa came home, waiting for the pleasure to start. Little Tessa, who one moment would be marching about like a tiny *Kommandant*, the next following Sheila around bleating that she 'only wanted to play'.

But that was before she discovered the joys of doing it for herself . . .

She hovered outside the fig tree house. Christmas Eve, with carol singers trilling in the distance, somewhere near the tube station. Was this really the time to have it out with Mr Tanner? Some of the immediate neighbours had already moved out, and she needed to know. How did he know her and John? Why did he want this house? Why did he pay off her mortgage? Was her beloved house really going to fall down? Would he sit in his car and suck her clit ever again?

She'd still not even seen Tanner's face. But every time she thought about what he'd seen through the window, through his cameras, how he'd licked her in the street, how he'd come right in and seen her lodgers torturing her with Alan's gourmet food, even announced that he knew her special birthmark, she would look out, see his car purring up and down the street, and want him.

Sometimes she couldn't wait till she got upstairs to her window, hoping he'd see her. She'd found a new thrill, the quick, secretive play with herself when her thoughts made her too horny to carry on with the housework. She'd be behind the sofa sweeping and would double over, thinking about Olga's violet-blue pussy coming down over her face, the lips split by one of her vicious thongs, Olga squatting over her face, thighs squashed large and wide over her, the popping initial drops then the salty taste of her wee gushing into her mouth.

It had happened several times, though Tessa didn't know. Olga came home from work, found Sheila tied up somewhere, checked no one else was around, then released a warm wet jet all over her.

So she would slide up and down the long handle of her broom, let the wooden column slip between her legs to nudge open her pussy lips, then she'd get down on her hands and knees and ride the rough handle, ride a cock horse, until she was panting and gasping, maddened by the harsh sound of her own ecstasy. And then came the thrill of flipping her skirt up, pulling down her knickers, still kneeling there on the floor, bracing her legs, her knees grinding into the hard floor, getting the handle of the broom, the rounded end of it, and nudging it in there, to hear the wet slurp of her pussy, nudge, nudge. Then she'd go a bit further. The length of the handle was quite terrifying, but she dared herself every time to push it further, her body closing round it, bucking as it pushed inside. She'd gasp, laughing at the noise, taking the broom handle and thrusting it up her cunt from behind, in, out, slippery with her juices, in a little further and finally a long, winding moan as she came.

OK. OK. Time for Mr Tanner. She stood under his wide porch, the double front door luminous with stained glass. She rang the bell pull, and it sounded somewhere deep inside, like a church bell. Footsteps rang out on flagstones, coming to answer.

She closed her eyes, imagining what he would look like. Not short and bald like Mr Brown, please, not black brooding eyes like John's, not spindly and cheeky like Alan.

'Sheila! What are you doing here?'

She opened her eyes. 'Olga?'

Olga held the door like the lady of the manor. Her leopard-skin coat was open over the green mini dress, her red hair smothered by a familiar white Cossack hat and teetering thighboots. Piled up in the hall were suitcases.

'Tanner's not here, Sheila. He's gone to a party.'

For a moment, Sheila's heart sank. She looked past Olga, into the hall. It looked like the entrance to a castle, all pale stone arches and alcoves, candles flickering and Christmas ivy winding about like an indoor forest. Steady, even floor. Straight banisters. Not like the crooked house hers had become as Messrs Tanner and Brown's gloomy predictions started to come true. You couldn't even stand upright in the bathroom now, since the ceiling caved in. 'I didn't know you were moving in with him for good.'

'I'm not.' Olga tapped one of the suitcases with her toe. 'I'm all packed up to leave.' She pulled Sheila into the sitting room, which was empty and dominated by an enormous, baronial fireplace. There were a couple of black and white photographs on the mantelpiece, in silver frames. 'This place needs a woman's touch, Sheila. It's dead.'

'No need to leave, Olga. Come back to mine. You can sleep in my room!'

'It would get a little crowded!' Olga put her hands on Sheila's shoulders. Sheila could smell her perfume and her breath, heady with mulled wine. 'And I don't want to be buried in falling bricks!'

'My house will never fall down. It's all a big lie. I can't trust John, and I certainly don't trust Tanner. That's why I came here to talk to him. I need to know how he knows me. Why he paid for my house.' Sheila pressed closer. 'But if Tanner's not in, and Tessa's gone to her parents, no one will ever know if you come over and bunk in with me – come on. It's Christmas.'

'Darling, I don't need your little house any more. I certainly don't want to be part of his big plan for this street. Anyway, he's paid me enough to go back to Prague.' Olga laughed, all low and sexy. 'I'm rich now!'

'Why did he pay you so much? I thought you only fucked him on the side?'

'So rude!' Olga laughed. 'He paid so much because I'm very, very good at it.'

I want to be you, Sheila thought. *I want to be very, very good at it.*

'Just be you,' Olga replied, and I realised I must have spoken the thought out loud.

The revelation burst over me like a hot shower, sweeping away all the confusion and doubt of the past weeks. As simple as that, the prim and proper Sheila Moss who had first come to Spartan Street was no more. She had experienced too much ever to be the same person again. She knew who she was at last, and all she wanted now was to be very, very good at it. Like a curtain being drawn aside, or a blindfold finally being lifted, "she" had become me.

'Besides,' Olga went on, 'it wasn't just the great blow jobs he paid me for.' She tossed a set of keys on to the hall table. 'I was spying for him, too. Not just the cameras. I nicked your photographs. Clothes. Letters.'

I went quiet. 'Spying on *me*?'

'That day he met me on your doorstep, when I came about the room. He knew me from work. Asked me to

207

report if John came back. And his ex-wife, Roxanne. Very angry. He told me how he saw the threesome through the window, how you were so shy! God, look at you now!' Olga shook her head. 'He wanted to know first when John left, second if you were still here. He's in big trouble. He conned everyone, Sheila.'

'Tanner?'

'John. He never paid for any of it. It's lucky Tanner kept a lot of his money back. Your half of the street is, how would you say it? Doomed.'

'Bollocks.' I looked at Olga's obscenely sexy mouth. 'I love you, Olga. I'm going to miss you like crazy. But I want to be fucked by a man. Like you are, every day when Tanner pays you. In fact, I want Tanner to fuck me.'

'He wants to fuck you, too. He tells me he's wanted it for fifteen years.' Olga stood in front of the mirror, already painting her lips. She pointed at the photographs on the mantelpiece. 'See?'

And then I saw it at last. One photograph, cracked across the glass, of Roxanne in a white veil tossing a bouquet at the camera. Next to it, a photograph of me laughing over my shoulder in the vineyard in France, wearing tiny white shorts and a striped Gallic T-shirt. And in the background, his face a blur of agonised longing –

'Of course, of course. I never even knew his surname.' I sighed at the picture, practically feeling the sun on my skin as I kissed it. 'Little Toby.'

Eighteen

Alan, not Daphne, opened the door of number 69. 'Christ! You're dressed as Olga in that scarlet number! It suits you!'

'Where's the action, Alan? And what are you doing here?'

'The food, of course. I couldn't prepare it in our kitchen. One of the French windows has broken, and there's dust everywhere.'

Olga had laced the dress as tight as possible, so I had to take little sipping breaths. I was horny and light-headed with the lack of air. The dress smelled of Olga. Olga's bare skin had rubbed inside it. Her tight, waxed pussy had nudged against it when she walked, or sat down, or hitched the dress up to open her legs, glance about furtively, squat over my face, open herself up, sticky layer by sticky layer, and let a teasing little trickle of pale yellow urine dribble into my eager mouth . . .

A set of double doors opened, letting out a stream of dazzling light, and a tall figure in totally see-through white chiffon came out.

'So you've come!'

Daphne pecked me on the cheek and I could smell alcohol on her breath. She seemed taller than ever. She led me into an enormous drawing room. I was blinded by dazzling lights, a total contrast to Toby's flickering candles at number 43.

'Am I the only one who wasn't invited?' I glanced over her shoulder. 'I'm looking for Toby.'

'But now you're here you must stay.' Daphne handed me a glass of champagne. Her ice-queen eyes were wide and glassy. 'This is my husband, Guy, so keen to meet you.'

Cherie, Flora and three tall men were standing in the middle of the room, totally still. The women all wore the same white chiffon, skimming over bare breasts, nipples, hips. The men were in loose white trousers and white shirts. They turned to greet me, all with wide smiles, all lifting one hand in greeting. A tall man with blond hair shook my hand. 'The mysterious Mrs Moss from number 44!'

Cherie and Flora came up on either side, pressed their cheeks for a kiss. 'So sorry to hear about your little house, Sheila.'

'Cherie!' Cherie's skin felt powdery, and cool. They all had the same glassy expression in their eyes, like dolls. 'You've lost weight!'

'We're all perfect now!' Cherie trilled. There was the same dimple in her cheek, but her hair was long and white-blonde now, just like Flora and Daphne's, and there was no sign of the plump stomach and pendulous breasts. 'Just like our darling husbands wanted us! Just like Tanner wants this side of the street.'

'Where is he? Toby Tanner?' I asked, looking around. Alan had disappeared. I could hear clanking from what must have been the kitchen, miles away.

'Are you ready to begin, Mrs Moss? We've heard so much about you,' another husband said, chinking my glass with his.

'Begin?'

'We want to get to know you. We don't know any of the poor souls from the other side of the street,' one of the other men said. 'I'm Jamie, by the way. Cherie's husband.'

'But of course we all share when we're bored!' Flora curled her fingers round my arm and pulled me down to the floor. The others were sitting down slowly, crossing their legs neatly, making a circle.

'Our first Christmas in the street.' Daphne took out a champagne bottle and placed it in the middle of the circle. 'And what better way to get to know you than by playing truth or dare?'

'But you already know me –'

Guy spun the bottle, deliberately making it point straight at me. They all smiled, and shuffled closer to each other, leaving me isolated as if being interrogated. The men edged behind the women.

'Truth,' I said, gulping my champagne.

'Who's the most *verboten* person you've ever slept with?' Flora asked, twirling her hair round her finger. 'Say, like a postman. Or someone else's husband, for example?'

'Not one of ours, I hope!' Cherie snuffled, patting her new, extended hair. 'We could never entertain you for cocktails again if you slept with Guy or Jamie or Graham.'

'In fact, we'd have to kill you,' Flora stated, wriggling into her husband's lap, pushing her bottom down on to his legs.

'None of us would dare stray, petal, would we?' Guy or Jamie or Graham said, stroking at her breasts and squeezing them hard. So hard that Flora's little nipples popped through the muslin between his fingers. So hard that Cherie winced.

'I thought you said you shared?' I swallowed more champagne.

'Oh, we might take turns behind closed doors.' Graham looked directly at me. 'But that doesn't mean we'd go across the road and fuck the starchy neighbour, would we, darlings?'

'Language!' Daphne exclaimed. The three women gasped and rolled their eyes. The men had squeezed in

211

even closer to their women. Six blank faces closing ranks. The more plastic they looked, the more alive I felt. I squirmed about in my tight red dress. Olga's tight red dress.

All three men started fondling the breasts of all three women, who tilted their heads back against their husbands' shoulders, stretched their arms up to tangle their fingers in their hair, and started to make little cat-like moans of pleasure.

Like Tessa. I jolted. Just like Tessa. The little girlie noises that so turned me on.

'Go on, Sheila,' Cherie urged, pushing her breasts up into the air. 'Tell us the truth.'

'Who have you slept with that you really, really shouldn't?' pestered Flora, spreading her legs to wriggle harder on her husband's legs. 'And don't say your neighbours!'

'Her brother. John Moss. He was my best friend.'

There he was, leaning in the doorway. He wore a white suit, shirt open, hand in pocket. He looked like Daniel Craig, about to open fire.

'Toby!' I yelled, trying to get to my feet. Olga's red dress held me back. 'Little Toby!'

'Little Toby!' They all echoed drunkenly. 'Toby Tanner!'

He looked at me. The last time I'd seen him he was sweaty and sixteen and punching John in the jaw. 'Tell them, Sheila. About the man you lived with, fucked, for fifteen years.'

'Your brother, John Moss.' Daphne nodded.

'Half-brother,' I said automatically, then gave in. I wanted to slap them all across the face to crack those polite, plastic masks. But most of all I wanted to chastise myself. 'We had the same dad,' I began wearily. 'John was my lover, and we lived together for fifteen years.'

They all gasped obediently. Cherie leant forwards, her round breasts visible beneath her white gown. Jamie's

212

hands were still clamped round them, kneading and fondling.

'Remember him, Cherie?' I asked. Wickedness coiled inside my chest. 'He fucked you in the show home.'

'Brother!' Cherie's eyelids rolled like a doll's, as if she was stoned. 'Never said he was your lover.'

'So I guess that makes me a liar, as well as guilty of incest.'

The room was quiet for a moment. The carol singers I'd heard earlier were closer now, a couple of doors down, singing *O Come All Ye Faithful*. They'd have no comfort or joy or mulled wine from number 43, would they, or number 44 for that matter.

'Yeah, all these years Mrs Moss here – *Miss* Moss actually – she's been fucking her brother. The first time I saw her was in their dad's wine cellar. Moss was fucking her from behind, and that's when I saw her arse.'

'Toby, calm down –'

Toby stepped forward and wrenched at Olga's red dress, tearing the laces open to show my bottom. 'See? The England birthmark! What do you think all his cronies in the building trade would think about that on top of all his other scams? Or rather, his fellow jailbirds, once they've caught up with him.'

There was more crashing from the kitchen. I couldn't help it. I was still high on my encounter with Olga. High on seeing little Toby again, gorgeous and angry. I wondered what Alan was making in there. Chocolate sauce, blended passion fruit? How would that look smeared all over these pristine women, all over their white clothes, white limbs, up their legs, pushed into their bleached-blonde pussies? How would their smooth husbands like to lick it off?

'That's disgusting, as well as illegal!' breathed Graham, the quietest of the husbands. His eyes glinted. 'So. She looks like a maiden aunt. Ruts like a goat.'

'No wonder she's dressed like a hooker,' Guy scoffed, pushing Daphne off his knee and standing up. 'I thought you said she was a school marm type?'

'This is me,' I said. 'This red dress. These boots. The black cashmere isn't me.'

'Not for long,' said Daphne. 'You have to wear white to live in this street.'

'I heard that between consenting adults it's not incest, it's genetic sexual attraction.' Flora took a little sip of her champagne. 'They're related but they're strangers.' She looked at the blond men, the blonde women, the white identical clothes. 'Like looking in a mirror.'

'Like fucking a mirror, you mean!' spluttered Cherie, choking on her champagne.

'Language, Cherie!' Graham pulled me roughly up by the arm. 'I'm not sure we should be entertaining people like this in our house.'

'Guy, calm down,' soothed Daphne. She took my other arm. 'She's not to blame. Look at her. You just dressed as a hooker tonight for fun, didn't you? You'll look beautiful in white. The man was a bastard, wasn't he, Toby? He's shafted the lot of you over that side of the street.'

'Tell us why him, Sheila.' Toby had blue eyes, not dark like John's. His face was stony with anger. 'I've been wanting to know for fifteen years.'

'What's it to you?'

'I wanted you,' he said. 'You silly bitch.'

'You were just little Toby!' I shouted. 'I wanted John!'

'This could get ugly.' Cherie fanned her face. 'Perhaps Mrs Moss should go home.'

'She doesn't have a home to go to,' muttered Toby, turning his back and picking out a couple of piano notes on the grand in the corner. 'Her precious brother's seen to that.'

'OK, so let's carry on.' Flora's husband Graham came behind me and started to peel off the tight dress.

214

'It looks like she needs teaching a lesson about what's acceptable in this street. If you'll permit, Toby?'

'I've waited this long,' he said. 'Be my guest.'

'How about the dare part of the game, then?' Daphne suggested. 'As I'm the hostess, and as the bottle chose you, Sheila, I'm going to let you choose a dare.'

The carol singers started up *Good King Wenceslas*. They sounded as if they were next door. Someone was tinkling sleigh bells. Impossible to tell if anyone in Spartan Street was paying attention. As for me, who wanted a bunch of people in bobble hats waving lanterns when you could stand here with a bunch of kinky neighbours and the man you should have chosen fifteen years ago?

'Nipple clamps,' Toby said, tossing a little box across the room. 'She likes those.'

'I thought we were supposed to be punishing her?' Graham pulled the red dress down.

'Makes me hard seeing how they pinch and hurt her. Put them on.'

'I am sorry, Toby.' I looked across the room, but he was hunched over the piano keys. Could easily have been a sulky sixteen-year-old again. 'I had no idea.'

'Just do what you're good at, but go lower. Then I might think of forgiving you,' he said. 'Starting with some more girl on girl stuff.'

'My neighbours could help me with that, couldn't you, Cherie? Flora?'

'No way. These girls lie back and think of England like good little wives.' Graham pushed me. 'But you, toffee-nosed slut? Let's see if you rut like a goat, shall we?'

Guy laughed softly at that. He bent his head, and suddenly clamped my nipple with the little metal vice so that the pain sang out. Jamie looked stunned for a moment, flushed red, then bent to do the same, squeezing my other breast hard, pulling the nipple out with his

215

teeth and biting on it hard so that I reared up with the jolting pain of excitement before the clamp bit down.

'Enough!' Daphne came to, yanking at the two men. 'Get off her! We're your wives!' She whipped aside her chiffon kaftan to show her round, pale breasts. 'Suck *our* nipples if you want to!'

'But that's just it!' scoffed Jamie. 'We don't want to! You'd just lie there like a corpse.'

'That's because they prefer the girls to do it,' I murmured.

'But Mrs Moss?' Jamie pinched the nipple and sharp pain shafted through my belly. 'She likes it every which way!'

'Whatever happened to punishing her? She's enjoying it!' whined Cherie, tugging at her husband.

'He's a naughty boy, isn't he?' I laughed. 'So punish him. Spank him, Cherie! And I dare you to spank your husband, Daphne.'

'Spank him? I couldn't lay a finger on him!' Daphne fluttered her hands about in horror, but there was no mistaking the glint of temptation in her eyes. 'It's degrading.'

'Because he's your lord and master?' I glanced across at Toby. So handsome. So angry. Reduced to watching. 'Because it's OK to play with the girls, spank them even, when hubby's not around, so long as you act the Stepford wife when he's home?'

'We like it that way.'

'They like it missionary.' Graham had my arms locked behind me so I couldn't move. 'On their backs, staring at the ceiling.'

'That's why we have mirrors up there!' Cherie giggled. 'So we can watch our boys going at it, you know, like those porn movies we saw at that club –'

Daphne was glaring at her.

Flora nudged Cherie. 'It's only so we can check on our fake tans at the same time!'

216

The Three Fates looked like vestal virgins. Where were the big dildos, the blindfolds?

I so wished Olga was here so I could stand over her, in front of everyone, and push her pussy into my face. Olga would push her tongue into me, suck me, lick me, then I'd kiss her, taste my own cunt juices slathered all over her mouth –

'So you're the one who needs punishing!' hissed Daphne. 'Not our boys.'

Olga's thick red lips, the violet slick of her pussy, how Olga's tongue had tasted before the taxi arrived and she'd rushed off in a cloud of scent wearing my clothes.

The carol singers had stopped. Maybe they'd given up singing to an empty street.

'Oh, loosen up, girls. Mrs Moss doesn't look strong enough to break a twig. How hard is a slap from her going to be? Come on. I'm game,' Guy said, sticking out his bottom. 'It'll be a laugh. Then the good bit is I choose what we do to *her*.'

The others shuffled away to make room. Graham let me go. I stepped forwards, Olga's boots forcing me to swagger, my legs parting like a cowboy's. Toby was watching me. I kicked Guy hard on the backside so that he fell forwards on to his hands and knees.

'Oy, you stupid cow!' he yelped, and started to get back up, but I kicked him again, driving my sharp heel into his buttock.

'You're squealing like a girl, Guy!' scoffed Jamie. 'Still think this is just a bit of fun?'

The wives were bunched together, their arms round each other's waists. They wore identical looks of naked fascination at the lord of the house grovelling on all fours.

'You stay where Mrs Moss puts you, boy,' I ordered.

'*Miss* Moss,' Toby snapped. 'Never married, remember?'

I flushed. I yanked Guy's white trousers down. He wore no pants underneath, and his bottom was taut and

217

tanned, two sexy round buttocks too lovely to hurt. I wanted to hit him really hard. He started to swear and pull his trousers up and I felt horny anger and pushed him down, digging my high heel into him to pin him there.

'A whip, Graham. Get me something. Anything. Something he prizes.' I held my hand out like a surgeon awaiting a scalpel. 'He thinks this is just a joke.'

'You're perverted,' whimpered Cherie, straining to get at me.

'Yeah, she has changed, hasn't she?' whistled Flora, holding Cherie back. 'We'd never think of it, would we, Daph? Getting a little innocent down on her knees, blindfolded perhaps, maybe stuffing a great leather cock up them till they squeal?' She wrapped her arms round Cherie, rocking against her. 'What would your Guy think to that leather dildo?'

'Shut up, Flora.' But Daphne moved towards her two friends, sandwiching Cherie between her and Flora.

Graham handed me a badminton racket from behind the sofa. 'He's unjustifiably proud of his backhand return, as I recall.'

'So you think it's smart to play badminton, do you?' I gripped the worn leather handle and leaned over Guy. I licked at his ear lobe, saw him smile, relax. Felt the evil surge of desire. I wanted him. Wanted all of them. Mostly I wanted Toby. But I'd have to earn it. 'What do you think the committee would say at the club bar if they saw you being whipped like a puppy? Where's your shuttlecock now?'

'I can see his shuttlecock from here!' Cherie giggled, rubbing herself against Flora. Flora opened Cherie's dress, grabbed her breasts.

Guy started to kneel up, and I lifted my arm then brought the racket down on Guy's buttock, making a satisfying, swiping sound. He jerked, yelling in surprise. The Stepford wives twittered on the sidelines.

The blow reverberated up my arm like an electric shock. Must have hit hard. I was panting with the exertion. A neat criss-cross pattern rose on Guy's buttock. The sight made me flip my arm back and smack the racket down once more, on the same buttock, so that Guy jerked again. The red marks grew darker on his skin.

Graham whistled, came up behind me and cupped one of my buttocks. 'The wives had you down as some kind of little mouse who looks like Miss Moneypenny. But you're nothing like they said! More like Barbarella!'

'Yeah,' yawned Toby from the piano stool. 'What happened to that lovely girl?'

'It's all in the dressing up,' I replied softly, bracing for another strike. 'I go into my lodgers' rooms. I wear their clothes. Sometimes they wear mine. Then I can be whoever I like.'

'Kinkier and kinkier.' Graham stroked my bottom. Goosebumps rose as his fingers crept into the crease under my cheeks. 'So, how many strikes do you think, Mrs Moss? I don't think you've hurt him enough, pompous bastard. He barely flinched.'

I raised my arm. 'Oh, six of the best, don't you think?'

'Do me! This is better than any sex club! She looks just the part.' Jamie knelt beside Guy, sticking his bottom up in the air. I caught a scornful look pass between him and Guy.

'You better believe I'm the part!' I kicked the back of Jamie's knee so that he fell forwards. 'Stop sniggering, worm. Time for you to experience real pain.'

A single voice was rising, a lovely clear soprano, over the hedge, out on the pavement, *Once in Royal David's City*.

'Can you hear that?' I shouted at Toby. 'Can't you tell them to go away?'

'Hear what?' His eyes were on my breasts.

'Carol singers!'

'Well, it is Christmas!' Flora wandered over to the window. 'God, there's dozens of them.'

'Yeah, go on then, Matron, do me! Please, matron, do me!' Jamie was still sniggering, nudging at Guy with his elbow. 'You're so strict, Matron, coming into the dorm in your sexy boots and those sharp heels. Ow. I'm so naughty.'

Cherie knelt down on the floor beside him and grabbed at him, tried to pull him up. 'You sound stupid. Don't lower yourself, darling!'

'It's a game!' shouted Jamie, shaking her off. 'She's the one who's going to lower herself!'

'Go lower, Sheila!' shouted Toby. 'Much, much lower.'

'Pull his trousers down, Cherie!' I ordered 'Or shall I start on you too?'

Grudgingly, Cherie obeyed, pulling her husband's trousers down and exposing his cute backside. He had no idea how hard I was going to whack him.

'OK, witch,' Jamie taunted, pushing his buttocks out, so tender, widening the crack between them. 'I want the witch to smack me, too. Smack me, nanny, smack me!'

I looked over at Toby. His hand was on his crotch.

'You boys have no idea how ridiculous you look,' I said in my best school marm voice. 'You'll be licking my boots for mercy by the time I'm finished with you.'

I leaned my heel onto his bottom so that the flesh gave, grew tight and red around the sharp heel as I drove it in deeper. 'The game's not over yet.'

'Here. Try this.' Flora sidled up and handed me something, then dodged backwards as if I might take a swipe at her.

The two men were still sniggering like schoolboys, pinned down by my shoe. The muscles were tensed in Guy's already bright-pink buttock. I glanced again at Toby.

'I'm doing this for you, Tobe,' I said. I opened my knee, spread my legs, tilted my warm pussy to balance better, then smacked the sole of Flora's first little shoe on Guy's waiting buttock, then the other onto Jamie's waiting bottom.

They both jerked upwards with the force of the blow. I was thrilled. How easy it was to subdue them.

'Note, ladies, they're pissed off with me now because I've got the upper hand. They feel stupid. Humiliated, don't you? On hands and knees in front of Mrs Moss,' I gasped, thwacking each little shoe down hard on the exposed male buttocks.

'*Miss* Moss.' Toby's voice was rough. His fingers were round the big bulge in his trousers.

'They like it, don't you, boys?'

The two men were shaking in weak denial, but their eyes had glazed over. Sweat was shining on their faces, eyes fluttering closed as I kept hitting them, saliva dripping over bared teeth as they hunched on all fours, heads twitching loosely with each stroke.

'Again, Matron. So good. Like you did at school.' Jamie was gibbering now. 'Like you did when I was naughty, took me into your room when everyone was outside playing rugby, told me off, took me across your knees, pulled down my shorts, remember, Matron?'

'Yes, Vixen. I remember. The naughtiest boy in the class, weren't you?'

I sounded like a Wimbledon champion serving an ace, cunt twanging with pleasure to hear the thwack and the grunts of shocked pleasure, knowing how fierce the initial smarting pain was, how hot it grew, how it spread until your whole body felt red raw and defeated, how it drove spikes of lust straight to your cunt.

'But then you made it all better, Matron. So sexy. Spanked me first, then the loving. God, so sexy, Matron.'

'Jamie? What are you talking about?' Cherie broke away from her friends, bent closer to him. 'Did you really have a thing with your matron?'

'How kinky is that?' breathed Flora, shoving her hands between Daphne's legs.

My breath was keening with the effort. Now I was hearing things. Two men grunting like pigs on the floor in front of me. Choral singing and sleigh bells jangling through the window.

The two men squirmed, white shirts sticking to their backs. They moved more slowly now, spread their legs wider, shouted obscenities. Their hands reached for their big cocks growing harder with each blow.

'Oh, Mrs Moss, harder, please!' moaned Guy, slumping forwards on to his forearms, one hand working on his stiff cock. 'I admit it. I don't want you to stop!'

His words shattered the moment.

'For Christ's sake stop her, Graham!' Daphne announced coldly, darting forwards in the brief hiatus while I caught my breath. Daphne pushed me. I fell easily to the floor. 'She's humiliated us enough. She's had her fun.'

'Their fun, you mean. Let's ask them, shall we?' Graham laughed, went round to jeer at his mates down on the floor. They just looked blindly round, gasping for breath. 'On second thoughts, let's keep them quiet. No more calling for Matron!'

He took a couple of napkins from the table and gagged first Guy, then Jamie, pulling the cloth tight between their teeth so that they looked like a couple of dogs being muzzled. 'They like it, Daphne. She's teaching you something here. I could get off just watching the way Sheila sucks her cheeks in and goes red every time she hits them.' He grinned, standing up again. His cock was a stiff outline in his trousers. 'Bloody hell, who would have guessed these two knobs had a thing about spanking!'

'Get up, Guy. Do you have any idea what you look like grovelling about on the floor like this? I'm ashamed of you. Jamie, you look like an arsehole!'

'She used to be so innocent,' Toby said, over by the window.

Daphne pushed me again. My face banged up against their bottoms. I could feel the heat of their smarting cheeks.

Both men were sucking and dribbling at their muzzles. They were clutching their cocks now, pulling at them frantically, their bottoms still thrusting up in the air.

'I want to be Matron!' Flora leapt up from her sofa and grabbed the shoes out of my hands, started thwacking both men as they grovelled on the carpet. When they tried to crawl away from her she deftly tied their wrists together with more napkins and lashed them round the heavy legs of the huge white grand piano. 'Now beg!'

I sat back, exhilarated. Toby was looking away from me. But I didn't care just then. We'd be together in the end.

'You were supposed to be punished, not rewarded!' Daphne's voice shivered in my ear. I turned so that Daphne's mouth smeared on mine. Wicked lust flashed through me. I was on my knees again. I pushed my tongue in between her pale lips. Daphne snatched away, but the contact made my pussy squeeze impatiently.

Suddenly there was a sharp thwack on my arse. It was far harder than any of Tessa's strikes, perhaps another shoe, the blow smarting hard and hot, tenderising my bottom.

And from somewhere in the white room, Alan said, 'Canapés, anyone?'

'Not shocked, Alan, are you?' Daphne glided towards him, her white dress flapping open to show her naked body.

Alan took a long green stem of raw asparagus wrapped in parma ham. 'Let's show them, Sheila, what we would do with canapés at our house.'

223

'Show them, Sheila.' Toby's voice was very quiet. And right behind me.

'No? Our hostess, then.' Alan handed the asparagus to Daphne. 'Trust me, I'm a chef. You can eat it. Or you can stick it in your husband's arse.'

'Alan! I thought you were a nice boy!' Daphne took the asparagus. Opened her mouth and slid it inside as if sucking it off.

Alan laughed, enjoying the attention. 'That's what we do at home, don't we, Sheila? Tell them what Tessa makes me do, usually just before I'm going to work!'

I glanced behind me. Toby was right there. 'He puts food up me. Usually fruit. Something he's spent all afternoon preparing. He's a pastry chef, you see.'

Flora giggled. 'Like bananas, you mean? Long, yellow curved bananas with that hard skin, just like a –'

'Better than that. Bigger.' Alan walked over to where Flora was sitting on the grand piano. She had her high heels planted on each man's back as if she was about to ride a chariot. Alan pushed the tray at her, and she took a wrap of smoked salmon, fastened tightly round a column of goat's cheese. 'She can take a melon up there, now. She's well trained. Chunks of pineapple and cheese, seventies style, on a very sharp stick. Like this.' He picked up a vicious looking cocktail stick, jabbed it at Flora's mouth.

'He leaves them in there.' I felt Toby's weight shift from behind me. He crossed the room to where a camera and tripod were set up. 'Those long fingers are so good at making pastry, whipping cream, slicing strawberries. They stick food up my bottom. Just think. The very fingers which roll out filo pastry and flay passion fruit for an entire restaurant full of guests.'

Daphne gave a gasp of laughter and looked at Guy, his trousers round his ankles, his bottom bright red, his hair flopping over his face.

'Try it,' Alan said, pushing the tray at her. 'See if they fit up his arse.'

A look of triumph gleamed in Daphne's eyes. She took two more stems. 'Open him up for me, Flora.'

Flora grinned, pulled open Guy's buttocks to reveal the purple whorl of butt hole closed up tightly. Guy made a token effort to resist, shaking his head and grunting into his muzzle, but Flora just smacked him again. Daphne pushed both sticks of asparagus a little way up his anus, forcing the hole to accept the invasion, then close tightly round the stalks.

'Mrs Vixen? What about you? Would you like to, ah, decorate your husband?'

Cherie giggled and went over to Alan's tray. She picked some delicate cheese straws, twirled like barley sugar, and pretending to make a disgusted face, pushed these up Jamie's bottom. The hardened, cooked cheese would scratch, I knew, at the sensitive lining. My own hole squeezed with longing.

Both men pulled at the bindings round their wrists, shook their heads, trying to loosen the gags in their mouths, now dark and wet with their saliva.

'They look disgusting,' said Daphne, snaking an arm round Alan. 'Who would have thought it? City sharks, grovelling about on their hands and knees like this –'

'And liking it!' Alan licked his lips. 'Our Tessa always makes a threat, you know, if her victims try to complain. So just think what the boys up in the Gherkin would say if they could see you now!'

Guy and Jamie pulled more violently at the grand piano, but it didn't budge.

Cherie was dancing towards Alan. 'Let's give a canapé to Sheila. See how good she is at this. Can I, Alan? Put one in Sheila?'

Cherie took a chipolata-length sausage off the tray, stuck her tongue out and licked it suggestively before tossing it in her mouth. Then she took another.

225

'Sure, Mrs Vixen. Why not dip it in this pretty little bowl,' said Alan softly. 'It's chilli sauce.'

Cherie dipped her canapé into the bowl, several inches of sausage meat now dripping in dark-red, tangy sauce flecked with green peppers.

'Hey, Sheila,' she said, eyes sparkling with excitement. 'How about that? Chilli, he said!'

Cherie knelt down, stroked my buttocks for a moment.

'He does it like this, does he? Opens you up like this?' Cherie scrabbled at my buttocks, slid her fingers inside the warm damp crack and pushed the thick sausage in, the little blunt end nudging at the hole, making me groan out loud.

Cherie pushed harder. 'Remember how big that dildo was?' she whispered, fingers spiralling up my anus to make space for the sausage. She pushed it up, right up, so that it wasn't sticking out. It was right inside, the sauce slithering inside me, my pussy giving a spasm of envy as my anus closed round the invasion.

Daphne pushed Cherie out of the way. 'Over to the piano!' she ordered quietly, smacking me hard on the bottom. Her hand print fanned out on my sore butt. The blow jolted the sausage so that it moved further up inside like a worm burrowing its way. 'Your final dare is to eat the canapés! Yes, that's right. Out of their backsides.'

'Oh my God, that's revolting!' squealed Flora, kicking her heels with delight.

Guy and Jamie were still wriggling in futile attempts to dislodge the canapés from their bottoms, shaking their heads, growling furiously, gritting their teeth against their muzzles.

The chilli sauce was seeping right through the pores of my skin, like liquid fire.

'Get your mouth in there, and eat!' Daphne pushed my face right into Guy's bottom. 'Open him up, Flora.

Let's all see the disgusting spectacle she's making of herself!'

My nose was buried in Guy's crack, the dull, dank smell of his bottom thick in my nostrils. The fire inside me was intense, but the pain was intoxicating, silencing me. As it burned up I instinctively closed my mouth to avoid the prospect of tasting another person's bottom.

'Eat! Alan's made them specially!'

'No! I can't do that! Never done that –'

'Not what we've heard. We've heard that under that prim exterior you'll do anything for a few crumbs of affection.' Daphne held me by the ears while Flora opened up Guy's buttocks. The smell, mixed with sweat and his sex, too, was rough yet musty. I closed my eyes, fought the gagging in my throat, breathed it in, all the while my own anus squeezing desperately to expel the sausage burning with chilli sauce. I was dancing about on my knees, agonising fire spiking inside.

Someone pushed me, and there was the asparagus tip, nudging like a tiny cock against my lips. I got it between my teeth, Guy's bottom warm, almost stifling, wrapped around my face as I pulled it out, felt the pop as it emerged, sucked it into my mouth, felt it rest on my tongue before the taste seeped out, the taste of asparagus yes but also the dense, earthy taste of another person's bottom.

'I can't go on with this!' I tried to spit the asparagus out.

'You dare be sick, and you'll be eating all your meals like this for a week!' Daphne hissed. A hand came over my mouth, shoving the asparagus in, clamping my lips so that I was forced to swallow the green shoot. Then with no time to take a breath Daphne shoved my head back inside Guy's bottom to take the second stem, drooping out of his hole.

This time I took it quickly, sucked it in and swallowed it, a rush of shame filling me along with the rush of

227

saliva as I realised Toby, who used to worship me, was watching.

'Now clean him up.'

I shook my head, gasping for breath. 'No, that's enough. I'm in agony here – this chilli sauce – burning me!'

'That's the way you like it.' Alan reminded me. But now someone was singing. Several people. On the doorstep. Something slow and droning, in German. *Stille Nacht.* 'The more pain the better.'

I was dizzy with confusion, the stinging heat of the chilli sauce torturing my backside, the residue taste of Guy's bottom harsh in my mouth.

'Now lick him clean.'

More than one person had hold of me. My face was shoved into the squashing softness of Guy's bottom, the boniness beneath.

I rubbed my nose quickly against the nub of his hole, turned away.

'With your tongue, Mrs Moss.'

Daphne cranked my jaw open, pushed my face against Guy's bottom. My lips and tongue made contact. The taste was rough in my throat. I couldn't breathe, the smell in my nostrils strong like dope. I kissed at the little hole, felt it twitch. Mine twitched in response, setting off another ripple of fire inside, mingling pain with unbearable excitement. My pussy was wet and pulsing. The hot sauce had seeped in there, somehow. I needed to get my fingers inside, claw it out.

'We're waiting, Sheila.'

'And then I give you your reward,' whispered Toby.

'I don't deserve a reward,' I moaned, turning towards his voice. 'I went off with that bastard, lived in shame for fifteen years –'

'Don't beat yourself up,' he muttered, stroking the birthmark on my butt. 'He'll be rotting away soon. Just like all his houses.'

His voice never used to be so sexy. My pussy was loosening, juices trickling out, juices mixed with chilli sauce.

'Lick him!' ordered Daphne. I'd forgotten who, what, where. I stuck my tongue out. It nudged Guy's hole, which opened, even as he was trying to pull away. I followed him, my tongue stuck to him. I pushed it further up, felt the soft lining of his anus, the squeezing of it like a fist, the sharp tang of his smell coating it. I realised I was pushing my tongue in and out, like a cock, and he was pushing back against my face, the smart tycoon reduced to a jerking, whining piglet rubbing his arse urgently as he started to come.

What would the boys in the Gherkin say? He juddered, the force of his climax pulling my tongue inside again. I swiped round the tight ring and felt my pussy contracting. I tried to touch it, but someone was yanking my hand away so I couldn't reach myself.

The room had gone quiet. Flora with her legs crossed on the piano, hands stuffed down between them. Cherie on the stool, fingers right up herself. Guy slumped on his front, one eye visible over his shoulder. Jamie leaning against the piano leg, milking the thick drops of come from his cock. Alan leaning on the other side of the piano, smiling. Daphne close up beside him, scooping food into her mouth. Where was Toby?

'It's burning me, Alan!' My tongue was stiff with the exertions of licking out the man's arsehole, the taste of him coating it, my voice thick with shame and lust. 'Like having a hot poker up there. The chilli. I need water, ice, anything! Get it out of me!'

Still they didn't speak. Flora got down off the piano to untie the two men, who started to stand up stiffly, wiping their behinds. Daphne was whispering to Alan, her tongue flicking in and out of his ear.

'Cool sensation, isn't it? Like being bitten by red ants. So get a grip, Moss. It was only a mild sauce,' Alan

229

remarked, taking a chicken satay gleaming with peanut butter off the tray. Daphne, still not speaking, opened up her dress to display that ice-white body, the waxed snatch, the hint of scarlet between the lips. I thought of Olga again, of her violet-blue cunt, bearing down, opening to release a stinging jet of piss.

'Make you feel better?' It was Toby's breath, cold on my bottom compared with the rampaging heat inside me. Alan was pushing the satay between Daphne's legs, up into the unfolding red slit. Daphne stood there, smiling slightly, staring straight at me as her hands rested lightly on her hips and Alan pushed it in. My cunt tightened. I was desperate to touch myself. My sex lips were so swollen.

'I'll get it out for you,' Toby murmured, pulling my buttocks apart. Every touch was excruciating now, like salt in a wound. 'Keep still. I've never done this before.'

His fingers made a funnel and pushed into my ring, forcing it open. The pain did seem to be receding. I was washed with harsh desire, flowing up with Toby's fingers, pushing down, pushing the sausage easily down the damp, sticky passage –

Somewhere in the house a bell rang. Not a sleigh bell. A doorbell.

But now the sausage was slipping out, dropping somewhere, and now Toby's mouth was sucking at my ring. He was sucking my arse like he started to do the other day through the car window and it felt wonderful, wet saliva slurping round, fingers still up there where the sausage was, exploring, going higher, my bottom pushing onto Toby's firm, wet mouth, the slippery length of his tongue pushing in. I opened my legs to let him, whichever part of him wanted to come in, my cunt throbbing furiously as my anus tightened, squeezed, and here it came, rushing down, Toby's tongue fucking me now, Toby sticking something up my pussy now – what the hell, oh God, the chilli sausage, he'd sucked

230

the sauce off the sausage and now he was shoving it inside my cunt!

The doorbell rang again, someone leaning on it, determined to be heard. Tessa, come to claim me. John, come to apologise. Olga, come to try again.

Toby pulled the sausage out and shoved it into my mouth. I tasted myself, my own smell, my own cunt juice, other juices, and I choked and groaned and came at last.

'Where's Alan?' I wondered, hitching up the scarlet dress.

'Bringing in the *pièce de resistance*, I hope. That's what we're paying him for,' drawled Daphne. She was sitting on the sofa with her knee bent, her fingers idly fingering her bare, almost pale blue pussy. 'The icing on the cake.'

'He's taking his time, isn't he?'

'Just answering the door! Guy, visitors!' Alan came back into the room.

I looked around for Toby, but suddenly all the men lifted me and plonked me on the grand piano.

'No, not the chilli again!' I wailed, tossing my head from side to side. 'Toby, I thought you'd forgiven me!'

'I have,' he said, his face whirling with the others above me. 'I'm just making one last film for Johnnie.'

In my dizziness there seemed to be far more people in the room than I remembered. There was a smell of mulled wine and pine cones, too seasonal and cosy for this icy house.

'OK, let me through.'

'So what's on the menu, Alan? You're a pastry chef for God's sake!' Flora asked, running her finger down my pussy, nails skimming between the swollen lips. 'Where's the famous pudding?'

'I'd say Mrs Moss here is good enough to eat. Or she will be when I've finished with her.'

The lights were blinding me. But no one had tied me. No one was forcing me to lie there, naked and spread open like a sacrifice.

The remnants of chilli sauce were still biting with heat round my arse and cunt, the arsehole taste of Guy still thick in my mouth. And now something cold was drilling into my hole, the little ring opening shyly to let it in, squeezing closed frantically to make sense of yet another invasion, muscles loosening obediently. I flung my arms up, my clamped nipples like tortured raspberries.

What's on the menu for tonight, Sheila? That's what Maureen had asked me. Maureen's fat face, those obscene purple baboon lips glistening and gobbling like a fish.

'Will mince pies and some mulled wine do?'

Guy's voice sounded far away, the tramping of feet in the hall like a sound effect playing on a CD.

I lifted my bottom, waggled it obscenely for my audience. Then I saw what Alan was holding. His precious piping bag, bulging with something, cream or custard. He was inserting the biggest metal nozzle of his piping bag into the tight ring of my anus, screwing it round deliberately to get it in.

'Looks like a torture instrument,' Flora remarked in her husky drawl, opening up my buttocks like a magician's assistant.

Toby's camera whirred and beeped. The nozzle rotated just inside and my muscles squeezed round it to pull it in. Jamie and Guy leaned on me, pushing a leg each, bending my knees up so that they were spread, showing my pussy, the lips stretched apart as Alan pushed the nozzle in further.

Then he squeezed the bulging piping bag. Warm, yellow custard, pumping until my anus hole tried to close like a little trap, but of course it couldn't close entirely, and while Alan transferred the nozzle to my cunt, my arse was convulsing, squeezing out the custard, and now all the men were there, bending their heads to lap at it, smear it across their faces before pushing custard into their wives' open mouths, rubbing it over their wives' white dresses, pushing it in between their legs.

And I was being fucked by a metal nozzle and I came, bucking there on the grand piano while my perfect neighbours licked and sucked and left me there to fuck each other senseless.

And, whispering *We Wish You a Merry Christmas*, a group of stunned carol singers, all bobble hats and waving lanterns, waited for payment.

Nineteen

I stand on the pavement outside my house. Or at least, outside the hoardings where my house used to be. All that's left of it, and all the others on that side of the street, is a jagged pile of dusty rubble, a stick or two of scaffolding and the faint whiff of gas. Only a pair of redbrick columns stand side by side like sentries where my garden gate used to be.

It's like one of those World War Two documentaries. Behind me, a perfect row of houses with nicely even rooftops, clipped hedges, freshly painted doors, sumptuous curtains hanging in the windows. In front of me, ruins. My lovely house – gone. And not a single lodger left to brighten the scene. No lights flickering in the windows, no music blaring through the door, no one dancing about in the hallway to greet me wearing nothing but an old netball skirt. No one flitting past in a flash of fake fur and fishnets to get to the club before she was sacked. No one shouting from the kitchen to get me to taste his *pannacotta* before he chilled the moulds.

Not even a door to slip my key into. And all because of my *fucking* brother.

But in my curled fist there is another set of keys safe in the pocket of Olga's fake fur. Along with the skimpy white dress, it's virtually become my uniform now. No more mourning weeds and tight black sweaters for Miss

Sheila Moss. This is the new me. The real me. And I'm getting to like it.

I turn and cross the road to number 43. Stretching away on either side, the smart houses stand calm and empty behind their dark box topiary. They will occasionally flower into life, bulging with fun and God knows what kind of sleazy thrills behind drawn curtains. But I am never invited any more, and since Christmas I've seen almost nothing of my raucous neighbours – which is odd, considering we once used to see everything. I'm sure if we ever passed on the street now we would avoid each other's eyes and pretend we'd never rolled naked in each other's arms, or slurped piss from each other's cunts, or tongued each other to a frenzy on the deep white shagpile in the living room. What kind of people did that sort of thing, for God's sake? This is a respectable street.

I slip the key into the door. It wasn't so long ago that I'd flounced out of that horrible job at the planning office, rushed home to cook harissa chicken for John, thinking he was back for good, thinking he was all I wanted, dancing with desire as I let myself in, thinking my key was like a cock in a lock. Now it's a different key, a different lock. And an oh so different, oh so better life.

Carols are playing somewhere softly in Toby's house, but it is all in total darkness. I shuffle through the pitch-black hallway, still unfamiliar with the dimensions – though there will be plenty of time to remedy that – searching for the stairs.

'Not allowed up there yet, Moss! Along here.'

Soft hands land on my shoulders and push me forwards into a big space with cool tiles. The sharp edge of something on my thigh. Something bulky, giving slightly as I bump it, my elbow sinking into something squashy like dough.

There is a click and spotlights dazzle me. I cover my eyes for a moment, nervous and excited.

'Happy New Year, Moss! It's me! And look what I've brought you!'

Tessa is behind me, pulling my hands away from my face. But before I turn to embrace her, I look at what she's brought me – and stagger back in shock. Trussed like a turkey across Toby's kitchen table – *my* kitchen table, rescued from number 44 – is John.

He is stretched face down and naked, his torso flat against the surface, his legs spread and strapped firmly by the ankles to the table's stout wooden legs. His wrists are similarly attached at the other end. His cock and balls hang limp at the apex of his thighs, and his skin glistens with sweat – whether from fear or cold, I can't tell. And neither can he, because his mouth has been tightly gagged with a vivid strip of lacy cloth which draws his lips back from his teeth in such a way that it looks as if he is grinning a terrible smile. But his eyes are haunted as he gives me a beseeching, hurt look. I just stare back at him, stunned.

'You can practise on him, when you want to be *really* debauched.'

I giggle as Tessa slaps John's rump, leaving a dull red patch, like a faded rose petal. As John flinches, his bottom opens wide to expose his anus hole, which in this light looks black.

'I've coated that bit in some of Alan's Belgian cooking chocolate,' crows Tessa, running a finger over the glistening hole and sliding it into her own mouth. Now I look at her. Her baby-blue eyes glitter demonically. 'Moss, you know what to do.'

'Yes, but what is this, Tess? How did you find him?'

'Oh, it was all Toby's doing,' Tess says airily, hoisting herself up to sit cross-legged beside my brother's heaving ribs. Her naked cunt flashes brightly at me from underneath her tiny skirt, and I suddenly realise what the gag in John's mouth must be – her panties. 'He was still pretty mad at this fuck-wit here, so he tracked him down to France and sweet-talked him into coming back. Told him he's done some kind of deal with Mr Brown and the council. He'll be let off with a warning this time so long as he agrees to design the new development for nothing. And this time –' she turns to spank John's gleaming buttocks to emphasise each word '– you're going to be a good boy and do it right, aren't you?'

A deep, wounded groan issues from John's throat. I feel my stomach lurch with excitement – to have him back here, in my house, naked and bound and helpless and at my mercy, when I thought I'd never see him again – thought I'd never *want* to see him again . . . No. I may be a reformed character, but I'm not that reformed. Not yet. I swing my hand and bring it crashing down on John's quivering backside.

'We can't hear you!' The words catch in my throat. 'Answer the pretty lady!'

John groans again. I leave my hand on the flesh of his arse, soothing and caressing, then move it down to cradle his balls. They hang heavy in my hand, and almost at once, to my delight, his big beautiful cock is suddenly stirring against the edge of the table. As I continue to massage his balls and arsehole, the swelling tip scrapes hard against the sharp edge of the tabletop, and he groans again, this time in real discomfort, shaking his head uselessly from side to side.

'It was all Toby's idea,' Tessa goes on gaily, twirling a strand of my new, ash-blonde hair round her fingers. 'After all, he owns the street, he can pick who he wants to work on it. And not only that, he says we can all come and live with him here, now that we're homeless.'

'We?'

'Not Olga. She refused to join in. Not our kind of people.' And she pulls a mock-grim face, then bursts into peals of laughter.

'Tessa, I could eat you,' I begin to say, but then

Toby's voice suddenly booms out from the cavernous hallway.

'Ready for the show!'

'Show?'

'Oh, you'll love it. We're going to show your ever-loving brother here your film.'

'My film?'

'It's all there. Your old house. You masturbating in the window. You thought you were behind the curtain, but Toby saw all of it. How it used to be in the bad old days. But it's all going to be so brilliant now.' Tessa slaps John's arse. 'And Toby knows *exactly* what he'll be wanting us to do with this meaty bit of beefcake here, Mr Big-Shot Property Developer – *not*.'

The doorbell rings.

'That'll be Mr Brown,' Tessa says, giving John's sweating bottom another vicious slap.

She drags me round to the other end of the table, to where John's goggling eyes can get a good view, then nudges open my mouth with her slippery tongue. 'Look, John, see how I like to kiss your pretty little sister? And I'm not the only one. She likes to do it with Toby. And not just kiss him. Fucks him too. You'll be seeing a lot of that later. I'm sure they'd love to perform a duet for you, right here in the kitchen among all the fruit and veg. Maybe use some of it on you as a finale, if you're lucky.'

Her hands are on my tits, squeezing and kneading. My nipples are standing out like bullets. I'm sweating bullets too, my skin almost as wet as John's with the thought of Tessa, and the forthcoming film show, and what we'll be doing to teach John a lesson. My cunt is slick with juice and I can feel my head begin to swim helplessly in the familiar aroma –

And then my eye is caught by something equally familiar, but completely unexpected.

'Burgundy!'

238

A case of wine stands in the corner of the kitchen, the wooden crate branded with the family insignia.

'Toby brought that back with him too, thought you might like to toast your revenge in style.'

'You little darling.' I bend over and pull her white T-shirt up. 'Now watch, closely, John,' I say sternly, turning to my brother lying so helpless and forlorn at my mercy. 'See what I've learnt in the months since you ran out and left me in that crumbling ruin across the street. Little Tessa's going to lick my arse, and then I'm going to do something a whole lot nastier to yours –'

Tessa slaps me hard on the bottom. It stings beautifully.

I lean over on the counter, thinking not of Tessa as she spanks me, but of number 44. My house. In ruins. The window where I stood, behind the curtain, looking out, exposing myself, pleasuring myself while the hand across the street pulled on his cock and people passed along the pavement below, my audience. The sleek businessman marching along the pavement with his briefcase, always stopping by my gate at the exact same time. The postman who, one morning, finally looked up and saw what I was doing. The milkman, the group of students. All those perfect neighbours, dressed in white . . .

Tessa, finally finished with my bottom, rushes to open the door. Her giggles fill the air. There is Mr Brown. No clipboard now, or dirty raincoat. A white shirt, baggy white trousers. They suit him. Tessa winds herself round him like a cat, her plump thigh in its white stocking hooking round his leg, and then, without further ado, she grabs his wrist and scampers upstairs, dragging him after her.

I open the window for a moment and breathe in the cold air. In the few minutes I've been in the fig tree house the ruins of number 44 seem to have receded even further into the past. There'll be nothing left to even remember soon. Along the road, a digger is scooping up bucketfuls of 48 to 60 and dumping the wreckage into giant skips.

A movement behind me. Warm hands circle my waist then slide swiftly up my body to tweak my nipples. I press my buttocks back into his groin, where the firm rod of his cock is already stiffening in expectation. Toby lifts my heavy dark hair and blows on my neck, just like John used to do. Shivers run all over me. The boy from the vineyard who watched John fucking me. Who wanted me, and has watched me, and watched over me, ever since.

'So if my old house was the brothel,' I say, smoothing down my skimpy white dress and patting my hair, 'what was yours?'

He laughs and gives his former rival John, still lying naked and quivering across the table, a none-too-gentle slap on the shoulder. 'The convent, of course!'

'Then let us pray,' I reply and, kneeling down, shove the neck of a wine bottle up my brother's arse.

nexus

The leading publisher of fetish and adult fiction

TELL US WHAT YOU THINK!

Readers' ideas and opinions matter to us so please take a few
minutes to fill in the questionnaire below.

1. Sex: Are you male ☐   female ☐   a couple ☐?

2. Age: Under 21 ☐   21–30 ☐   31–40 ☐   41–50 ☐   51–60 ☐   over 60 ☐

3. Where do you buy your Nexus books from?
☐ A chain book shop. If so, which one(s)?

_____

☐ An independent book shop. If so, which one(s)?

_____

☐ A used book shop/charity shop
☐ Online book store. If so, which one(s)?

_____

4. How did you find out about Nexus books?
☐ Browsing in a book shop
☐ A review in a magazine
☐ Online
☐ Recommendation
☐ Other _____

5. In terms of settings, which do you prefer? (Tick as many as you like.)
☐ Down to earth and as realistic as possible
☐ Historical settings. If so, which period do you prefer?

_____

☐ Fantasy settings – barbarian worlds
☐ Completely escapist/surreal fantasy
☐ Institutional or secret academy

- ☐ Futuristic/sci fi
- ☐ Escapist but still believable
- ☐ Any settings you dislike?

_____

- ☐ Where would you like to see an adult novel set?

_____

6. In terms of storylines, would you prefer:
- ☐ Simple stories that concentrate on adult interests?
- ☐ More plot and character-driven stories with less explicit adult activity?
- ☐ We value your ideas, so give us your opinion of this book:

_____

_____

_____

7. In terms of your adult interests, what do you like to read about? (Tick as many as you like.)
- ☐ Traditional corporal punishment (CP)
- ☐ Modern corporal punishment
- ☐ Spanking
- ☐ Restraint/bondage
- ☐ Rope bondage
- ☐ Latex/rubber
- ☐ Leather
- ☐ Female domination and male submission
- ☐ Female domination and female submission
- ☐ Male domination and female submission
- ☐ Willing captivity
- ☐ Uniforms
- ☐ Lingerie/underwear/hosiery/footwear (boots and high heels)
- ☐ Sex rituals
- ☐ Vanilla sex
- ☐ Swinging
- ☐ Cross-dressing/TV
- ☐ Enforced feminisation

☐ Others – tell us what you don't see enough of in adult fiction:

_____

_____

_____

8. Would you prefer books with a more specialised approach to your interests, i.e. a novel specifically about uniforms? If so, which subject(s) would you like to read a Nexus novel about?

_____

_____

_____

9. Would you like to read true stories in Nexus books? For instance, the true story of a submissive woman, or a male slave? Tell us which true revelations you would most like to read about:

_____

_____

_____

10. What do you like best about Nexus books?

_____

_____

11. What do you like least about Nexus books?

_____

_____

12. Which are your favourite titles?

_____

_____

13. Who are your favourite authors?

_____

_____

14. Which covers do you prefer? Those featuring:
(Tick as many as you like.)

- ☐ Fetish outfits
- ☐ More nudity
- ☐ Two models
- ☐ Unusual models or settings
- ☐ Classic erotic photography
- ☐ More contemporary images and poses
- ☐ A blank/non-erotic cover
- ☐ What would your ideal cover look like?

_____

15. Describe your ideal Nexus novel in the space provided:

_____

_____

_____

_____

16. Which celebrity would feature in one of your Nexus-style fantasies? We'll post the best suggestions on our website – anonymously!

_____

THANKS FOR YOUR TIME

Now simply write the title of this book in the space below and cut out the questionnaire pages. Post to: Nexus, Marketing Dept., Thames Wharf Studios, Rainville Rd, London W6 9HA

Book title: _____

NEXUS NEW BOOKS

To be published in July 2007

MOST BUXOM
Aishling Morgan

One thing rules Daniel's life, voyeurism. A desire far too strong to be denied, despite all the guilt it brings him. He knows the risks and is determined to give up his filthy habits. But when he finds himself as landlord to four voluptuous young female students the opportunities for peeping are far too good to resist. Unfortunately he has bitten off far more than he can chew.

Most Buxom should be a delight for all those who enjoy the female body in its full, opulent glory, while there is also plenty of the sort of kinky sex we have come to expect from Aishling Morgan, and even a splash of male submission.

£6.99   ISBN 978 0 352 34121 1

THE UPSKIRT EXHIBITIONIST
Ray Gordon

Mark and Anne have been tempted by the idea of wife swapping since their first shared sexual fantasies. They have the desire, the determination and a watertight relationship. Only thing missing has been the right couple to swing with.

But that small hurdle is overcome when they move next door to the sexy and exciting Johnny and Lisa. Their new neighbours are avid swappers and engaged in organising the season's largest swinging party.

As Mark and Anne take their first tentative steps into the waters of swapping they are soon immersed in a tidal wave of new experiences. The only thing left for them to discover is whether or not their relationship is truly watertight.

£6.99   ISBN 978 0 352 34122 8

If you would like more information about Nexus titles, please visit our website at www.nexus-books.com, or send a large stamped addressed envelope to:

Nexus, Thames Wharf Studios,
Rainville Road, London W6 9HA

NEXUS BOOKLIST

Information is correct at time of printing. To avoid disappointment, check availability before ordering. Go to www.nexus-books.com.

All books are priced at £6.99 unless another price is given.

NEXUS

☐ ABANDONED ALICE	Adriana Arden	ISBN 978 0 352 33969 0
☐ ALICE IN CHAINS	Adriana Arden	ISBN 978 0 352 33908 9
☐ AQUA DOMINATION	William Doughty	ISBN 978 0 352 34020 7
☐ THE ART OF CORRECTION	Tara Black	ISBN 978 0 352 33895 2
☐ THE ART OF SURRENDER	Madeline Bastinado	ISBN 978 0 352 34013 9
☐ BEASTLY BEHAVIOUR	Aishling Morgan	ISBN 978 0 352 34095 5
☐ BEHIND THE CURTAIN	Primula Bond	ISBN 978 0 352 34111 2
☐ BELINDA BARES UP	Yolanda Celbridge	ISBN 978 0 352 33926 3
☐ BENCH-MARKS	Tara Black	ISBN 978 0 352 33797 9
☐ BIDDING TO SIN	Rosita Varón	ISBN 978 0 352 34063 4
☐ BINDING PROMISES	G.C. Scott	ISBN 978 0 352 34014 6
☐ THE BOOK OF PUNISHMENT	Cat Scarlett	ISBN 978 0 352 33975 1
☐ BRUSH STROKES	Penny Birch	ISBN 978 0 352 34072 6
☐ CALLED TO THE WILD	Angel Blake	ISBN 978 0 352 34067 2
☐ CAPTIVES OF CHEYNER CLOSE	Adriana Arden	ISBN 978 0 352 34028 3
☐ CARNAL POSSESSION	Yvonne Strickland	ISBN 978 0 352 34062 7
☐ CITY MAID	Amelia Evangeline	ISBN 978 0 352 34096 2
☐ COLLEGE GIRLS	Cat Scarlett	ISBN 978 0 352 33942 3
☐ COMPANY OF SLAVES	Christina Shelly	ISBN 978 0 352 33887 7

NEXUS CONFESSIONS

NEXUS ENTHUSIAST

NEXUS NON FICTION

- - - - - ✂ -

Please send me the books I have ticked above.

Name ....

Address ....

....

....

.... Post code ....

Send to: **Virgin Books Cash Sales, Thames Wharf Studios, Rainville Road, London W6 9HA**

US customers: for prices and details of how to order books for delivery by mail, call 888-330-8477.

Please enclose a cheque or postal order, made payable to **Nexus Books Ltd**, to the value of the books you have ordered plus postage and packing costs as follows:
    UK and BFPO – £1.00 for the first book, 50p for each subsequent book.
    Overseas (including Republic of Ireland) – £2.00 for the first book, £1.00 for each subsequent book.

If you would prefer to pay by VISA, ACCESS/MASTERCARD, AMEX, DINERS CLUB or SWITCH, please write your card number and expiry date here:

....

Please allow up to 28 days for delivery.

Signature ....

Our privacy policy

We will not disclose information you supply us to any other parties. We will not disclose any information which identifies you personally to any person without your express consent.

From time to time we may send out information about Nexus books and special offers. Please tick here if you do *not* wish to receive Nexus information. ☐

- - - - - ✂ -